ANOTH

Tracey Scott-Townsend

Second Edition
This edition published by Wild Pressed Books: September 2018

First published by Inspired Quill: March 2015

Paperback ISBN: 978-0-9933740-8-1
eBook ISBN: 978-0-9933740-9-8
Wild Pressed Books Ltd, UK Business Reg. No. 09550738
http://www.wildpressedbooks.com

To Phil, for the silver horse

Prologue

The story of Another Rebecca was inspired by the painting 'There is no Night' by Jack B. Yeats.

I STEP OVER something hunched on the floor like a sleeping beast – the thin blanket off the bed – that bloody headache pressing relentlessly on the back of my skull like a thumb. A woman moans in her sleep. Loads of others are snoring, and there's a smell of pee. I hate it here. I want to go home. The nurse at the desk huddles over her computer.

The rash on my neck itches. Mine's the last bed in the ward, my hand rests on the surrounding curtain for a moment – wondering why I am out of bed – but something propels me forward. I push the curtain aside and stand pressing a hand over my mouth.

I have to bite my fingers just to feel real.

The shelving unit and bathroom at the end of the ward have gone. Yeah, really. Or maybe it's a dream, and perhaps I haven't actually got out of bed at all. But my cold feet on the warm floor and the pinprick itchiness of my rash tell me I'm awake. They've gone, the shelves and the door to the bathroom. They're just not there anymore. What?

One, two, three, four, five... *counting sometimes takes away the feeling of rising panic. Like when Mum's at her worst and...* never mind. *Fingers of fear creep up my spine. Keep counting...*

Whoa.

I'm in a grey, dusty room with a small armchair in the centre. The curtain swings closed behind me, only now it's heavier. Velvet. Thick carpet pushes up against my feet in swirly shapes – grey, like everything else in the room. I haven't enough energy to be worried about where I am, so I sink into the armchair, surprised to find how comfy it is.

A burst of impatience. My fingers tap on the wooden arm of the chair. I wish I had my iPod or a sketchpad and pencil; something to listen to or do. My knee jiggles restlessly inside my pyjamas. After a moment I realise my eyes must have been closed without me knowing because I find myself opening them. Time rocks about.

Where am I?

In front of me a huge window takes up a whole wall of the room. A landscape on the other side of the glass comes into focus, like at the start of a film. A hint of light touches the sky. My hands tingle – it goes all the way up my arms and into the back of my neck, then down again to the base of my spine where it settles in a warm pool. Comfort, like my mum's arms when I was little, envelops me.

Yes, I'm waiting. . . but what for?

The landscape is flat in the grassy foreground, hills in the distance, the sky a deep indigo streaked with rose, crimson, and viridian. Painterly and rich, all the techniques I've been studying at college. Closer to, the colours are cadmium yellow and vermillion and ultramarine. It really does look more like a painting than solid land and sky, with thick, crusty paint nearest to me and thinly diluted streaks on the horizon. My paintbrush hand twitches, bringing to mind the hospital art therapy room. I half-rise from my chair but the curtain swishes open and a lady comes in with a cup of tea on a saucer.

"Hello, Rebecca dear, how lovely it is to see you."

I don't know you.

The lady leans over, her scent flooding my nostrils. It's familiar. She offers me the cup of tea.

"Thank you."

"You're very welcome, dear. He'll be here soon."

Who will?

There's something insubstantial about this woman, dressed in a soft grey sweater and matching cardigan. Her smile's friendly but her gaze goes right through me. She moves noiselessly back towards the curtain, silvery curls bobbing, her smile fixed in place, not quite real.

Wait! But she's already gone.

I sip the tea; hot and perfectly real, slipping down my throat. My attention goes back to the landscape in front of me. I jump, nearly spilling my drink because I see a figure on the other side of the glass, resting on their elbows, a man or a boy looking out over the landscape. . .

Ah, now I can see what he's looking at; a horse, a beautiful shimmer of white amidst the blues and crimson, galloping in the direction of the glass. The thunder of hooves rattles the window, echoes in my stomach. I put the cup and saucer on the carpet and lean forward.

Hurry, hurry, hurry, I want you.

Now I see him properly, blond hair brushing his shoulders, lifting and falling all over the place as the boy springs to his bare feet. He wears a billowing white shirt and jeans torn off at the knee. He gives a long, low whistle and the horse snorts in answer. Tosses its head and lets out a high whinny, coming to a stop right in front of him, shaking its mane. He puts his hand on the horse's neck and leans forward, breathing into its nostrils. The horse stills, one brown eye looking sideways through the window at me. So close its eyelashes are visible through the glass.

I stand up. I feel hot. Wiping my hands on the legs of my pyjamas, I'm conscious of the unsightly rash on my arms and wrists, so I pull the sleeves of my top as far down as I can. Then I press my face to my own reflection, looking out into the indigo-dimness.

He enters the room, the boy, through the window as it slides open. I'm shivering inside but it feels good. Before he looks at *me he raises a hand to his horse, ordering it to stay where it is.*

A cool breeze blows in from the landscape but heat moves up from my chest to my forehead. My legs tremble so much I have to keep shifting from one foot to the other. My tongue's stuck to the roof of my mouth.

"Rebecca. It's so good to see you!"

I love you, I love you. *Ridiculous but true. I've never seen him before in my life but I knew it the minute I saw him. His name's on the tip of my tongue. It will be so familiar when I hear it.*

I feel myself smile, no longer caring about the rash.

"How are you?" *The first thing to come out of my mouth.*

"I'm very well, thank you, Rebecca. But what about you... you've been ill?" *He hasn't touched me yet but his brow furrows with anxiety.*

"Oh it's this... Scarletina thing. I didn't respond to the antibiotics, so..."

I've been weak for a long while, spent a lot of time off college.

Before I've realised what's happening I'm in his arms. His chin digs gently into my shoulder and my head rests on his chest. All I can hear his heart. I could cry with relief and it's the nicest feeling ever. My wooziness makes it impossible to think beyond the moment. His hands stroke up and down my back. "I missed you so much..."

Oh My God. What does he mean?

"I missed you, Rebecca. Did you miss me?"

And yet when he pulls his head back and I tilt my face up to see his eyes I know exactly what he means. Yes, I did miss you. I don't know how but I did. *I'm too choked up to say it.*

"You've cut off your beautiful long hair, Rebecca. But I like the way it curls around your ears. It shows off your big brown eyes and your elfin face. It suits you."

My hair's been short as long as I can remember; how strange that he should think of it as beautiful and long. Ahhhh, his hands move on my face and neck, a finger trails across my cheek and under my ear; back up into my cropped hair. I have an overwhelming feeling of lucidity.

"And you," comes out of my mouth.

"And me?"

"You too. You're..."

"I'm?"

"Still beautiful." It's almost as if someone else speaks through me, doing the things my hands have started to do. Massage his spine through the rough fabric of his shirt, press gently into the lean covering of flesh.

"I always loved it when you did that. I've missed you so much."

I've never done that to anyone before...

Rosy light permeates the grey room. He tips my chin up to meet his descending lips. It's not like being kissed by Edward Docherty at the college party. I'd hated the way his body trembled, and the hard lump pressing into my belly before I pulled away, wiping slime from my face with the back of my hand. He called me 'frigid' and told everybody I was a lesbian.

This boy kisses my mouth so gently, cups the back of my head in his hand. He eases away the headache that's been there so long. Ah. The tops of my thighs ache; the place where I've recently been experimenting with my finger burns. I know where I want his hands to go next, I want it so bad a whimper breaks out of my throat.

"Rebecca."

The boy's lips curve into a smile. "Rebecca." Everything about him seems utterly familiar. His name won't come to me. It's not allowed yet.

"We have to go, honey."

"Go?"

"To Oblivion. It's time to take you there."

"Oblivion?"

Outside the horse stamps its foot. The boy takes my hand.

"There's nothing to be afraid of, my love. I've been waiting for this for a long time. I'm so happy you've finally come."

I want to kiss him again but he laces his fingers securely in mine and tugs me gently over the threshold of the room. Stepping off the grey carpet we walk into the shifting landscape. The ground sinks, adapting to my weight. Grass brushes at my ankles, cool drops of dew on my ravaged skin. The air carries a static charge – it's in the roots of my hair, the sparkles of electricity snapping back and forth between me and the boy. The horse stamps and snorts; steam shimmers off its coat. Fear rises in my chest. The boy tightens his hand around mine, the safest feeling in the world.

"Breathe deeply. He won't hurt you."

I do as I'm told and the horse watches me. A sweet, strong smell comes off its skin. It's huge; a powerful, mythical creature easily eighteen hands high. A pinkish tone sets over the landscape, bathing the horse in colour. I have the strangest feeling I'm in a painting.

"Trust me." The boy places his hand on the horse's neck. The creature twitches its muscles, blows hot blasts from its nostrils, like a dragon.

"Come closer."

Taking another deep breath, I let him draw me forward.

"Put your hand on his neck."

"He's so warm." I'm close enough to see the individual hairs that make up his coat, feel the heat off his skin. His long strands of mane have the texture of rope. I push some aside from his eyes and he gives me a gentle snort.

"He likes you. He remembers you."

"Does he? How?"

"He has a long memory."

The horse nuzzles my pyjama top.

I give his muzzle a gentle rub. "It's like velvet."

"Rebecca?"

I turn to the boy. The headache returns, knocking at the base of my skull. A sense of what's coming next makes me say, "Don't leave me now..."

"I'm not leaving you, my love, I've come to take you with me."

"To Oblivion?"

"To Oblivion."

"For good?"

"Yes, if you're ready."

Memories break like waves. Mum reading me stories when I was little, making me a fairy dress for my birthday, taking me to meet my dad even though she couldn't stand the sight of him.

But then.

Cleaning up her sick, bathing the cuts on her face, picking her up when she fell. Having to call my personal tutor; going with her to collect Mum from the police station. Me, ill for so many months; hopeless, useless. Fearing I'll never get better, not even wanting to.

"I'm ready."

He's up on the horse already, reaching down to grasp my hand.

"When I say 'jump' I want you to take a leap. I'll pull you up at the same time." A rumble disturbs the atmosphere. It sounds like thunder. The horse shifts impatiently.

"We're gonna have to hurry," says the boy.

Our eyes meet for a second.

"I love you."

"I love you."

"Jump!"

In an effortless movement I'm up on the horse's bare back, the boy behind me.

"Grasp with your thighs and hold on to his mane," instructs the boy. "I'll hold you."

The animal takes off with a resonating thud of hooves. The sound connects with cracking rolls of thunder, breaking from an iridescent dome of sky.

"I'm falling off!" Panic stiffens me so the horse's strides bump and hurt between my legs. But the boy's voice is in my ear. "I've got you, Rebecca; it's okay – don't try to resist – move with it. Feel me behind you, enjoy it, my darling!"

His voice makes me trust him. I relax in his arms, move as he moves. We race across the landscape, the ground reverberating through the galloping body into our bones. Laughing out loud, my laughter transmutes into something else, as a juddering cry is forced from my lungs. Sensation gathers in my toes and tingles up my legs, catalyses into a ball of fire in my belly, explodes outwards. I crumple, helpless, against the boy. His strong arm supports me. I hear him groan.

The horse has stopped and is now pawing the ground, a foamy coating of sweat on its shoulders. The boy has his face pressed into my neck, making it damp. It takes me a while to realise he's crying. I twist my body around as far as I am able, stroke his face.

"What's the matter?"

He sniffs, wiping his nose on his sleeve.

"What's the matter. . . my love?"

He allows his wet eyes to meet mine, but he still can't seem to speak.

"Are we there. . . are we at Oblivion?"

He speaks in a flat voice. "I've realised something."

"Pardon?"

"I've realised something; you're not the right one."

"I don't understand."

"I am so sorry, we can't go together."

Oh my God. What does he mean? He's supposed to be taking me to Oblivion.

"My love." I've only just got used to those words on my tongue. Now the dampness in my pyjamas feels uncomfortable and embarrassing. He's no longer touching me, leans as far away as possible on the broad back of the horse.

I'll try the words again. "My love. . . what?"

He hangs his head, mumbles into the collar of his shirt. I only now notice the landscape around us has bled its colour, diminished into tones of grey. The brightness of the horse, unsettled beneath us, has dimmed.

"I'm so sorry, Rebecca," the words finally come out.

"I don't understand what's happened."

"I can't take you to Oblivion. I didn't mean to deceive you – please forgive me."

He leans forward and for a moment it seems he's about to kiss me again but he only swings his leg over the back of the horse and slides to the ground. He stands, looking up at me.

"It's not the right time for you, Rebecca. Come down now."

I could stay here on the horse, I could gallop away and then he would have to come and find me.

But even the huge creature seems despondent, dropping his head low to the ground, nosing desultorily at a grey-looking tussock of grass. There's nothing I can do except lean forward as the boy did and struggle to slide my leg behind me over the back of the horse. I kick away the boy's waiting arms and jump to the ground by myself, pain shooting up my leg, not caring even if I've just shattered my ankle.

"I thought you were mine, but you're not. I'm so sorry, sweet girl."

We're back outside the grey room. The boy stands with his arms around the horse's head, human forehead pressed against equine. I give him a final look, then walk, stiff-backed, into the grey room and slide the massive glass door shut behind me. The only thing I want is to curl myself into the smallest possible ball in the grey armchair and cover my head with my arms to try and stop myself hearing, feeling in my bones, the thunder of the horse's hooves as it gallops away – carrying my boy.

The smell of my own vomit rouses me. The room is stifling. Grey. I retch again. Fever sends rivulets of sweat streaming down my face and neck. Cold. The room's walls are oppressive; there is no window anymore. I would cry out but my throat feels swollen. Weird lights vibrate at the corners of my vision. I push myself out of the chair and get unsteadily to my feet.

I need to get out of here!

Where's the door? It was behind the grey curtain. But the curtain is too heavy to move and it's all dusty. Let me out!

I can't produce a sound from my swollen throat. When I turn back to the armchair it isn't there anymore. The walls are closer together! I wobble back to where the window was, lay my cheek *against solid wall. I drag in deep breaths, trying to pull in fresh air. My fingers scrabble for cracks, or a lever that might open a window again.*

I want to go to Oblivion. I promise I'll be the right one. Please take me to Oblivion with you.

ANOTHER REBECCA

One

Bex

February 2010

THE BRRRINGING TONE hurts my brain.

"Yeah?"

It's the hospital. They found Rebecca collapsed in the bathroom. She's had some kind of convulsion; they reckon because of her high temperature. Fuck. Can't concentrate. Can't place myself. I just want oblivion. Take me there, someone. Or something, preferably something from a green bottle.

Got this weird weakness in my right arm. I can barely hold the phone.

"Don't know what you want from me."

Bloody hell, what are they saying?

"She's in good hands in't she?" I say. "Come in, at this time of night, what the eff for?"

I switch the phone to the other ear. The nurse is giving me a right telling-off, making out I don't love my daughter. 'Course I do, whatever she wants to insinuate. "It's the middle of the night." I feel dizzy. "You should be giving her a sleeping pill or something."

No reply, it's a fucking heavy-breather. *Try again.*

"How about I come over first thing in the morning?"

Shadows in the darkness. Scary. But they can't break through the thorns around my bed. Breathe out. The voice

3

on the phone has gone away.

Guilt bites. Spreads a black hole in my side.

Shifting up in the bed, my elbow slips in saliva. A bigger stain wets the middle of the bed.

Damn cat. Fuck you.

It was only a bit of a drink. Just a drop, but I mustn't drive. Ain't got enough money for a taxi. Wonder if I could manage the twenty-minute walk to the hospital. Sweat slithers down my forehead. Suppose I should go, shouldn't I? But she'll be all right. She's the strong one, Rebecca. Looks after me, she does. But I will. I will go in.

A sudden, disturbing recollection hits and I look down: the damp t-shirt riding up my thigh shows a finger-mark-shaped bruise. No.

It can't have been me that happened to. I won't look.

My head swings and my feet hurt when they touch the floor. Cars go past with a flood of yellow light. It's comforting, that and the traffic sounds, they're the only company I got.

I pull on a jumper and the first pair of jeans I find. *Takes forever.* Where's my hairbrush? I push my arms through air that is thick like treacle. Time falls away; minutes last longer than they should.

I'm still sitting with the hairbrush poised above my head. Fuck it. I'll put on a bit of lippy, eyeliner; there you have it. Respectable mum.

"Not too much blusher Mum." Her voice comes to me as I zip the make-up bag shut. Another thing she always says is *have some breakfast. Line your stomach at the beginning of the day. With food.* She feels more real to me when she's not here.

My head's banging. Could really use another fag, but the packet's empty. Shit.

It's nearly 2am. When did they ring? I'm in the living room – got a feeling I might have been sitting on the arm of the settee a while. Shit, I'm shaking all over. Should I ring the hospital back? Rebecca might be asleep by now. Best not disturb her, eh?

Light outside. The window rattles in its rotten frame, jolting me upright. I'm still on the settee, wearing my trainers. Two thick-bottomed glasses glare at me from the coffee table. The rings in their bases add yet another shade of brown to the room.

I rub my eyes. Rub them harder.

A siren blares by. I stand on trembling legs and walk over to the narrow window, smeared with salt and grime behind the thin curtains that I drag open one at a time. The right one sags loose in the middle and I have to tug it inch by inch. Oops. As my head lurches, my fingers tighten on the fabric and another curtain hook detaches itself from the rail.

Our flat looks out over Sea View Road, not that there's any view of the sea here at the back end of Skeg-Vegas. Living room isn't much to write home about: poky and drab. Except for Rebecca's paintings, the only colourful things in it. I haven't got the energy to redecorate but hey, a glass or two of my favourite tipple is cheaper.

Speaking of, I'll have a quick livener before the day starts properly. Clear the head a bit.

I could have lived in a nice place in Nottingham: red brick Victorian or a brand new house on an executive estate. If I'd played my princess part properly and kept him happy. But that would've been a betrayal. Rebecca and me, we're all right. More like best friends than mother and daughter. We like the same music and clothes, enjoy watching TV together. We look after each other.

We didn't need him after all, Jack.

This time I remember to lock the front door when I go, not leave the key in it like I did last time. I make sure to put it in a safe pocket.

Two

Jack

"I'LL FUCKING SWING for you one of these days."

I'm shouting even as the click on the line means she's cut me off. She's a selfish, evil bitch who thinks of nobody but herself.

Edna stares at me across the trays of hinges, arranged neatly on her desk ready for the Millington order, her mouth hanging open. Veiny hands hover over the keyboard, shoulders hunch around her cardigan-wrapped chest. When she sees me looking her jaw snaps shut. A single, thick hair sprouts from the bottom of her chin and I can't take my eyes off it. It trembles with the effort she puts into keeping her mouth in a tight line.

Arthur shuffles into the room carrying the box I've been waiting for all afternoon. He starts to dump it on my desk.

"Watch the fucking Johnson contract!"

I just manage to rescue the sheaf of papers from underneath. The boy's an idiot. I put the contract safely into the envelope Edna handed me before the phone rang, then go over and slap it on her desk unnecessarily hard because I can't stand the expression on her face. She sucks her lips even further into her mouth.

Red creeps up from the collar of Arthur's neatly buttoned shirt; his face floods with colour right up to the roots of his ginger hair, like a paper towel absorbing spilt juice. I loosen my shoulders, try and breathe slowly the way Wendy taught me. Arthur's standing in front of me now, running the tip of his tongue over dry lips. The way he carries himself you'd think he was sixty, rather than seventeen. It's not normal.

"All right, you can go."

He won't do anything unless given a specific instruction. I don't know why I let Edna persuade me to take her grandson on, or why I took her on for that matter. Disapproval slices the atmosphere in the office.

"Open that window, will you Edna?" The combination of the mustard-coloured walls and the thick, recycled air makes me feel sick. That and the echo of Bex's drunken voice still ringing in my head. I slump into my seat, angle myself so the monitor cuts off my view of Edna - and hers of me. The screensaver picture of Wendy and our twin sons acts like a temporary tranquilizer. My hands grab the cardboard box on my desk and I attempt to pull out the object inside, jammed in over-tightly. But while my hands struggle with wood and cardboard my head replays the conversation I just had with the mother of my daughter.

The hate for Bex is so strong it twists my insides into a knot. *Don't think about it now.*

Bitch.

The object I've pulled from the box is a smooth wooden scale model of a door, set within a frame on a solid base, like a trophy. I run a finger over the polished metal of the locking panel and fish around in the bottom of the box for the plastic bag containing the shiny new keys.

My favourite part of the job is when the commissions become reality. I designed this one for a high-security hospital. Playing with the key in the lock, I open the miniature door and close it again. I'm proud of the adaptable locking system.

'Doorphenalia' started off as my dad's market stall selling locks, hinges, door handles and rubber seals. We also sold brass polish and chamois leathers and a whole host of other things at the beginning.

While my older sister went off to join the new age travellers in a covered cart pulled by a gypsy horse, I spent weekend after weekend hollering at my dad's stall.

"Two for the price of one!"

I resented Iris being able to choose her own lifestyle while I had to stay in Nottingham and help Dad. But when he died. . . well, it was me who got the lion's share of the inheritance.

"Mr Portman."

Edna's decided to put on her *nothing if not polite* persona. I ignore her martyred expression.

"Yes, Edna?"

"Just a reminder that you promised to pick the twins up early from school. They have their dental appointment at three thirty. Wendy is busy with a client this afternoon."

Not a Doorphenalia client: Wendy runs a cupcake business. Edna closes her lips again. My fingers start to construct an aeroplane out of the scrap paper littering my desk. I should aim it at her head.

Not only does Wendy keep me organised at home, she's planted Edna in the office to do the same thing. Today I fucking resent it.

They go to the same book group; they're meeting tonight. From what I can make out they don't talk that much about the books they're supposed to've read. Edna'll be asking her, all concerned like, whether there's anything the matter with me.

Glancing up at the planner on the wall I slam the model door shut on its plinth and lock it from the inside – the inmate side. My hands clench, the right one curling into a fist around the cool metal of the miniature key. The ranted conversation with Rebecca's mother on the phone won't go away.

I can't believe that bitch didn't tell me before. The kid's been in hospital nearly a week. She's been asking for me. What the fuck am I going to tell Wendy? Book Group's only on once a month, she'll give me the silent treatment for the whole of next month if I tell her I can't babysit tonight.

"Daddy, you promised!"

Joshua tugs my sleeve. Bobby kicks me and I have to make an effort not to hit him back. They're spoilt. They've had everything my daughter didn't get. Rebecca was picking her mother up off the floor when she was their age.

"If you ever. . . "

Wendy speaks in a low, cold voice. She must have seen the way I was flexing my hand. She watches us from the cloakroom doorway, arms folded under heavy breasts. Her face is red from crying.

I look down at my sons' golden heads. Joshua bursts into tears. Bobby gives me another hard kick before moving over to his mother.

I stifle a curse, make myself breathe deeply.

"Don't be bloody stupid."

"So you're going to let the boys down as well as me?"

Wendy tucks her book into the artfully constructed understairs bookcase with elaborate ceremony. She's had to ring her friend Karen and tell her she can't come to book group. She's also reminded me I'd promised to take the twins to gym club.

"They were really looking forward to going with you, Jack."

"Wendy." I go over, risk putting my hands on her shoulders. She only flinches slightly.

"I have another child. You know that. I can't let her down again. The boys have me all the time and so do you. But Rebecca's in hospital, for Christ's sake."

The problem is Wendy can't stand the fact of Rebecca's existence. She doesn't want me to have had a past at all, not one that contains a child and especially not that child's mother.

Wendy shrugs away from me and blows her nose. "Well you could have let me know before. Nobody can babysit at this short notice."

"I didn't know before."

I say it gently but I'm thinking what a selfish cow she is. I'm not stupid enough to mention Bex's name and set her off again.

"Look, I have to go now. It's a couple of hours' drive. Don't wait up. I'll see you later. I. . . "

She wants me to say I love her. She's hanging her tearful gaze imploringly on mine but it gives me a shrivelling feeling. Sometimes I can do it, when I'm full of one of her good dinners or after we've had sex, but I can't seem to push the words out tonight. I just want to get away. I've got to go.

The TV's on. At least the boys have settled. Wendy won't take them to gym club now; she won't be seen out with those red-rimmed eyes. She turns right away, shoulders stiff. That song comes back in my head, the one with the heart-breaking lyric that insists two out of three things in a relationship aren't bad. It was always all Wendy was ever going to get.

When Bex got pregnant I knew she'd never be motivated enough to leave me or get rid of the baby. She'd need me, which was what I wanted.

I was twenty-one, still living at home, working my fingers raw on the market stall to save for a place of my own. The night I first saw Bex she looked like Audrey Hepburn, purple dress fitted like a sheath and dark hair piled up on her head.

Watching her, nobody would've guessed the way she was living, already heading towards alcoholism. We were in a nightclub for her brother Dave's birthday.

Dave and I played in the same football team. Meeting him in the toilets after I'd repeatedly danced with her, he warned me.

"You wanna steer well clear of my kid sister, mate. She's off her head at the moment."

"What d'you mean?"

I zipped up and went over to the sink to wash my hands. Dave followed me. He swayed slightly on his feet, peering at a zit on his chin in the mirror. When he'd given his hands a quick swill under the tap he ran them, still wet, through his hair. He belched and rubbed his stomach.

11

"She's out of control, mate. Her fiancé got killed. She's only nineteen and hardly ever comes home, sleeping God knows where and taking God knows what."

Bex's huge dark-brown eyes loomed in my mind, looking as they had on the dance floor while she curled and twisted her body around me. Dave gave me a pitying look.

"Yeah, yeah, I get that she's a looker but I'm telling you, she's dangerous at the moment. I reckon she needs psychiatric help."

I moved over to the hand drier.

"I'm telling you as much for her sake as yours, Jack," he said on his way out. A rush of hot, clammy air and a blast of noise hit us when he opened the door. He raised his voice and I turned so I could hear what he was saying.

"She don't need no more complications in her life right now."

Dave and his other mates moved on to a different nightclub shortly after that, but I decided on going home. I had to get up early for the stall. Worried I might puke up standing in the queue for my jacket, I leant over, arms crossed at the waist. Couldn't stop thinking about Bex.

A girl in line kept pinching my bum, calling me peachy cheeks. Anger flared up. Swivelling my head round I snarled at her, a pretty girl. Any other night I'd have thought I'd got lucky. What was wrong with me?

But she didn't have the dark haired, dark eyed beauty of Bex. I'd avoided Bex for the rest of the night. Now I might never see her again, if what Dave had told me about her lifestyle was true.

But she was there on the street when I left the club, leaning against the wall, stubbing a cigarette out on the pavement with her high heel. The doorman stood watching her from the entrance, running a hand over his bald head. A voice on his radio crackled loudly but he made no move to respond to it, his eyes fixed on Bex.

A surge of protectiveness rose in my blood when I thought of that ugly shit getting his meaty hands on her. I stumbled forward, the cold making me realise I was more drunk than I'd thought.

Bex's thin arms wound around her body like wire, her long neck looked as vulnerable as a swan's. When she lifted her head I saw the raw emptiness in her eyes. But by the time I'd closed mine and opened them again she'd managed to replace her lost expression with an amused flirtatiousness.

"What happened to you? I thought you were never coming out of there."

———◄○►———

Rebecca looks up at me now with those same eyes her mother had. I thought I could rescue Bex from her sorrow, really believed it. But maybe she would have got over it better if I had left her alone. Rebecca should never have been born. She's a tough kid, but she's lost all her spark.

She's a pixie, sharp ears poking out of her short brown hair. At first I think she's wearing eye make-up but they're shadows, the blue of her veins pushing up through translucent skin. She has spots on her face; loads more on her neck and chest and arms. In the yellow of the overhead light she looks as stark as a Dickens character. My insides contract. You see kids like her on those adverts for children's charities.

For the first time I truly see it: how badly I've failed her.

Three

Rebecca

I'M IN HOSPITAL for another three days. I don't remember the convulsion really, except for the flashing lights at the corners of my eyes, the grey floor tiles, grainy up close, and a smell like burning. Oh, and that disgusting pile of sick.

There's a window across from my bed and I've sketched the view from it so many times I could do it in my sleep. There are three trees in a perfectly straight line across a patch of lawn surrounded by a border of pebbles. I sketch the interlocking branches with tiny strokes of a pencil from the set Dad got me.

There's a bench in the middle of the square, next to a drinking fountain that looks as if it's been standing there forever. I'm not sure if it works; I've never seen anyone drinking from it. But people come and sit on that bench. Eat their sandwiches or snog or cry on each other's shoulders. Some come to have an argument.

Once, an old man sat there for the longest time without moving. I was sure he'd been given some terrible news about his wife, wondered how he'd manage without her for the rest of his life. Sad.

I hang out in the Art Therapy room. Someone who works here says they're going to put up a painting of mine in the Maternity Wing. They're looking for pieces that will help the mums-to-be relax when they're in labour. Apparently the one I did has exactly the right feeling for that. I'd prefer to have another go at it with acrylic paints, but they tell me they love it just the way it is. They're going to give it a deep cream mount, cover it with glass and add a gold-coloured frame.

I don't know what made me do the painting; it just came to me. The image is always there in my head now. It's an abstract landscape made from as many colours of blue as I can mix with their rubbish poster paints. Adding a touch of red and a streak of vivid green helps, but it still isn't exactly what I'm aiming for.

Some streaks of white in the middle ground, just a few marks, resemble a horse. I add strokes of colour in the foreground too, and squinting just about reveals it represents a human.

A bluey landscape with a horse and a human figure. Not the kind of thing I usually paint, but maybe it's the start of my 'blue period' or something. Picasso had one of those.

A woman from the hospital management team says my painting reminds her of a work by some famous painter in the past; she can't remember his name but she says I should have a look through some art books and find it.

Rodin's 'The Kiss' sits on a plinth in the corner of Dr Parrish's office. I saw the real thing when I went to The Tate with my art class. The original is much bigger and is made from marble, unlike this small bronze copy.

Dr Parrish is telling mum about the tablets I have to take when I go home, and she's at least pretending to listen. I catch her eye and we both try not to be the one to smile first. She looks away but her lips are already curving upward at the corners.

Part of me is scared about leaving. There were no responsibilities in here.

In the car park, I watch Mum carefully as she puts my bag in the boot of the car. She doesn't look like she's had a drink today.

I'm tired out by the time I get myself strapped into the seat beside her.

"All right babe?" She traces a finger over my cheekbone. "You're so pale. You have violet hollows under your eyes, Rebecca Jane, but to me you are still the most beautiful girl in the world."

She gives me a sad smile. When she says things like that I wouldn't change her for anything. Sometimes her dark brown eyes remind me of the seals at the sanctuary where I had my Saturday job. I used to stare at those seals' eyes for ages. But if Mum catches you looking into hers she puts on that gormless expression she's good at faking.

I can't relax in the car, haven't been able to since that time we had a crash. The sound of the other car hitting us when Mum wasn't paying attention felt like it cracked my skull open. It didn't count as drink driving on Mum's part because nothing showed up on the breathalyser but you could smell it if you were cooped up in that small space with her. The worst thing about it was, she couldn't stop laughing afterwards.

People've asked me why I insisted on going back to live with her when I could've stayed with the Marten family. I was happy there, it's true. But I guess the simple answer is: she's where I belong. I can't just pretend she's not. And I'm afraid she'll end up dying of some stupid accident if I don't stay with her. I sneak a look at her face while she's driving, tongue tucked into her cheek and her eyes narrowed, fastened on the road. At least she's more careful these days.

We manage to get a parking space near our flat. There's the tang of sea air as I swing open the car door. Pity my stupid body wouldn't make it as far as the beach. Getting out I'm shivering. I should have worn my hoody.

My legs are hollow; I weigh nothing.

There is no solidity under my feet, as though I'm about to float upwards like a balloon.

The people who live in the upstairs flat've left bags of rubbish right in front of the gate. By the time we're in the hall all I want is to go and lie on my bed. I'm just about to escape when

Mum insists we watch a rerun of Casualty on the sofa, as if I haven't had enough of hospitals.

"Mum I'm really tired. Dr Parrish told me to get as much sleep as possible for the next few weeks until my immune system's fully recovered."

"Don't be mean," she says, "I've had to do without my right hand woman for a week already." Seeing my face she starts up with that wheedling voice of hers. "I'll be off to work soon anyway. Sit with your poor old mum for a while, ducky. Go on. You can have a nice sleep later."

She rubs her hand over-hard on the back of my neck, fingers digging in. I shrug out from under them but do as she asks. It's not worth upsetting her.

The fawn walls of our tiny living room crowd in as we tuck ourselves up on the beige sofa and pull the brown blanket over, nursing mugs of hot chocolate. We curl our legs under us and lean against each other. Actually, she leans against me and I wish she wouldn't. Strands of hair escape from her ponytail and tickle my cheek. Blowing them away with the side of my mouth makes her move off my shoulder. She sniffs loudly.

All my paintings on the walls remind me that they're going to put my latest one up in the maternity unit. My future could include having exhibitions in galleries. But there'd be so much wine lying around. I'd have to keep an eye on Mum the entire time or get somebody else to do it.

The weight of that thought pushes my body into the sofa.

It's late in the afternoon. A sharp blade of light slices at a low angle through the gap in the half-closed curtains, transforms itself into a shape like a cross on Mum's lap. She's asleep. I could get away now if I had the energy, but I don't. The green and brown carpet reminds me of a forest floor and my eyes become slits so I can more easily perceive the grass and trees, the mushrooms that bloom under rocks.

Buses rumble by, the sound as comforting to me now as the washing machine was to me a baby. A sweet feeling of safety descends on me and I half-close my eyes again. My home is much cosier than the hospital.

Now I'm back here I'm okay.

Her head's flopped onto the back of the sofa; she's snoring now. I should wake her up ready for work. But just for a minute it's nice to appreciate the peace.

Let sleeping mums lie. I force myself to slide out from the nest of cushions and test the weight on my legs before I take the first step away. In the kitchen I put the kettle on.

"Wake up. Mum."

Dandruff nestles in her hair. I feel sick. What if she never wakes up? I give her shoulder a shake.

She makes a sticky sound with her mouth before she finally stirs and looks around, confused. Her eyes flick over to the bookshelf but I've removed the bottle that was there. She doesn't say anything but her frown deepens.

Avoiding her eyes I say, "I've got your uniform laid out ready, and your comfortable shoes."

She hates them but she'll be on her feet for hours.

"Have a wet wipe."

There's no time for a shower.

"Deodorant."

She goes in the bathroom and brushes her teeth and I hand her the hairbrush. Her uniform hangs off her body. When did she lose so much weight?

"Try and get this down you."

I've made her a ham sandwich. She's supposed to get a meal at work but instead she has an extra fag-break or a "liquid repast" as she calls it. She takes a bite and gags. Hides the reaction well.

"I'm not hungry, love."

I ignore that, running a bottle of water from the tap.

"Make sure you drink this, you don't want to get dehydrated. Handbag?"

"Handbag."

"Keys?"

"Keys."

"Phone?"

"Phone."

"Purse?"

"Purse."

It's a routine we've played out every time she went to work at whatever job since I was tiny. In those days she left me with one of her mates or occasionally on my own.

I heave a sigh of relief once she's made it out the door, in time for work if she walks quickly. Then I go into my room and collapse on the bed. I let go, can't stop myself from crying.

Four

Bex

"HERE'S A FIVER, duck; you'll have to get yourself sommats for tea. I'm going back to bed for a bit."

Rebecca tucks the money into her pocket and inspects her reflection in the hallway mirror. Feeling shaky, I back off. I watch her from behind the door and see how she winds that curl on her forehead around a finger, fastens it in place with one of her flower slides. The only make-up she ever wears is eyeliner and it makes her eyes too big for her pixie face. She would have gone down well in the sixties she would, with her Twiggy eyes and Mia Farrow hairstyle.

"I'm off in a minute, Mum."

I snap back into my body. She's been at the toilet all morning and has butterflies in her tummy; she doesn't know I know that. But I feel her emotions like I once felt her movements in my own tummy. Yeah, it's true, despite how I might come across. I'm still her mum.

Her portfolio is propped up by the front door.

"What time's your bus, did you say?"

"8.55."

"Is it warm out?"

She opens the front door and sticks her head out. Sunshine pours into the hallway, bathes her in a pool of light like an angel. That's when a shiver goes through me. I'm bent double

21

with this cold sick feeling that I seem to have all the time lately. She's leaving me.

"It's a lovely spring day," her voice calls back.

She comes into the room, searching my eyes to see what I'm thinking.

"You ready, chuck?" I offer.

I stink of morning breath, cigarettes and coffee. She leans towards me for her kiss.

"Yeah. I'm looking forward to going back."

I press my hands over my belly. Time swings backward. I've just put her down on the floor to take her first steps.

"Change of plan, Mum," she hefts the portfolio strap onto her shoulder and makes towards the pool of sunlight in the hall. "I've decided to walk up to North Parade and catch the bus from there. It'll be lovely on the beach at this time of morning."

She turns at the door to give me a wave. I think of her first day at school. The door closes. I feel sorry for myself for not being young. For my life being fucking over and hers just beginning.

There's a smell coming off me: something past its sell by date. Into the bath I go, empty the last few drops of that scented stuff in, mask over my rotting odour.

Sun brightens the room and the patches of mould on the tiles look almost pleasant. The light on the water dances, gives my boobs an exotic appearance. I push a finger between my legs and have a stroke to see if it has any effect, trying for a minute just to persuade myself I'm not dead. But my heart's not in it. I'm all closed up, a renewed virgin.

Nobody has touched me since you Sebastian, honest. (Funny how easy it is to forget it was sex that caused Rebecca.) *You're such a liar, Bex.*

Water sloshes off me like a giant waterfall when I stand up. My big white towel is still draped over the rack in the kitchen, so I'm stuck with the small pink one that hardly covers my rude bits. In the hall I take my illegal peek into Rebecca's room. The PRIVATE sign warns me off but I'm compelled inside this time.

That painting; is it something she's been studying at college? Seen on the internet? It's almost a direct copy of the picture I used to love.

The bastard painting that ruined my life.

The Great Grief rears up and clonks me on the head. I have to run out the room because if I don't I'm gonna be sick all over Rebecca's clothes, never mind the pink carpet underneath them.

My towel's fallen off on the bathroom floor.

Naked and squatting, I empty myself out from the top end but then still need to sit on the toilet and shit. I feel better now.

It's no good, I'm gonna have to have a drink if I want to stand any chance of getting through the day. I'm shaking all over, can't even move.

Just a little bracer.

It's not my fault.

There're still a couple of hours before work, I'll have a sleep now I've settled my stomach with a tipple from the green bottle. Don't want to think about the memories that painting brought back. I get under the covers and pull my knees up to my stomach, squeeze my eyes shut tight.

Before I drift off to sleep I find my libido's not quite as dead as it seemed. It creeps up on me unexpectedly. I want him so bad. So I have him for a while, invisible as always but I feel him with every nerve in my body. *Are you angry with me, Sebastian?*

Later, I wish I hadn't bothered. My grief pours back into the gaping hole he's left behind. Sebastian. *Ihateyouhateyouhateyou.* I empty the remaining drink from the bottle and I furrow my way into the deepest, darkest sleep it's possible to find.

Five

Rebecca

We get a notice of eviction from the landlord *and* Mum loses her job. She was on her third warning for being late or not turning up at all. We're not sure what we're going to do.

A new word, *homeless*, settles on my tongue. I can't even make myself care. At least it feels like a way out.

"Break the circle." That's what my counsellor used to tell me.

Calling Dad, I don't get an answer on his mobile. So I pluck up the courage to ring his home phone.

But his wife answers and she doesn't like speaking to me. She says Dad's taken the twins to their football match and they're going for a burger afterwards. I get a funny feeling thinking of them all together; weird that those boys are my brothers. Half-brothers; Wendy's not my kind of mother anyway.

I sometimes imagine having days out with them all, but it hasn't happened yet. I've wondered what it would be like to go and live in Nottingham with their family. I picture their house with a basement flat or an attic apartment that has its own entrance via a staircase up the outside of the house where maybe I could live.

More realistically, it's probably one of those crowded together detached residences on a new estate like the ones springing up on the outskirts of every town. I don't know, I haven't seen it.

I send Dad a text: 'we r being evicted. I'm sorry but can u help?' I'd rather not ask 'cause I know he's offered lots of help in the past and Mum always refuses. Or she'd take the money and spent it on something else.

No prizes for guessing what.

Dad met me in Lincoln the week after I came out of hospital. He gave me an extra £50 to spend on art materials, so I bought some new brushes and oil paints.

"Promise me you won't give my money to your mum, Rebecca," Dad said. "She gets enough benefits as it is. Bitch."

I heard him say that under his breath and it gave me pins and needles.

"I'll cancel the standing order if you do, you know. I mean it. I'll set up a trust fund for you instead."

Red burned my face. It was like he knew Mum went through my purse looking for my bank card. Dad says I should buy clothes with the money he gives me but Mum always ends up borrowing them and I never like them as much after that.

At college we're studying the Pre-Raphaelites. To be honest I can't see the potential for developing a similar brotherhood in Skegness. We never discuss Art or Great Ideas outside of college.

I've kind of fallen in love with Dante Gabriel Rossetti. He had so much passion. It's stupid of me, right? He was a bastard the way he treated Lizzie Siddal, not marrying her until she was practically dead and then having an affair with his best friend's wife.

I can't stop thinking about Lizzie rocking an empty cradle after the stillbirth of their daughter.

I'm in the room with her, actually there, listening to her crying, pale and ethereal.

Get away from Gabriel; I want to tell her, *while you still can.*

"Don't take that crap from him. Listen, it'll be the death of you."

But she raises the draught of Laudanum to her lips, sinks even deeper into despair. And then I want to go and scream in Gabriel's face.

"How could you have treated her like that?"

They all used her.

She nearly froze to death in a bath of cold water modelling for *Ophelia* by Millais. But it's Rossetti's painting *Beata Beatrix* that really gets to me.

I don't know why death is so romantic.

Did you know Rossetti dug up the body of his wife years after she died so he could get back the book of poems he buried with her? He must've felt like such a shit afterwards, taking back the last gift he ever offered.

If I died, it'd be just like my mum to dig me up to get back something she would've put in the coffin with me when she'd been drinking, all sentimental.

Most likely it'd be her stash of gin.

"*Rebecca,*" she'd wail at my funeral. "I'm so sorry, it was all my fault. I'll never drink again! Here, take these with you, I'm gonna be a reformed character from now on."

... Until the next time she ran into some sort of problem. When only drink could solve it and she'd stop at nothing to get it back.

I play with paint on the canvas in the college studio long after the other students have gone. Every stroke of colour, and the way you apply it, matters. Being involved with the colours and the thick, buttery texture of the paint is the best feeling ever.

Almost.

There was something better, I know it.

As I lay in a smear of titanium white, the hot breath of a horse momentarily warms my neck; a faint purple glow covers everything. I shake my head and carry on loading the brush. I flatten it onto the canvas, tip first. This is more or less the same as all the paintings I've found myself making since I was in hospital, a bluish landscape with a white horse galloping towards the viewer and a human figure in the foreground.

A shadow hovers at my shoulder.

I've been sensing her a lot lately: a flash of a girl with dark eyes like mine. My imaginary friend. No wonder I haven't got any real ones.

"Moved on to Irish Modernism have you, Rebecca?"

It makes me jump, because of being so engrossed in the application of paint. I didn't hear my tutor, Tom Moran, come over.

The shadow vanishes. Did I hear a rustle as she went?

Tom's standing behind me, a mug of tea in his hand.

"Pardon?" I clear my throat.

He takes a sip of tea and winces, blowing out hard through his lips. "Hot."

Putting the mug on a trolley he comes to stand at the side of my easel, touching his lips with his tongue. I keep my eyes on the paint, catching the tang of sweat, not entirely unpleasant, when he moves back to look at my painting from a different angle.

He has thick brown hair tied behind his ears in a short ponytail, and wears one earring, a silver parrot. His eyes are almost black like a bird's. We're lucky to have Tom at the college in Skegness because he once won a quite important national painting prize.

"Irish Modernism. It's a transcription of *There is no Night*, isn't it? I've noticed you tackling the same subject a lot recently."

"Irish Modernism... I'm not sure what you mean." My face gets hot; I'm such an idiot sometimes.

He looks at me as if I'm stupid, then purses his lips and brushes the pointed beard on his chin with his fingers.

"Do you really not know the painting I mean?"

Head hanging, I say, "I don't think so." I want to say 'sir' but we use first names for our tutors in college, which I find difficult.

"Hang on a minute."

He goes to one of the computers along the other wall and taps about on the keys for a minute.

"Here it is!"

I wipe the excess paint off my brush with a rag and then dip the brush in turpentine, stroking it repeatedly on the neck of the jar. Lines of colour run down the glass sides and make blossomy shapes in the pool of clear turps at the bottom.

On the screen is a painting that looks just like mine, or rather, since Jack Butler Yeats's was made first, mine looks like his.

"Member of a group known as the Dublin Painters," says Tom. "There's actually an exhibition of his work on at the National Gallery in Dublin around about now. He's a celebrated Son of Ireland, Yeats is. Ever heard of the poet William Butler Yeats?"

"Hmm, I might have."

I haven't but I don't want to seem even more stupid. Tom nods.

"Well, that's his brother. Very artistic family."

He gazes at the screen a moment longer and then turns back to my painting and gives a low whistle.

"Can't believe this isn't a more or less direct copy of the Yeats. You must have taken in the image subliminally at some point. Amazing coincidence otherwise."

I start to hate my painting, but at the same time feel incredibly protective of it. That image is mine. The boy in the picture is *mine*; the horse is mine. I know it. I've seen them somewhere and it wasn't in any painting. I've been there; it was *real*.

The more I think about it the more I'm sure and although in my painting the boy is constructed by a few smears of paint there's a solid picture of him in my head, a sensory memory in a secret place in my mind. But I don't know where it comes from.

I don't say this to Tom. I take a scrap of paper and a pencil and write the name of the artist and the title of his painting.

"You ought to have a look at the rest of his work," says Tom. "I don't suppose you could get over to Dublin?" His voice peters out.

He's met my mum.

I think about the money that goes into my bank account from my dad. A wild idea slips into my head.

"When is the exhibition on?"

Tom's picked up his tea again and is sipping it with a thoughtful expression, his eyes scanning my painting.

The idea of flying to Ireland fills me with an overwhelming lightness and I have to hold on to the edge of the trolley where all my paints are laid out to stop myself wafting away.

Suddenly I want to see the paintings by Jack.B.Yeats more than anything; or perhaps I want it just a bit less than how much I want to be somewhere else, in a place unrelated to the life I have with Mum. That sounds awful, but it's true.

It's a stupid idea anyway; we don't even know where we're going to be living next month. But there's nothing wrong with asking.

"It's on right through the Easter holidays, I think."

About the time we're being evicted from our flat. I could just go.

I have a relative in Ireland, my dad's sister Iris. She settled there in the late eighties after joining a band. I don't even know her but I *am* her niece so she might want to see me.

A bubbling sensation starts in my stomach and I have to stop myself clapping a hand over my mouth because a sound is trying to work its way out and I'm going to look even more of an idiot than usual.

Tom's not looking at me anyway. He's swigged the last of his tea and is collecting his jacket from the boxed-in office in the corner of the room, hurrying home to his wife or to the pub, whatever he does after college.

"Caretaker'll be here to lock up in a few minutes, Rebecca. Best make sure you clean those brushes properly, good ones will last you years if you look after them. Have a good weekend, see you Monday!"

Six

Jack

Spring 1991

"I THOUGHT YOU were never coming out of that place," she said. "Makes me feel like I'm being strangled, the air in there does."

In the streetlight and the car headlights flashing by and the flickering neon sign over the door of the nightclub, Bex's face looked green. She clutched her stomach, bent forward. Strands of her dark hair had come away from the arrangement on the back of her head, making her look less Audrey Hepburn. My hand went out involuntarily and touched her skin; it was cold.

She shivered, bit on her lips.

"Don't you have a jacket?" I was trying to be practical. I fought to ignore the hard-on straining against my trousers. Leaning over her to arrange my jacket on her shoulders, her breasts gave softly against my chest as she straightened up, the puff of her warm breath in my ear.

It was the breath that did it; I couldn't restrain the moan I'd been holding back. Stepping away, embarrassed; turning it into a cough.

"S'alright," she murmured. "C'mere." She pulled me towards her again, fingers digging into my shoulders.

Bex wrapped her hand round the back of my neck and brought my head down. Her tongue probed the corner of my mouth, searching for a way in. Her other hand caressed my chest and belly, caught in shirt buttons on its way to my erection. She traced through the fabric of my trousers. I let out a breath. Her hand cupped the shape of my balls, squeezed gently, still working my mouth with her tongue.

But it was all too professional.

She broke away after a few moments. "What's up?"

Her eyes had gone flat.

My face was wet from her exploring tongue.

I could've had her, up against the wall in the alley between the club and the neighbouring building, but I would have been fucking a blow-up doll for all the emotion she showed.

"Nothing," I said. "It's just. . . "

On the dance floor I'd been attracted by her vibes; the vivid sadness that made her warm and sexual and human – exciting. A challenge. I wanted to soothe her pain. Her fiancé had been killed; I could make her forget him. She was young still.

She slumped back against the wall, head hanging; forgetting about me already.

I couldn't just leave her there.

And anyway, she was still wearing my jacket.

The bouncer with the crackling radio had gone back into the club.

Bex was drunk. Anyone could take advantage of her.

A group of clubbers swerved past us, arms linked, the girls' heels clicking on the pavement. Shrieking voices rang out against the noise of traffic. A few streets away a siren blared: police or ambulance. It was that time of night.

I put my arm around her. "Where can I take you?"

She fitted against me perfectly. Her head rested on my chest.

"I dunno, my Mum and Dad's house, I guess." Her voice faded. All vivacity had drained away.

We walked slowly and after a while she stopped to slip her feet out of her high heels. Like a child, she handed them to me to carry and the simple action made her seem human again.

I hooked the straps of both sandals over one finger and took hold of her hand. I squeezed it, hoping for a response and she fitted her fingers more carefully around mine, but didn't squeeze back.

At least we looked like a couple now. She kept her face angled towards the other side of the road as we walked and didn't speak to me at all.

I scanned the pavement ahead to make sure she didn't walk on anything dirty or dangerous, worrying that her feet might get too cold. While we walked back to Dave's parents' house I built up fantasies of taking her out on dates, getting to know her slowly, making her all right again.

She was only nineteen. She couldn't possibly be the lost cause Dave made her out to be.

We'd left the town centre behind us and were walking away from the main road into the linked streets of a council estate. Most of the houses were in darkness. Music blared loudly from one and people stood about in groups on the wide area of grass in front of the house. Scrunched-up beer cans had been thrown over the hedge.

I guided Bex away from the potential of cut feet. Someone shouted something as we passed. As we drew level with another front gate a dog suddenly lurched, barking, out of some bushes, making my heart pound. My fingers had tightened around Bex's and she squeezed mine back. We both laughed in a nervous way.

The walk could have gone on indefinitely and I would have been happy.

"It's just up there," Bex said.

She slowed down and tucked loose hair behind her ear. Then she put her hand on a gate.

"It's this one."

Her white feet glowed under the street lamps.

I didn't know whether I should follow her in or not.

A light was on in a front bedroom. She stood still and faced me, letting go of my hand to unclick the latch on the gate. Her sandals clacked together as I trembled. She reached out to take them, her eyes on mine.

In the dark I sensed a spark in hers, felt her gaze slide to the bulge in my trousers. Her not touching me made it worse, made me want her more. I tensed my stomach. She breathed fast. Then she spoke.

"You can come round the back."

I let her lead me, expecting to enter the house by a back door, but instead she indicated to the path leading from it. Bex stopped to put on her sandals, holding onto my arm, walking carefully on high heels. Skirting something on the dirt path she stopped to explain.

"Dog shit."

As if in answer a low growl came from the door behind us. Bex took my hand again.

"It's all right baby," she said, her voice slurring. "He can't get out. You're safe with me."

She seemed now like yet another person, different from the sad, passionate girl on the dance floor and the mechanical one who tried to have sex with me outside the nightclub, or the child-like creature who walked home holding my hand.

My erection twitched and I thought how it would feel to release myself inside her. The goose pimples on the exposed skin of my arms conducted a thrill of electricity through me.

At the end of the path Bex pulled open a shed door and clicked on a light fastened to the inside wall.

The space was ordered. A camp bed stood under the small window. A large bottle of water and a glass were on a shelf. A Mickey Mouse rug covered part of the floor.

Bex wound her arms around my neck, falling against me, her eyes half-closed and her lips brushing my cheek.

"It's only temporary," she said in a sad way.

Dave had said she was sleeping 'God knows where' and despite the aching in my balls I pushed her away from me but

34

still carried on holding her. My fingers stroked the skin of her neck.

"Don't you have a room in the house?"

"I haven't really lived there for a long time."

She tried to avoid my gaze. "Haven't lived at all for a long time," I thought she muttered under her breath.

Heavy earrings dangled against her neck. She was so damaged and beautiful. The aching in me spread across my stomach. Too perfect to be true and yet so flawed. It showed in the hopeless look she gave me. This was after I moved her face towards mine, cupping her chin with my hand. It made me even more determined to fix her.

A girl this young shouldn't have a look in her eyes like that.

She'd gone limp again. I wrapped her in my arms, lowered myself carefully onto the camp bed; folded her into my lap. This time I didn't try to calm my breathing. She shifted until her face was above mine, kissed me with her perfect mouth. My lips opened to let her in. She moved in my lap until the pressure on my cock was unbearable. My hand slid between us and wrenched open my zip, pulled her dress and knickers aside to make room for her to ram herself down on me hard.

"Wow, oh –*wowohwowohwow*," I heard myself crying out.

She called somebody else's name as she came but I was too lost to notice at the time.

I stroked her and held her for hours afterwards, both of us somehow crammed together on the camp bed. She cried inconsolably and I told myself I was embarking on the long journey towards making her well again.

2010

Looking back at how I behaved then I have to laugh. Or cry. I was so confident of my ability, and that I would have the patience to 'cure' Bex.

No matter how much I hate her now in real life, dreams like the one I just had about her cut me up every time. I remember that, in her way, she was as innocent as I was when we first got together.

The truth is she never pretended to be anything other than what I saw, but I insisted on keeping my blinkers on.

Wendy stirs beside me in bed and I try to control my agitation. If she picks up on my sadness she'll only want to comfort me, or expect me to comfort her if she picks up on what I'm upset about.

It will inevitably turn into her pain then. She'll want to make love, re-establish her hold over me.

I haven't got the strength for it right now.

I love her, but not in the way she wishes I did. Not in the way I loved Bex. Or Bex loved Sebastian.

My mind's filled with the lamplight eyes of my daughter gazing at me from the hospital bed. Even now, I'm convinced I can save Rebecca the way I was convinced I could save Bex. Stupid, stupid man. Tonight all the fury I had towards the mother of my child is superseded by the memory of that first night I held her. When there was still enough of 'Rebecca' showing through to make someone like me want to love her.

1991

I called her by her given name: "Rebecca" and she uncoiled in my arms like a snake.

"Don't ever call me that," she said. "Rebecca's dead, you have to understand. She's never coming back. I'm Bex. Rebecca stopped living when. . . it's over now. Bex is what you get. And believe me you won't want her once you find out what she's really like."

She pressed her face into the single pillow, muttering that she was a bad person, a hopeless case. I couldn't understand what she was saying – *'I've stopped living even though my body is carrying on.'*

I pulled her back towards me. Her face was blank.

"I've stopped all the clocks. My life is over."

She reminded me of a poem.

I murmured, "Shh, honey," stroked her hair.

She stopped talking, resumed the quiet crying. I thought if she cried long enough she'd get it all out.

I wrapped her long, dark hair around one of my wrists. My throat was parched, my trousers stained with semen and her juices had dried on my thigh.

We were both naked now. I would have to get dressed, walk the streets smelling of our sex, put the key in the lock of my home and slip in undetected. I'd have to get to the house before Mum and Dad woke up, put my clothes in the washing machine to avoid comments on the state of my laundry.

Mum couldn't help herself. Living at home I was still her boy. I had enough money saved for a deposit on a rented flat and decided there and then to forget my dream of buying a house and to look for somewhere I could move into as soon as possible.

I took another look around Bex's shed. It was no place for her to be living. I'd ask her to move in with me.

She'd cried herself to sleep. With difficulty I manoeuvred out from under her, nearly tipping the camp bed up by crawling off the end of it. She slept on.

My elbows bumped the walls as I pulled on my clothes. When I bent to retrieve my jacket from where it had slipped off her shoulders and onto the floor, I spotted the bottles, some lying empty on their sides; some full of amber or clear-coloured liquid, crowded under the cupboard at the side of her bed. I concluded that she needed me even more than I'd realised.

I was determined to be her knight in shining armour.

Seven

Bex

"WHAA..?"

Shit, it's cold. What's the point of bringing me a cup of tea if she doesn't wake me up properly? Makes me retch, drinking cold tea, she knows that.

I give my head a shake, makes the room spin. I shudder. Sweat pours off me and my hand snakes back under the covers, feeling like it don't belong anywhere near me.

"Rebecca!"

The cat pushes the bedroom door open. It's only got half its teeth left but that don't affect the volume of the yowl it gives me. When I move, wet seeps through my t-shirt.

"Oi, you bastard cat," I accuse. "You've peed in my bed again!"

Milly gives me a withering look. Who am I kidding? She jumps up and starts pummelling my stomach through the quilt, intensity in her eyes.

"Gerroff!"

I jerk my leg and she goes flying, twisting onto all fours as she hits the floor. Dust motes hover over the dirty orange carpet. The cat chases a fly. It stinks in here.

"'Ere, don't. . . "

Too late. In her pursuit Milly knocks a couple of boxes off the top of the cupboard. It's time I started packing for the move anyway. That's a joke, seeing as we don't even know where we're going yet. My hand disturbs an acrid tang on the damp sheet. Rebecca's face flashes through my mind, S'alright, I won't tell her, can stuff it in the washing machine before she notices.

All through the night my veins pulsed and throbbed. Thought they were gonna burst.

I must be ill.

Where did I go last night? I only had a couple of quid.

But it don't matter if I let a bloke buy me a drink every now and then. It's not like I get out much.

I promise I didn't get up to anything, Sebastian.

The social won't give me a payment 'til the end of next week. I'm gonna have to ask Rebecca if she's got any money for bread, some milk and my ciggies. Don't think I've got the nerve to ask her for money for drink as well though.

Is it Saturday? Think it is. Wonder where Rebecca's gone.

The room rocks. For a minute I can't make my body move – that scares me. When I promised Sebastian all those years ago I was gonna stop living even though my body would carry on I was young, didn't realise what it would be like. There was life and there was death; I knew that. But I couldn't've known then about all the stages in between. Stop all the clocks, I thought, cut off the telephone. Walk away from everything. That would be it.

"Having you was cheating," I say into the air, talking to the Rebecca that shouldn't have been born. Jack's Rebecca.

The dust motes swirl and for a weird second I think they're gonna spell out words or something. Sebastian, maybe. But then it settles again and everything's still the same as it was before.

She's put me out a sandwich with a bit of cling film over the plate. Milk's in the fridge and some orange juice already in a glass. Must've been shopping, her.

But I can't face it.

That nagging pain in my side goes on and on, little devil jabbing me with a knife. Head banging like a steel band.

I go to the kitchen drawer but the painkiller box is empty. Shit.

"Drink some water, Mum," her voice says in my head, but I feel sick.

The floor lurches. I can't feel my hands.

I take a sip of orange juice, gag, and have to rush over to the sink. It's pointless living like this. I've got to have a drink.

"Look in my eyes while you say it."

Rebecca made it seem like we were playing a game but she was dead serious.

"Repeat after me: I promise not to drink during the day anymore."

Just a little stiffener, that's all I need.

Ah, my friend from the green bottle hits the spot as usual. See, I've stopped shaking. It makes no sense to give it up.

After shovelling half a tin of cat food into the bowl on the floor I straighten up, pressing a hand to my head.

Rebecca comes in the back door with bright cheeks, hair glossy as a polished conker. Her freshness takes my breath away but at the same time anger stabs me in the chest.

She's wearing a new jacket, grey with some kind of fluffy material in the hood. Her old one's stuffed in a Fat Face carrier bag. She didn't buy that with the Child Benefit I give her. Come to think of it, I can't remember when I last did give her any. She stares me out.

The last finger-full of gin wavers in front of my eyes. After that it'll all be gone. Rebecca's purse pokes out the top of her bag.

It wouldn't be stealing; she'd get it back when the Social send me that cheque.

"Where've you been?"

"I had a chance to meet Dad in Lincoln." She pauses. "He only rang this morning."

She looks defensive. My nails curl into my palm.

"You were asleep," she says, "so I couldn't tell you. I tried to wake you but I had to go catch the bus."

Sneaked away, more like.

"I made you a cup of tea though," Miss High-and-mighty says. "Didn't you drink it?"

"Give you some money again did he?" I hate it when she calls Jack 'Dad'.

She looks evasive.

"He bought me this jacket, do you like it?" She fingers it possessively. She'll hide it, soon as she gets it out of my sight. "Do you like my new haircut as well?"

Flaunting her purchases; rubbing it in. I fold my arms.

She gathers her stuff up from the counter, turning to go to her room.

But at the last minute she adds, challenging my silence, "He brought the boys with him."

"You what?"

"He brought the boys to meet me – my brothers. They're so cute!"

"They're not really your brothers."

I'd do anything for a drink. She's not bothered about me. After everything I've done for her.

"They're only your half-brothers, and not even really that seeing as you don't even know them."

She tilts her chin up, slides her eyes off to one side. "Yeah, well, I'm getting to know them now, aren't I? They're great boys and they really seemed to like me. We went bowling. It was me and Josh against Dad and Bobby."

She's being deliberately provocative.

Suddenly they're all so much better than me.

But it's not them who've looked after her all these years. I want to give her smug face a slap, the bloody bitch; dig my fingernails harder into my palms.

"What did he say about the eviction?"

I manage to get it out before she has a chance to disappear into her bedroom.

She stops at the door, holding onto the handle.

"He said he couldn't do anything."

She doesn't know I can see the reflection of her profile in the mirror on her bedroom wall. Cast in violet from the purple netting on her window. She bites her lip; half closes her eyes. I guess she's praying I'll leave her alone.

"He'll soon get fed up of you anyway," I say. "I'm the one who's always been here for you, not him. He's got one of them glamorous wives now, a couple of sons, and a posh house. He'll always think of you as a hanger-on from a life he walked out on a long time ago. He just feels sorry for you, that's all."

She doesn't react. She's closed her door. Already put her music on.

I could try tapping on the door, tell her some jokes. We could watch a rerun of Casualty together. That's what usually happens.

She'll apologise for upsetting me later, like she always does.

I finish the last drop of gin in the bottle, fish about in the sideboard drawer for a number. My cousin Rick. I'm going to have to ask for his help otherwise I don't know where we're going to end up bloody living.

Eight

Rebecca

PUSHING ASIDE THE layers of netting I lean over the windowsill, my head outside in the darkness. It's a clear night with lots of stars. Mum used to tell me they were pinpricks in a huge black blanket that God puts over the sky at night. I don't know why she mentioned God because she isn't religious in any way, and we never went to church.

Those little boys I met today. My brothers. They don't seem surprised that I'm their sister. Sweet Bobby climbed up on my lap so trustingly at the bowling alley.

I felt immensely protective of him in my arms, my nose in his clean-smelling hair. I'm sure he'll never get nits or be given special shampoo by the health visitor for crusty scalp conditions.

It's not just Mum and me anymore.

I have a safety net. A family.

I finger the metallic stars on my curtain, pondering this.

I haven't spoken to Mum all evening but when I went for a shower, she was in my room. Damn! Don't ask me how I know; I've got a sixth sense about stuff like that. Anyway it's all quiet now. She's probably gone to the amusements, or maybe the Sea View up on the corner to blag a drink off someone. Tonight I don't really care as much as I usually would, I'm happy with having music on and the new book about Irish Modernism Dad bought me and the fact that he's going to call his sister Iris and arrange for me to visit her over Easter. He said he'll give her my mobile number so she can ring me.

Oh my God.

I'm crying again. I feel like Alice in Wonderland, stars reflecting in my pool of tears.

I listen to all my favourite songs, and then I realise they're actually *her* favourites. They were only ever mine because they were hers; she told me they were mine, I inherited everything from her. And I'm scared because I don't know where the boundaries between us begin and end.

Dad said, "You've got to start living your own life, Rebecca; you're not responsible for your mother."

And later when I mentioned that I really want to go to Ireland but I can't because of needing to be there for Mum he got irritated and started pulling Bobby along by the hand so fast I had to pick Joshua up and run to catch up with them.

"It'll be the best thing you could do for her in the long run."

We'd stopped to rest on a bench because Bobby was crying.

"She's spent her whole life expecting to be rescued. It's not fair that she wants you to be her knight in shining armour. Her neediness made you ill, for God's sake, can't you see that?"

He took me into Fat Face and insisted I let him buy me the jacket.

It's not about the money, it was the look on his face when he saw me wearing it, and me knowing he'd never want to borrow anything he's bought for me. We went into Waterstones and I read to my brothers while he looked for a title Wendy had asked him to buy. We couldn't believe there were so many books about cupcakes. He let the boys choose one storybook each but they both wanted 'Percy the Park Keeper', the one I'd been reading them, so our dad said they could have it but they would have to share nicely.

"What about you, Rebecca?"

"Pardon?"

"What book would you like? I've bought one for Wendy and one for the boys and I'm getting this boating one for myself. It's only fair that I get one for you as well."

So we went to have a look in the Art section and I found the book on Irish Modernism. It's more of a history book than an art one and it seems to contain a lot about the poet William B. Yeats, the artist's brother, and not much about the painter himself, but it'll give me a background on the culture of the country I'm going to visit. My tutor says that context is the important thing in art. Dad seemed to approve of my choice.

There's a chill in the air. I pull the window to and draw the curtains, tuck my feet under the purple furry blanket on the end of my bed. I'm about to settle in for a read of my new book when I hear the door handle flick up. The next sound is mum falling into the hall – three clattering footsteps followed by the crash as she hits the floor. She ought to be in pain but she just screeches with laughter.

I check what I'm wearing in case she vomits on me; decide the old vest top I've changed into is dispensable. Ironically it's one of hers that I borrowed from the clean laundry basket when I was putting mine in the wash.

Propped up like a doll against the sofa, she cackles when she sees me.

"Ahhh, if it isn't me Rebecca. Look at the face on you, so disapproving of your old mum. I've only been out having a bit of fun, me duck, you should try it sometime!"

Her ugly laugh turns into a vicious cough, leaving her covered in sweat. The look she gives me once the spasm subsides is proper poison.

"Fucking bitch. You're a killjoy, you."

I hold my breath against the alcoholic gusts rasping from her mouth and try to haul her up. Straightaway she slumps sideways into a heap on the floor. She'd quite happily lie there for the rest of the night, not notice how cold her body gets. A pile of sleeping bones is all she'd be.

Let her rot.

I brace my knees; drag her into a sitting position again. She's heavier than she looks for someone that scrawny.

She spills out sick and whines.

"Leave me alone, interfering cow. Miss goody-bloody-two-shoes!"

And I would like to. Oh, I would.

Keep the thought of Ireland in your head.

I smell the urine a second before the steam drifts up. It hits the back of my throat. God help me.

Don't let yourself cry, she'd only laugh.

I'm panting with the effort.

"Help me then, Mum, you're all wet."

Some instinct makes her help drag the wet knickers over the ends of her skinny legs, catching on the buckles of her sandals. She won't remember any of it in the morning but I will. I give one last heave under her armpits until she's on her side on the sofa in her damp skirt. I'm not moving her any further.

I wish I could get some water down her but it would only dribble back out. I fetch a bucket to put under her face and a blanket to cover her. I tread sheets of newspaper into the pool on the carpet and gather them up with rubber-gloved hands; shove them with the knickers into a carrier bag which I tie shut and stuff in the kitchen bin. I'm not going to the trouble of unbuckling her sandals. I just want to wash my hands.

Turns out, she's not quite unconscious.

"Rebecca," it's only a murmur.

"What?"

I'm not prepared to have one of those maudlin 'you know I love you baby girl' conversations. I head towards the bathroom. But it's not about that. She's muttering about moving. Saying 'caravan'. I go back over.

"What did you say?"

Her words are so slurred I can only just pick them out.

"Caravan."

I wonder if she's managed to get us a temporary pitch on one of the many sites around here. We lived in a caravan with Dad when I was little.

I wait a moment longer but no more words come out. So I lean forward, hold my breath, bring myself to push back a strand of long hair from her sweat-sheened face. Don't want it to get in the way of her mouth if she's sick again. But nothing.

I go to the bathroom and scrub myself.

Back in my room the book lies open on the bed. I place it on the shelf of my bedside cabinet. My latest blue landscape painting with the white horse and the boy seems to beckon me into it from the easel in the corner. I fix my gaze on it; *forget that old hag is out there in the living room*. I wish I could go to that landscape. I know, impossibly, that it's a place I've been happy before.

I sense the pale, oval face of my shadow-companion at my side as I settle into bed. "Who are you?" I want to ask but when I turn my head she's gone, never really there. It leaves me feeling lonelier.

Just after midnight my mobile goes off. A voice I don't recognise says my name with a questioning tone. I realise straight away it's my Auntie Iris.

Nine

Bex

ARRGHH. HEAD HURTS. Think I'm gonna die. I used to call this a hangover but to tell you the truth, I don't get them anymore. I just feel shit until I drink again, so this is different. This is agony, right behind my eyes. And I haven't even opened them yet. But that's nothing compared to the pain in my side. I'm a fish being gutted. Maybe some fucker slipped something into my drink last night.

Don't seem to be wearing any knickers. Try remembering what happened, keep my eyes tight shut. I'm balanced on a narrow plank of wood. Don't move, Bex, or you might fall off. Rootle through the tattered scraps of my mind. Huge gaps glare through the explanation of my shenanigans last night but it reminds me I went to the seafront with the money I took from Rebecca's purse.

⸻ ❦ ⸻

There's something exhilarating about the strength of the wind battling in off the sea. It bashes its way through the shifting metal structures of the pleasure fair and they clank and sigh. It carries the scent of candyfloss and hot doughnuts, snatches of amplified song, the voices of bingo callers and canned music from the amusements on South Parade. I clutch my newly acquired bottle, something propelling me to totter towards the boating lake, circle round it to the deserted beach. I taunt myself with my fear of the sucking darkness of the sea at night. My heels sink into the damp sand and I pull them out, reinsert them one step at a time, slow steps forward. Beyond the dancing lights and relentless noise of fun, fun, fun, both the sea and the sky above it seem like a gaping black hole, filled with the bellowing crash of waves. Standing there in the dark I shiver, completely alone. I should let it take me.

But my body stumbles back up to the front where it's all noise and flashing lights. Head into 'All the Fun of the Pier', the bottle in my shoulder bag banging against my hip. I thrust silvers and coppers into the slots, listen to the crash of coins falling in the metal tray. I grab and feed them back in. When all my coins have gone I find Diane who worked with me at Funland Bingo. She's with her husband Jim, so I scrounge a lift back with them to The Sea View.

"'Ere, did you know, Jim," says Diane after they buy me the first double gin. "Our Bex has got the voice of an angel? Used to be a singer, she did. I bet if you bought 'er another double she'd show you."

After that it's a bit blurred but I remember a bunch of us went into a back room and they pushed the tables to the walls. Harry the landlord's nephew brought in his guitar and we had a bit of a sing-song. At the end of the evening there was only me and Harry left. The door had a bolt on the inside. Half my age, he is, but it didn't seem to bother him. He fetched another bottle from the bar.

I was known for my voice once. Used to get me out to sing at the parties we had every summer at Newtown Linford, they did. Sebastian'd be standing there watching me, tears in his eyes. Wouldn't recognise me now, he wouldn't. But that's the whole point, dummy. I stopped being her when he died.

Try opening my eyes.

It turns out I'm half-lying on the wooden bit at the edge of the couch. Can't remember how I got here. The orange bucket stares up into my face. A thin slime of green bile at the bottom makes a mirror for the Halloween mask I guess is me. My eyes still feel like they're being burned by a laser beam.

I manage to roll my head back and Rebecca looms into view, or rather a fuzzy-edged silhouette of her does. I sense her trembling with indignation.

Uh-oh.

"You fucking stole my money, didn't you?"

I've never heard Miss Prissy-bum swear before. It's a bit of a shock; my stomach lurches in response. One hand fumbles its way to my hurting side and I fish about in my brain for a recollection of where the rest of my body parts are meant to be, find another hand and press it to my forehead.

"Give it a rest, ducky," I manage to croak, "Your poor old mum's not feeling that great today."

"Oh my God!" explodes Miss Feisty-pants-this-morning, "And I suppose you reckon I am? I'm sick of having to pick you up off the floor, Mum. It's disgusting."

There, she's said it. My own daughter's sick of her mum. She thinks I'm fucking disgusting. After everything I've done for her. It's because of that bastard Jack getting his claws back into her, but that doesn't make her words hurt me any less.

What is the point of me being alive, I ask you? There's not a damned soul in the world that cares if I live or die.

"I was only having a bit of fun, duck, why would you want to deny me the only bit of pleasure I have, eh? It's not as if you're stuck in the house yourself these days are you? What with you always staying late at college getting up to I don't know what. And now you're spending more time with your father who's suddenly become so popular, even though he didn't give a shit all those years."

I struggle to drag myself into a sitting position and she don't even lean forward to help. She watches me in that holier-than-thou way. I wipe the sweat off my face.

"Mum. . . you can't go on like this. . ."

"Like what, would you care to explain exactly what you mean, *Rebecca*? I suppose what you're saying is I'm not good enough for you now."

She doesn't say anything. I bat aside the glass of water she tries to hand me. Some of it spills and lands in the bucket, disturbing the green film. I retch.

"You know I can't drink water in the morning."

"You need to drink it, Mum, if not you'll get dehydrated."

"Oh what would you know about it, Miss Goody-two-shoes, never put a foot wrong in your life have you? Well fuck you, should be a social worker you should."

She stares at me, giving the fucking sad-eyes.

She's wearing a mini-dress with flowers on over blue leggings. There's a flower clip in her hair.

She looks fresh and pretty. Shit.

"I'm sorry, duck."

Can't stand her going on at me all morning, can I?

"Pass me the water again and I'll try a sip just for you."

She perches on the edge of the armchair.

"I wish you wouldn't say that."

"Say what?"

What have I done wrong now, for fuck's sake?

"Say 'just for me'. I want you to do it for yourself, Mum. I can't be around every second to make sure you're all right, can I?"

I do my best to get the water down. Between sips my head keeps sinking forward, like my neck's made of elastic. Something niggles in my brain.

She said she can't always be around.

Her shiftiness reminds me of when she asked if she could go on the residential trip to Germany in Year 9 and I told her I couldn't cope on my own for a whole week, she knew that.

I catch her ranging gaze. Humph. I'll change the subject.

"I've got us somewhere to move to, by the way."

"You were muttering something about a caravan last night."

Pause. *Muttering* – cheeky bitch.

"I had to give your Uncle Rick a ring."

Another surge of bile hits my chest. I burp. Rebecca winces.

"Who's Uncle Rick?"

"Oh. I don't suppose you've seen him since you were a tot. He's my cousin. Lives on a bit of a farm the other side of Lincolnshire. He's got a caravan we can use on a stretch of land he's planning to develop. It's empty at the moment, all plumbed in and everything. It sounds okay."

Rebecca's silent for a minute. You can almost see her brain ticking over.

"Where is it?"

"I've told you, other side of Lincolnshire. A village about ten miles south of Lincoln. There's a pub across the road he says, where I might be able to get a job."

"But I'd have to leave college!"

"I've thought about that. You could transfer to Art College in Lincoln; there'll be a bus."

"Mum. I've only just got settled back at college. I'm enjoying it. I don't want to have to change courses, make new friends and start all over again. And anyway it might be a different course from the one I'm doing! "

"Sometimes we have to just get on with things even if they're not what we want. You can still do your art; you can still go to college; just a different one, and you can keep doing your English correspondence course."

I'm getting the shakes.

"I've sorted us out with somewhere to live which might not be up to your high and mighty standards, madam, but at least it's a roof over our heads and the possibility of a job for me. Your Uncle Rick can give me a reference; you know I've got no chance of getting a job around here."

Her head hangs. "When are we moving?"

"We've got until just before Easter so you can finish the term off at college here and get your tutor to help you organise a transfer to Lincoln. We won't be able to take everything with us."

I push myself up off the settee, totter carefully over to the sink, conscious of the lack of fabric between my legs. Where the fuck did I lose my knickers?

I still have my high-heeled sandals on, the straps pinching and rubbing. I catch a whiff of my armpits when I lean forward and grab the sink, fight nausea.

Life's so fucking shit.

Dunno why I bother.

"Anything you want that we haven't got room for you'll have to get your precious father to look after," I say. "Rick's gonna send us a van at the beginning of the Easter holidays and we'll follow on straight after in the car."

She's standing at the side of me, fidgeting. The nervous expression on her face pisses me off. I feel like crap, can't she just leave me alone?

"What's the matter now?"

She takes a deep breath, gives me a pleading look with those puppy-eyes of hers. Then she says it.

"I won't be here at Easter."

Ten

Rebecca

I'M SO EXCITED!

Dad's picking me up at nine o'clock. Nine o'clock, bloody hell, it's only half-past-eight. It feels like the longest half-hour ever.

Arrghh.

Oh yeah and I only just got my passport, was worried it wouldn't come on time. I keep looking at the picture on it, so surprised that it's really me. I look. . . hopeful.

Mum hasn't got out of bed to see me off but I didn't expect her to. Don't care anyway.

She was on another bender last night, here in the flat with her mate Diane. She knew I wanted to get to sleep early.

I look out onto Sea View Road as traffic goes by. Sea mist hangs in the air, and I know it's gonna be a lovely day...

Diane's going with Mum to the caravan on Monday to help her settle in. Everything in the flat is packed away. I didn't think Mum would get her act together but yeah, she's been on a mission. We're taking our beds and the living room furniture, but a lot of our stuff has been thrown into a skip the landlord provided. He would have done anything to help us get out. I guess he wants some new tenants who'll pay the rent on time.

Dad's furious that Mum's making me move to some obscure village.

He says they'll all be inbred. Not to mention we'll be living in a caravan. He offered to pay rent on a room in a shared house for me if I wanted to stay in Skegness. Some other students, Tara and Kelvin, are looking for a new housemate, but I'd better stay with Mum. For now. In a new place where we could actually make a go of it.

Dad said Art College in Lincoln'll be great though; it has a good reputation. Tom was sorry to see me go. He's told me to invite him to my end of year show in the summer and although he's impressed with my dedication to perfecting my transcription of what he thinks is the Yeats painting, he'd like to see me develop a new theme.

The cat jumps onto the back of the sofa. I stroke her absently, avoiding her stinky breath. She's nearly as old as me. Mum says we should have her put to sleep but neither of us can face it.

"See you on the other side of Lincoln, Milly."

Her real name's Matilda. She purrs and arches her scabby back when I stroke her. We ought to take her to the PDSA again for some more cream.

OhGodohGod, it's nearly time. I work my way around the boxes to Mum's bedroom door, push it open.

She's face down on the bed in the clothes she wore last night. Her hair's a collection of tangled clumps. Sorrow and fury forms a scream in my chest. I want to shake her, hit her, kick her off the bed, lift her by the hair, shout in her ear.

"Wake up, you bitch, I'm going to do something exciting, a good thing for me: why can't you be happy for your daughter, just for once?"

Instead I move closer and whisper "Mum?" in her ear.

There's no reply, only a moan. She turns her face slightly on the pillow with a scrunched-up frown, her clenched fist scuttering its way up the bedspread to her face where it presses itself into her cheek.

"Mum, I'm going in a minute, will you wake up and say goodbye?"

"Whaaaa?"

Her mouth makes smacking noises and another groan comes out. I grab a gin-smelling glass from her bedside table and go to the bathroom, fill it with water, don't know whether to pour it over her or try and get her to drink it.

Shit.

I can't leave her like this. I try to get her to lift her head and drink some but she pushes me away.

"Leave me alone. Go away to Ireland, why don't you?"

Her voice is a hoarse croak. Dribble slug-trails her neck. I dig my newly-painted fingernails into the palms of my hands, count to ten.

"I am in a minute, I just came in to say goodbye."

"Well you've said it."

She buries her face in the pillow, turning the other way. The doorbell rings. Dad.

"So, I'm going then."

She makes a tiny squeak but then with an immense effort raises her head again, puckering her mouth for a kiss.

Holding my breath, I barely make contact with the dry, cracked skin of her lips then draw back quickly with a long exhalation.

"Bye then."

But I can't seem to make my feet move.

It comes at last, a tiny smile managed without opening her eyes.

"Be off with you then; better not keep his majesty waiting on the doorstep. See you in a couple of weeks at the new place."

Dad helps me carry my art equipment and a few canvases to the boot of his car. He'll deliver them to our caravan once I've moved in.

"All set?" My case is on the back seat next to the twins.

"Can we go and see our Auntie Iris in Ireland as well, Daddy?" asks one of the twins.

We're heading for the A158 and Robin Hood Airport. I get a tickling feeling in my tummy to hear Dad reply.

"Not this time, buddies, but maybe we can all go back there with Rebecca in the summer, if she makes a good impression on Iris."

He winks at me and I only feel the tiniest pangs of guilt for Mum.

———�———

It's a small airport, really, but it's the biggest one I've ever been in and that's because I've never been on a plane.

I'm shivering. One of the twins takes my hand; I think it's Bobby but my vision's gone blurry so I can't really see.

Dad has to push me in the back to get me in the queue for security. My excitement is diminishing, replaced by fear. The ticket is clutched so tightly in my hand Dad has to prise my fingers apart. He smooths it open and passes it to the attendant, who also needs to check my passport. She studies the photo for a second then looks at me with a smile.

Someone tells me to take off my jacket and boots and put all my stuff in a tray and go through some kind of electronic doorway. Dad and the twins hug me goodbye. Joshua cries, begging me to come back. He thinks I'm going forever.

The scariest part is walking off on my own.

Light from the high windows hits the whitish floor, making a pathway, and it doesn't take me long to find the right area to wait in.

Then I can't believe I'm actually on a plane.

It's not much different from a slightly grubby bus inside except when it takes off, then I feel as if I've left my stomach and head on the ground while the rest of me soars into the sky. My hands grip tightly together and pressure builds up in my ears, but I love the thought that I'm flying.

———⋈———

Ireland

At Dublin airport my head spins. A woman from my plane shows me where I should go, and it's like a moving-pavement - an escalator that doesn't even go up. I roll my bag onto it and get carried along in the tide of people.

The main concourse is huge. Iris messaged me a photo of her but there are so many people around I don't know where to look. Just as the panic begins to start a tall boy comes striding towards me with a grin on his face as if he knows me. It's confirmed by him thrusting out a hand, speaking to me in an Irish accent.

"You're Rebecca, aren't you? Hi, I'm Connor O'Toole."

But it sounds like *hoi, oim Connor O'Toole.*

Okay. So he's gorgeous, more than.

He has dark curls and eyes that remind me of blueberries, a kind of smoky navy blue. He must be a year or so older than me. There's a flutter in my stomach; it's only natural. I return his greeting, confident that he must have been sent to meet me as nobody else here would know my name. There's a slight tingle in my fingertips as I take back my hand; must be a lot of static in this building.

"I'm Iris's godson," he says as we're hurrying towards the exit, him carrying my bag.

Too manly to pull it along, I imagine.

"She's just parking the car. She sent me in to find you 'cos she didn't want you to get worried. Fair play to you though, you've managed to get yourself over here in one piece... Ah, there she is."

He points towards a striking woman grinding out a roll-up on the paved area outside the main doors. She looks up as Connor introduces us.

Iris is wearing what I think is called a donkey jacket, like a man. She's tall like Dad and she has the same greenish eyes. Her hair's brown and wavy, again like Dad's. She looks familiar.

"Come here, girl," she orders me.

And she puts her arms around me in a hug. I allow myself to be buried in it.

Eleven

Jack

1991

I THOUGHT ABOUT her all day whilst I was on the stall.

"Buy one, get one free!"

Flourishing a bunch of car sponges, I pictured the way Bex dipped her chin in that graceful motion as she stood shivering outside the club.

I handed change to a customer.

"We need to get rid of these last few chamois," said my dad.

He coughed as he turned away from me to light up. I'd promised Mum I wouldn't let him smoke but what could I do? He'd ignored his own doctor's advice to give up smoking because of his heart.

"Here, madam," a woman rifled through a box of porcelain door handles.

"How about I let you have three of those for a fiver?"

The woman shook her head and moved on to the next stall. And at that moment I remembered how surprisingly soft Bex's belly was as I traced her contours with my trembling fingers.

Anticipation tingled in me all day.

"You look like you got ants in your pants, son," said my dad. "If you've got that much energy you can sort those nuts and bolts into pairs and pop 'em into paper bags, 20 at a time. Mark 'em up at a pound."

I couldn't wait to get home and examine the 'property to let' section of the daily newspaper, find a flat that would be suitable for us both to live in. At the same time I was terrified she'd be gone when I went to find her.

She couldn't have been living in that shed long or else Dave would have known about it. In fact none of it added up. There were no clothes in the shed, no signs that she did anything apart from sleep there, and drink. It occurred to me that she might only use the shed for sleeping with men. But that didn't make sense either. The Mickey Mouse rug on the floor suggested it was a place of comfort for her.

Anger gnawed at me. Why wasn't her family looking after her? She'd had a bad time. She was fragile and vulnerable. It made me feel cosseted, still living with my mum and dad. That made it more important to look after someone who needed me. I decided to give Dave a ring after work, see if he fancied a pint. Then I changed my mind. It'd be better to wait until the following evening after football practice. It'd seem odd otherwise. It wasn't like we were the best of mates.

"I can see you're not gonna take my advice, mate," Dave said as he picked up his pint.

We'd won our practice game so we were in a good mood, Dave especially since it was mainly down to him.

"I was just trying to save you from grief. Not that I'm not pleased someone's bothered about my sister. But our Bex, well, I reckon she's not quite right in the head at the moment. I don't want to give away the family secrets, it's up to her what she tells you, but she's been through a seriously bad time. Fuck, man." He took a long swig of his beer.

I said nothing, just waited.

"I told you her fiancé was killed in an accident, right? But some other stuff went on as well. Stuff even I don't want to talk about. Horrible. No wonder she don't seem to be getting over it. Like I said before, she needs psychiatric help, I'm convinced of it."

He finished the beer in another long gulp and put his empty glass on the bar.

There was an awkward silence. I ordered another two pints, slid one over to Dave.

"She been living at home?"

He squinted at me, picked up his second pint. I was only halfway through my first. Didn't want to seem like a lightweight so I took another swig. My stomach didn't feel right.

Dave was watching me funny. Probably seeing me properly for the first time.

"She's in and out." Dave said.

"She only came back home the other day 'cause it was my birthday. Got dressed up so pretty as well. She could make a lot of herself if she wanted to. Clever girl, you know, got her A Levels and all that."

He lifted a hand in greeting to a guy I vaguely recognised over the other side of the bar. His pint left an outline of foam on his upper lip, which he wiped with the tips of his fingers.

"Could have gone to university but the only thing she was bothered about was that Sebastian feller."

And now he's gone, I thought. Could she ever be that bothered about me?

Dave tapped the rim of his glass with a nicotine-stained finger. Lost in his own thoughts, it looked like.

"She's not really one of us, Jack," he eventually said. "Not a proper Nottingham lass. Spent her school holidays in a posh Leicestershire village with our grandma. Our mam couldn't cope, 'cause of her depression. Our Bex should've been adopted out permanently with Gran, I s'pose. Might've been the best thing for her. She don't know whether she's coming or going now."

My stomach curdled. Poor Bex. It intrigued me to learn she'd been planning to go to university. What could I give her that would match up to that potential?

"Couldn't she go back and live with your gran?"

Dave drained his second pint. I pushed my second one over to him, not a cat in hell's chance of me drinking it.

"Go to Uni and all that?"

Dave laughed. "Thought you were after her, mate. But no, you're right. Would've been the best thing for her."

Someone thumped him on the shoulder just as he lifted the third glass to his lips. Beer spilled on the bar. Dave laughed again and made a threatening gesture to the friend who'd greeted him. I sensed he was getting fed up of me asking questions.

"Our gran died not long after Bex's fiancé was killed."

He took enough time to finish off his conversation with me before giving the thumbs-up to the guy who was brandishing a handful of darts at him.

"And our granddad's just gone into a nursing home in the village. So she can't go back there. I s'pect she'll get herself sorted out eventually – she's a bright kid like I said. Just needs time. Or maybe you'll be the one to do it, mate. All right, all right." he said to the guys over at the darts board. To me, he said, "Sorry mate; gotta go, see you at the weekend."

My sense of urgency grew. The idea of rescuing Bex took over my life. I moved into a one-bedroomed flat two weeks after spending the night with her in that shed. I hadn't seen her since then, except in my own head. Mum and Dad thought I'd gone mad.

"You've ruined everything," Mum said when I told her what I was doing.

She hit my chest with the palm of her hand.

"Every penny you've saved up, pouring it away into a rental. You idiot. You'll never afford a place of your own now. You must really hate us to want to move out so desperately."

She sniffed and dabbed her eyes. Then she played her best card.

"First Iris leaves us for no reason and now you."

I felt guilty but I was sick of having to do everything Mum's way because of the choices Iris made.

"I can't tell you why I'm doing this at the moment, Mum, but once I get things sorted out I'll let you know. It's not because I don't like living with you. And I'm sorry you're hurt, but it's my life and you can't live it for me."

As soon as I got the flat sorted, I looked for Bex everywhere I could think of, more desperately each day. One night I even visited the shed in her parents' garden, opening and closing their front gate as quietly as I could; creeping past the side of their house in the dark like a burglar. I would have looked like such an idiot if I'd got caught, not to mention her dad would probably have set the dog on me. No light came from the shed, and it was only when I tried the door that I realised it now had a padlock on it. She could have been in the house I supposed, but it was around midnight and I didn't know which room was hers.

So I went home to the flat I'd only got because of her. I wondered how the fuck I could have made such a stupid mistake, perfectly aware it was my own fantasy I'd been acting out. She'd done nothing to suggest she'd wanted me for anything more than a one night stand.

But she waited for you outside the club that night, I kept telling myself. She must have liked you.

I masturbated in the new bed (the one I only bought because of her), fantasised about the sex we'd had. But I could never explode out of my body again the way I'd done when she was with me.

I always got up and changed the sheets in the middle of the night.

I started to think I'd imagined our connection.

"What's up, son?" Dad asked me at work. "Woman trouble, is it?"

"Something like that."

I ground my heel into the gravel under the stall.

"Usually is," he said. "Don't think there's any other kind. Oh by the way, pop in and see your mum won't you? She's been miserable since you left. Here you are, duck," His attention was taken by a customer trying to decide between two different brands of furniture polish. "I'll give you 50p off this one, that'll make it 25p cheaper than the other brand. Can't say fairer than that, can I?"

The customer went off happy and Dad carried on talking about Mum.

"Come back home with me after work, lad; she'd love it if you stayed for your tea. She's got, whaddatheycallit? Empty nest syndrome."

"All right, Dad." It'd save me getting fish and chips again.

He grinned and I moved to the other end of the stall to take care of a bunch of customers who'd suddenly crowded up. I served the first two and as I let the coins drop from my hand into my money belt there was a voice I recognised.

"So this is where you hang out all day."

Bex. She seemed different in daylight. Sadder than ever. Her long hair hung loose around her shoulders, fringe almost obscuring her eyes. She was wearing a knee-length denim dress with a thin, hooded coat that had probably once been brightly coloured.

"I was looking for some shampoo," she said. "Do you sell it?"

Her hair did look like it needed a wash. Thoughts of where she might be living, a shop doorway, an abandoned shed on an allotment, rushed through my mind.

"No," I said, "I'm sorry, we don't."

I wanted to say *come home with me and I'll run you a bath with the jasmine-scented bubble bath I bought, and light the candles I chose especially for you.* But she would think I was some sort of stalker. She seemed at a loss.

"Oh. Do you know where I could buy some?"

My dad had come over, looking her up and down.

"What's that you're after, love?"

Bex's eyes met mine.

I coughed.

"She's looking for shampoo, Dad. But it's all right, I can manage."

I had the urge to elbow him out of the way. It took him a minute to take the hint. Meanwhile, I could feel heat spreading up my neck and face.

Bex ran her fingers through the range of different-sized hinges in a compartmentalised tray. The tarpaulin stretched over the top of the stall flapped rhythmically. Dad stared at my face, then sucked air in through his teeth.

"Oh, I get it, lad. Right you are. I'll just be over there."

He looked over his shoulder at me as he crossed the walk-way to have a chat with the woman on the handbag stall opposite.

"I've been looking for you," I told Bex when he'd gone.

"Yeah, I know. My brother told me." She looked at me sideways.

"Was there something you wanted?"

You, I thought. Only you.

"I wanted to see if you'd go out with me. Take you for dinner or sommat."

She tucked her hair behind one ear and I could see her eyes at last, as deep and brown as I remembered. Her skin looked pale, fingernails were dirty. She pressed her lips together and the sensation I had when they opened over mine flashed through me. I hoped I wasn't going to get an erection.

I moved slightly so that I was standing behind a stack of boxes. She just looked at me.

"Not just that," I blurted out. "What it is; is that I've got this flat, you see. If you need anywhere to stay, y'know. You'd be welcome. Dave said – you were kind of between accommodation at the moment but maybe you've got somewhere by now."

The red flooded my face completely, I could feel it. What a jerk. No-one was that transparent. I should've stuck with the offer of dinner. She'd never want to go out with me now, let alone live with me. Idiot. I'd ruined my plan.

A new bunch of customers had come up and Dad was making his way back over from the handbag stall. Bex twisted her hands together. She stopped and shifted her bag further up her shoulder, trapping her hair beneath the strap.

"You might regret this," she said, "but I am in a bit of a fix at the moment."

She eyed Dad nervously, beckoned me to the opposite end of the stall from where he was serving a customer. She leaned forward and for a moment I thought she was going to kiss me but she just wanted to whisper something in my ear.

"I was staying with this friend of mine, Mary, sleeping on her floor. But she's kicking me out. Accused me of sleeping with her boyfriend. *Which is not true.* As if I would."

She widened her eyes at me. My heart pounded painfully.

"Says I'm not pulling my weight as well. Cheek of it." She wound a strand of hair around her finger. "Anyway, if you really mean it, I'd be grateful of a few nights. Just temporary, 'til I get myself sorted out, you know."

I couldn't believe it was happening. My dream was coming true.

"That's. . . it's brilliant," I said. "Of course, just a few nights as you say. Listen," I could see Dad getting impatient. The queue of customers building. "We'll be all packed up by about five o'clock. Meet me back here with whatever stuff you want to bring and I'll give you a lift to the flat in the van. After I've dropped Dad off."

I remembered I'd agreed to go back to his and Mum's with him for dinner. Damn. I'd just have to sort it out with him later. Buy Mum a bunch of flowers to apologise.

"Don't worry, Bex." She was already moving away as I rushed out the words. "I've got shampoo at the flat."

Twelve

Rebecca

I WRIGGLE OUT of Iris's strong grip. She comes across as way more assertive than Dad. Connor gives me a wink and a grin.

"Wouldn't want to get into a fight with this one now, would 'ya?" His accent makes me laugh.

"Well, look at you now; you're all grown up aren't you?" Iris says.

I can't believe it but she has tears in her eyes.

She catches me looking and makes a rough wiping motion with the back of her hand.

"Well, I haven't seen you since you was a little girl, have I?"

My cheeks burn.

I adjust the flower clip I wear to keep my fringe back, then shove both hands into the pockets of my new hooded jacket. The two of them are staring at me with benign smiles.

"Have we met before? I don't remember."

"Ah, you was only a tiny bit of a girl. I went over when your Granddad died. Not long before your mam and dad split up. I was trying to teach you to play the accordion, you probably don't remember. Your mam sang. She had quite a voice on her. Does she still sing?"

We head towards some uncomfortable-looking benches out the way of the crowds, perch on the edge of one.

"Give us your keys, Iris old bird," Connor says. "I'll put our Rebecca here's case in the car."

"He's a rum one, that boy." It's obvious Iris is really fond of him.

I bow my head, inspecting cigarette ends on the tarmac under the bench. My voice shakes.

"My mum doesn't sing much now." I mutter under my breath, "except when she's drunk, so I suppose she does."

Iris leans closer, brushing a hand on my leg.

"Jack told me about the problems she has. It must be really hard for you. She was such a pretty girl, your mam, only a few years older when I last saw her than you are now – you look just like her, Becky."

My head shoots up.

"I don't... can you not call me Becky? It's just Rebecca. Sorry."

I've probably ruined things with her already, spoilt the chance of coming back here with Dad and the twins in the summer. I should have just let her call me Becky, it wouldn't have hurt, oh why do I have to be so selfish? Inside the pockets of my jacket my hands coil up tight. I sneak her a sideways glance.

"Sorry," I mouth.

But she's laughing.

"I can tell you're my niece, the way you snapped at me then. We're going to get along fine! Rebecca it is from now on." She gets up off the bench, stretching. "My back's killing me. I got Connor to help me move the chicken run this morning; they've made such a mess of the ground where they were."

"You've got chickens?"

Obviously she has. She must think me stupid.

"Ah yeah. And a dog, a goat, and two horses. Connor and his brothers help me exercise them – the horses. Do you ride?"

"I've always wanted to but Mum couldn't, I've never... "

"Aye it's an expensive business if you have to pay for it. We all have horses around where I live. We'll be going back there tomorrow. I thought I'd treat us both to a hotel tonight though, have a night out in Dublin's fair city before you get tucked away in the countryside for the rest of the fortnight."

We're walking through the massive car park. Connor stands beside a dusty-looking dark red car several rows away, his elbow on the roof. He seems to be texting.

"Does he live near you?" I want to know whether Connor's staying in the hotel tonight as well.

"Ah yeah, just a way away. He'll be getting the bus back to Carrick this afternoon though after we've been to the Yeats exhibition. His mam'll pick him up from there. We all live half-way up a mountain."

It sounds so exciting to someone like me, from the flatlands of Skegness.

"His mam's an artist, like your dad tells me you are," Iris has put her hand on my back to help steer me through a particularly narrow gap between two cars. "You only just missed an exhibition she had in Dublin herself. It came down about two weeks ago. But I'm sure she'll be happy to show you her studio."

Just as we reach the car Connor slips his phone into the back pocket of his jeans. I can't help noticing his fluid movements. He turns with a flourish to open the passenger side door for me.

"Your girlfriend again is it, Connor?" Iris ruffles the back of his hair and raises an eyebrow, nodding towards his rear. I feel a twinge of disappointment that he has a girlfriend.

"To be sure, Deirdre can't leave me alone. It's not my fault if I'm irresistible."

"I love your accent," comes out of my stupid mouth, and my face is on fire. I duck quickly into the car but not before I see Iris and Connor exchange a glance.

"Get your arse in the back there, Connor," she says to him, still standing behind my open door.

She leans in close to my ear as the car rocks when he gets in.

"That Deidre's a tart but don't tell him it was me who said it, will you?"

She starts the engine, looks over at me with a grin I can't help returning. I feel as if enormous, heavy birds are letting

73

loose their grip on me and flying off my shoulders.

She curses and complains loudly at the cost of parking in the city centre but I'm entranced by Dublin and offer her one of my crisp five-euro notes, which she flaps her hand at.

"Don't mind me, you silly girl."

We do a walking tour and I ought to be embarrassed – any other teenager would, when Iris plants herself in front of the statue of Molly Malone. She opens her mouth to sing the popular ballad Mum used to serenade me with in the once-upon-a-bedtime of my childhood. Iris pulls open her coat, thrusts out white-shirted bosoms comparable to those of sweet Molly, curves her hands over her hips. They reveal themselves to be quite shapely. Her voice is rich and throaty and she draws quite a crowd. A few people throw coins at her feet and the three of us roar with laughter afterwards.

"You should have joined in, you naughty girl, if you've a voice anything like your mam's," says Iris. "Not Connor though. He can't sing for toffee but he does play a mean guitar."

She links one of her arms through mine and the other through Connor's and I try to match their big strides as we march together down Grafton Street.

We have lunch in this busy place called Pravda just off O'Connell Street. The bar's vibrant and thronging, Russian-themed, lots of young people. I look around me in amazement; there's nowhere like this in Skegness.

"It's not really my cup of tea but I thought I'd break you in to the Irish culture gently, niece. This is the Russian version of it. It's exactly Deirdre's kind of place though so Connor's quite the regular in here. Look, that's her, over there."

So Deirdre works here. My disappointment is only because Connor seems part of my new-found family now, kind of my god-cousin or even god-brother, since Iris is my auntie and she's his godmother. And I don't want to share either of them with the lovely Deirdre right at this moment. Which is a pity because she's coming over to us, planting a kiss on Connor's cheek, placing her hands possessively on his shoulders. I keep my head low, examining the menu, but she's not letting me off that easy.

"Ah, so you must be Rebecca. . . Connor's cousin from England isn't it?"

I notice Connor flashing me a glance. That must be how he explained me to her; great minds think alike. Deirdre reaches a hand towards me.

"I'm his girlfriend. Deirdre, how're ya?"

"I'm good, thanks. How are you?" I know I'm mumbling and I just want to crawl under the table.

Deirdre's got to go anyway, her boss is giving her funny looks and there are tables ready to be cleared.

"I'll mebbe speak to you later then, Rebecca?"

Not if I see her first, she won't. Connor goes quiet after she's moved off. I can't make out the expression on his face. Iris digs him hard in the ribs and he grunts.

"Eh stop that, it's child abuse."

"Yeah, yeah," says Iris. She turns to me. "So how's your daddy, Rebecca? Getting fat on all the cupcakes Wendy's making him, is he?"

There's a beautiful park and wide streets with huge, gracious buildings all around us. I'm so excited as we go into the museum. They have a big collection of European and Irish art, and I want to fill my mind up with it, take it all home, back to Sk. . . to my new home in a village near Lincoln. But shit, I don't want to think about any other home than here with Iris and Connor.

Before we go into the Jack B. Yeats room Connor suggests we look at some of the other Irish painters. It suits me because I want to save *There is no Night* until last anyway.

Connor seems to know everything about the permanent collection.

"I spent my childhood being dragged here by my mother," he tells me. "I used to enjoy the long bus journey into Dublin with her more than the trips to the art gallery. Especially after she had the twins, it was my only chance to get some time alone with her without a babby hanging off her tit."

I nearly choke on the toffee Iris handed me before she went back to sit in the café. With my eyes fixed on a painting of nuns in a convent garden by William John Leech I finally manage to speak.

"Twins? Are they boys or girls?"

"Boys; Riley and Fergus, they're nearly fifteen."

"Oh wow," I say, forgetting my embarrassment at the image he conjured up for me of his mother with an exposed breast.

"Wow?" Connor gives me one of his smiles.

"I have twin brothers too. Half-brothers, Bobby and Joshua."

"Ah now, well we have even more in common than we thought, then."

He puts the flat of his palm in the small of my back, guides me towards a painting he thinks I might like to look at, and the warmth from his touch spreads into my skin and muscle and spine, conducts into my belly and thighs. The feelings are vaguely familiar, but I can't think where from.

Thirteen

Bex

THE BROKEN BLISTER sticks to the heel of my stocking. My new sandals are rubbing something rotten, but they do match the vest-top with a diamante trim and the short blue skirt I borrowed from Rebecca's stuff.

Everything battles for space in my head: noise from the crowd of youngsters over at the pool table, the television blaring out from the snug on the other side of the bar, music from the jukebox on this side. This is my new workplace. It's called The White Hart, just across the road from the caravan.

. . . I'm sitting with Sebastian's bleeding head in my lap. Everything goes silent, inside and outside. Sun's shining on my face, birds sing in the green waving branches above as if nothing bad has happened. I don't know how long I sit here. . .

What?

Don's asking about Rebecca. He says there might be a job for her if she wants it, soon as she's eighteen. Next month in fact: May.

Don't want her working behind the bar with me though.

She rang earlier. Asked if I was doing all right without her.

I told her it's easier only having to worry about myself; well it is in a way – not having to put up with those superior glances, constant bloody disapproval. But I miss her an' all. I know for a fact she won't stay with me once she's finished at college. She's being sucked away from me now the outside world's got its hands on her.

Especially that Iris. . .

She's Jack's older sister. They weren't close, the family disapproved of her when she went off travelling in a horse and cart with her boyfriend. Got arrested for protesting against more or less everything, and she lived at Greenham Common for a year or two when those nuclear missiles were there. But I first met her when she was a member of that Irish folk-rock band, The Shanbos. Quite famous, they were. She played the accordion and when she came over for her dad's funeral, tried to teach Rebecca to play. I'd got really depressed again and I reckon she tried to help me but I was having none of it. I remember her getting me to sing, something I hadn't done for a while.

It's a pity the way things turn out.

But on the other hand. . . stop all the clocks, and all that.

I think I just had one of my absences. There's a three-deep tide of punters at the bar and I never noticed them coming. That other barmaid, Clarice, gives me the evils. She hates me anyway 'coz even though I'm new I get more tips than her. Don calls me into the kitchen.

"Now look here, Bex, I'm not saying you ain't good for business, 'coz it wouldn't be true. Your Rick wasn't lying when he said the punters would love you. But you've got to start pulling your weight, ducky. It ain't fair on our Clarice here if she's the only one doing the work, now is it?"

"No, I can see what you mean Don." I give him one of my smiles, "I'll get out there and collect those glasses, shall I, to make up for it?"

It's a job Clarice hates and I usually leave it to her 'coz I'm not that keen on it myself. But I've got a sixth sense when it comes to knowing when to ingratiate myself.

That's Don pacified for the time being. But I'm worried about these big gaps in my awareness. My absences. It don't seem right that things can just happen without me noticing.

It's important not to lose myself again for the rest of the evening. Also to make an effort to placate Clarice. She's got a lot of friends in this village and I don't want to find myself on the receiving end of a hate campaign.

"Have a drink with me, ladies," Don says at the end of the night.

The glasses are washed, the tables polished. He's only doing it 'coz he doesn't want to go up to his wife, Janet. Clarice and me pull up a stool each.

"Just the one then, Don," Clarice laughs with that funny snorting sound she makes, "some of us have got homes to go to, haven't we Bex?"

Afterwards we walk out into the darkness together.

"Settling into the caravan all right?"

"Not too bad, you know. My daughter'll be home end of the week."

"My brother-in-law has a few houses to rent if you're looking for something more permanent."

Everyone seems to be related to each other in this village.

"Thanks for that Clarice; I'll bear it in mind. See you tomorrow."

I'm turning left at the bridge while Clarice is heading off down the High Street.

What I miss most is a bath. It was great sinking into the bath in our old flat. Here it's just the shower in a right poky cubicle. The pressure's not much more than a dribble and it doesn't make me feel clean enough.

I check the caravan door's locked properly, I'm nervous living out here in the dark with just a flimsy sheet of metal between me and the world. In Skegness you could always hear the traffic and the funfair - except in winter. I liked that feeling of life around me, even if I didn't want to live it myself. But it's so quiet here. There's a few streetlights on the High Street, but none down Chapel Lane where my caravan is. Anyone could walk across this land and wrench open the door in the dark. I don't like it.

I pull Milly onto my lap after my shower. The fawn coloured settee reminds me of being back in our flat. Time for my bed-time tipple, feet up on the coffee table squeezed into the gap in front of the gas fire. The TV's pushed into the corner, the other side of the room from where I'm used to watching it but I couldn't put it where I would've liked it 'coz that's where the partition into the kitchen is. Some of the furniture Rick brought over in the van had to be stored outside in an old railway carriage 'coz there was no space for it in here.

Milly's not relaxed in this place at all. She seems to be shedding more hair than usual and she's not eating her food. "Come on old girl," I flatten my hand along her skinny spine, right to the tip of her tail, "don't give up on me now. Had you since Rebecca was a baby, I have."

A draught blows on the back of my neck from the metal windows. Milly gives one of her plaintive yowls.

"Two sad old things together aren't we, Milly?" If this was a fairy tale I would kiss her, disgusting creature that she's become, and she would transform into my prince and none of the bad stuff would ever have happened.

―――――◦◦◦――――――

I need an extra blanket on top of the quilt, and Milly to sleep on my feet. It's impossible to get warm. If I could be bothered I'd get out of bed and fill up a hot water bottle. The bedroom is clever with its limited space. There's a wardrobe with a sliding door at the foot of the bed and cupboards filling the wall above. Rebecca's room's even smaller than mine. The caravan has a corridor off the kitchen with the bathroom cubicle and her bedroom off one side of it, and my bedroom's at the bottom.

There's a thud on the caravan roof. Hair stands up on Milly's spine and she lets out an almighty yowl. Next thing, she's scrabbling manically at the window to be let out. There's a black shape dropping to the ground, streaking off through the darkness. Ah, but it's only another cat.

I put a curse on myself all those years ago when I made the pledge to stop living even though my body would go on. And back then, there might have been a reversal spell.

When I had Rebecca with Jack, there might have been a chance to reverse the curse. But I didn't take it and now it's too late. Here I am, still buried under the snow.

Fourteen

Rebecca

THERE IS NO NIGHT isn't even in the exhibition. It's disappointing, but it doesn't matter that much; my own vision of the landscape didn't come from the painting anyway.

Connor's at my side, talking me through each of Yeats' works. The later ones are similar in the handling of paint and subject matter to the picture Tom showed me on the computer screen, but they look so much more visceral – that's a word Tom taught me – in real life. The paint is laid on thick and unmixed in some places but it's no more than a thin wash on other parts of the canvas. Tom complimented me on the way I'd done that too and I felt guilty for accepting the praise. I hadn't planned it, my paintings just turned out that way. But as I study Yeats' paintings I'm mentally manipulating the brush and the palette knife the way he must have done.

"Have you noticed that Yeats' earlier paintings are of everyday subjects, and much more conventional?" Connor touches my shoulder lightly, steers me to look back at the earlier works. "But in these later ones, see, the paintings make you recognise visual elements that are only just there; he simply suggests them by a flick of colour from the end of a brush or a scrape of the palette knife through a buttery layer of paint, like so."

"You should get a job as a guide here," I say. "You know so much more about art than I do."

"Ah, but I'm no good with the brush meself. That's where

we differ, you and I. It's my mam," Connor grins at me. "She indoctrinated me. She can't get the lads to sit still long enough to listen to anything she says, so she goes on and on about it to me. And she makes me carry her bloody paintings everywhere an'all."

I'm hardly listening. There's a buzz in my ears. Being next to Connor provokes the same feelings I had when I was with the other boy. All the sensations are reawakened. It's going to haunt me until I know who that other boy was...is.

Connor's got a girlfriend anyway.

We're dropping Connor off at the bus station and he says, "Walk in with me, will ya, Rebecca?"

Iris says she'll turn the car round and wait for me outside. I'm sure he'll notice my twitchiness but he's looking at a text instead of me. He shakes his head.

"I know I'm irresistible but I'm getting a bit fed up of having to explain my every move to the girl."

Oh God, his accent is so sexy.

It takes me a second to register what he just said and when it sinks in I don't say anything, instead offer a compassionate look.

Inside the station the early evening light is blotted out by artificial overheads. We find the number 23 bus standing empty with a small queue of people waiting by it. We prop ourselves against a spare bit of railing.

"Two hours and forty-five minutes I've got to sit on that bus," says Connor. "I know the journey like the back of my hand."

I'm intensely aware of his presence. My skin prickles. The air's filled with the rumbling of buses, and I have to lean in to hear him.

84

"It was great having you explain things at the exhibition, it really helped," I say.

"Ah well," he gives me an amused look. "I think Iris was a bit nervous about meeting you on her own especially since you wanted to look at art, so she brought me along for the craic. I'm indispensable to her, I am."

His eyes are a dark violet in the bus station lights, his hair almost black. His skin's tanned; he strikes me as someone who spends lots of time in the fresh air.

"Iris, nervous?"

It seems unlikely.

"Aye. She does have a soft spot, believe it or not."

The bus driver's arrived. He pushes a button to open the doors. The engine chuckles to life and after a few seconds he beckons and the passengers start getting on.

Connor drops his rucksack and bends forward to give me a quick hug. For a moment his heart beats against my cheek through the wool of his jumper. I want to stop breathing. Then he brushes my cheek with his lips and releases me. I get the feeling he's used to hugging people.

I'm not.

"I'm coming over to Iris's when you get back tomorrow. I'll see you then, and we can talk some more."

"Ah, you're all right, don't worry about it," Iris says when I apologise for making her wait. She grinds her cigarette into the ground with the heel of her boot and tucks brown curls behind her ear. The action gives her an inexplicable vulnerability. She's tall and she has a big voice and personality so why should she be nervous of me? I feel suddenly exposed and get the impression she does too.

"Well," she says, "we'll get off and find our hotel, will we? This is a proper treat for me, you know. I don't get to stay in a hotel much these days, I can tell you."

Our hotel, Custom House, is right by the river Liffey. Iris has to park in a side street but when we walk back the sight of the wide river sparkling with reflected lights takes my breath away. As we enter the hotel she fidgets.

"I had to get us a twin room. I hope that's okay with you."

I'm surprised to find myself laying a hand on her arm. Maybe it's all the hauling about of Mum I have to do that makes me keep my hands to myself the rest of the time, but I want to stop Iris a minute, reassure her.

"Everything's all right with me, auntie."

The word feels soft on my tongue. Iris lets out a breath.

"Well. As long as you can put up with my snoring, niece."

I get the bed by the window. Iris uses the shower first. When I come out she's transformed. She wears a red turtleneck dress that swings against her knees, and embroidered leggings. She sees me looking.

"Morocco."

I raise an eyebrow.

"We were on tour, The Shanbos."

"The Shanbos?"

"It's the band I played in with Connor's dad."

After a pause I ask, "Do you think Mum'll be all right while I'm away?"

"Rebecca," she sits on my bed, red earrings swinging, green eyes glittering. "Let go of it while you're here. Think about yourself for once. We... your dad

and me, we just want to give you a bit of a break. Think of this as a respite – your life'll still be there, waiting for you when you get back." She swings her bag onto her shoulder and gives me a smile. "I'll wait for you in the bar while you get dressed. Put on your glad rags young lady, we'll have dinner in the hotel and then a night on the town."

I ought to remind Iris that I'm not eighteen yet, but decide not to bother. I'm in Ireland; everything is different here.

———◦———

Five o'clock the following afternoon. We're on the N4, on our way to County Leitrim. The sky's flat and grey but it's stopped

86

raining. My eyelids keep shutting and I'm tempted to let them go. Iris seems happy in her own company anyway. She said she spends most of her time alone and she likes it best that way.

"I don't mean I don't enjoy a bit of company though," she adds, "I love it. It's just that I'm happy by myself. Some people can't stand it."

"Did you ever want to have children?"

It's a personal question but she's said I can ask her anything.

She gives me a sideways look. "When I was young I expected to have children, but it was never a problem for me that I didn't. I've had a different life because of it, no better and no worse."

"Did you ever get married, or live with anyone?"

"I've had a few romances, never married though. I might have done but my man Pete died."

"I'm sorry."

"It was a while ago." She flicks her eyes over me. "He had a good rock 'n roll life and he paid the price for it, but I don't think he had any regrets. And neither do I, in the long run. There's no time for such useless emotions."

Iris is older than Mum but she seems younger, un-blighted by all the stuff that's happened to her. What's Mum really got to complain about? Okay, so she had a Great Grief when she was about the age I am now, but it seems so did Iris. It was no excuse for Mum deciding her life was over. It's not fair. She had me. She should have either made more of an effort, or got rid of me when she was pregnant. My two weeks with Iris suddenly seem more important than ever.

My eyelids are getting heavy again. So I let them fall.

———◦•◦———

We've collected wood for the range and Iris has put the electric radiators on. There's a dog flap in the back door of the kitchen, that's why it was okay for her to leave Gypsy alone last night. Iris wasn't joking when she said she lives half way up a mountain. As soon as we got here we had to go out and feed the heavily pregnant goat and take some hay to the horses. They came cantering towards us when they saw their food and the sound of their hooves jolted me into thinking I should be remembering something important.

Dusk falls quickly over the mountain and the chickens nearly trip me up when Iris sends me out to feed them, because I can't see them properly in the half-light.

"Sorry about all this work," says Iris, "but I didn't want Roisin to have to do it again this evening. You're gonna have to work for your living here I'm afraid, Rebecca."

"I don't mind at all. It's wonderful!"

"Ah, well, you haven't had to do it in the biting cold of winter. But mebbe you'll come back. Mebbe you could come here with your mam at Christmas."

She stops placing a few lumps of coal on top of the wood in the range and gives me a serious look.

"I mean it. I'd have your mam here. I reckon it'd do her the world of good."

I feel like crying.

"I'm not sure if Dad would like that. . . "

"I daresay he wouldn't. But my brother doesn't tell me what to do, young lady, and neither does anyone else. I'd like to help your mam, if only for your sake."

The fire roars away. We sit with plates of chips on our laps, glasses of wine at our elbows. Iris wanted to make me a hot whiskey but the smell of Mum's second-favourite drink makes me feel sick.

I feel warm and happy. Gypsy, a border collie with long silky hair, presses herself against my legs. The curtains are drawn against the fallen dusk and there's only one small lamp in the corner. Iris has left the range door open so we can gaze at the flames.

We hear the rattle of an engine in the yard out front and a smile comes on Iris's face. She gets up and collects our plates.

"That'll be your man."

I think she's saying 'Mam' and I go cold inside, stumble to my feet.

"What... how?"

"Calm down, Rebecca, he's not gonna bite you, is he?"

This doesn't make any sense. I rub at my forehead, wondering if I've fallen asleep and am having a dream. Footsteps crunch on the gravel outside. A sob tries to rise in my chest. I don't want Mum here. I know it sounds bad, but I realise how true it was, what Iris said about me needing a break.

Iris comes back from the kitchen and takes a look at me then tuts and sticks out a tongue-dampened thumb for a wipe of my forehead.

"You should've washed the coal dust from your hands before eating your dinner, you naughty girl."

Then the back door is pushed open. The dog-flap rattles as it's slammed closed again.

"Only me!"

I'm washed through with a sense of relief so strong I think I might faint. It's not Mum.

He comes into the room and we all smile at each other.

"You had the girl all of a tremble for a minute there, Connor," Iris says, "It must be that irresistibility you keep going on about."

Fifteen

Jack

1991

SHE WAS SOAKING in a bath of jasmine-scented bubbles. I'd given her the shampoo.

"I didn't know men used this type," she said. I said nothing, didn't want her to feel lured into a trap. I had to make it so good for her here that she'd never want to leave. She'd fall in love with me as time passed; it just required patience on my part.

I gave her the soft pink towel I'd bought. She teased me.

"Not a Nancy-boy are you, Jack? All these candles and stuff, never seen that kinda thing in a bloke's flat before."

It gave me a prickle of jealousy to hear her say 'before', and I vacillated between wanting to explain the reason for having all the feminine stuff and not letting her know how desperate I'd been to get her here.

It wasn't the first time I'd seen her naked but I stayed out of the way while she was in the bath, belatedly shy.

But I had her here. *She was here.* That was enough.

After a while she raised her voice over the sound of the running taps.

"'Ere Jack, you got any razors? Pits need a bit of attention. So do my legs."

91

Damn. My only shaving gear was the traditional kit my dad had given me for Christmas when I was sixteen. The kind you have to replace the blade in. she couldn't shave her soft skin with my used razor, could she?

"Jack!" she shouted louder. "You can come in, you know. Don't be shy."

I pushed the door open.

"You don't have to look away, you've seen it all before," she said.

Her cheeks were flushed. I could just make out the curve of her stomach under the water. Her brown nipples peeked out above a generous covering of bubbles.

I forced myself to meet her eyes once she removed them from my groin area. She dropped hers first, raised one knee, tutted.

"State of my legs. Look at 'em."

"Can't say I have any complaints," I kept my voice even.

This is the happiest day of my life, is what I thought. I finished replacing the razor and handed her the complete kit including the shaving stick and brush in its presentation case. She ran a soapy finger over the worn leather.

"Aww. That is so cute. You're really looking after me, you are."

———◦◦◦———

2010

"It'd do her the world of good, Jack."

"I don't know. Her mother'll never agree to it anyway, I'm sure of that."

"Have you even tried actually talking to the poor woman recently?"

"Poor woman! Iris, what are you on?" I sound like a real prig, but actually I'm fucking furious.

"I can't believe you're talking like that. Poor woman. Fucking hell. Have you not listened to a word Rebecca's told you about her mother? Bex is a drunk, evil bitch. Only interested in what's good for her. She's never put Rebecca first."

"And you always have?" Iris says softly.

"Oh my God. Iris. D'you think I'm not sorry for my mistakes? You don't have to rub it in."

I swipe my eyes with the back of my hand. They've started watering. Must've got some of that bloody chilli powder in them earlier. It was a lovely evening until Iris rang and ruined it. My sons are at their Nana's for the night. Wendy and I have been making an effort with each other.

Fuck. A picture of Wendy's expression when I return to the living room swims in front of my eyes. Reproach and accusation combined, it'll be. *Aren't our boys enough for you?* She thinks I'm obsessed with Rebecca.

"Jack," Iris says. "Remember how much you loved Bex once. It must have meant something."

There's no answer to that.

"You both care about Rebecca," said Iris. "Whatever you think about Bex. Give her a ring. See what she says."

"You must be fucking joking," is Bex's response to Iris's proposition. "This was all a plot, wasn't it, to get Rebecca away from me?"

I take a deep breath, my nerve-ends jangling.

"I can understand you not wanting to be left alone. It must be scary for you. But she's nearly eighteen. She can leave whenever she wants; she doesn't need your permission. Besides, she's much more likely to come back to you if she thinks you're willing to let her go."

"What do you fucking know about it?" Bex hisses into the phone, like an angry swan. "Child psy-pissing-chologist now, are you? You're in and out of her life like a bastard-yo-yo. Yeah, but you were willing to let her go when it suited you."

"I wasn't. . . " I begin. "I wasn't willing to let her go. . . "

I can't believe I'm getting into this conversation with her again. This is why we don't speak. All she ever does is accuse me. She's gone silent.

"Bex. . . "

What do I say to her?

Her voice is different from how it used to be. There's a rasp in it. I strain my ears for another word.

My head's fucked-up, I've been careful so long, kept my two worlds separate. It can't work, trying to communicate with her. Iris was wrong to get me to do this.

A long pause. . .

"What?"

I try and think but nothing comes.

"I don't know. I can't talk to you. It was pointless ringing."

"No. . . what? I want to know." Her voice has gone lower, sultry. Stop it, I think. Stop being Bex.

I hate you.

"Go on, you were going to say sommats, weren't you?" She has this wheedling way. It gets under your skin.

Where did we go wrong? I'd never say it. Where did I go wrong?

The misunderstanding was obvious from the start, at least to her. She kept trying to tell me. *I want you, I need you,* (or at the very least I'm prepared to stick around with you,) *but there ain't no way etc.* Ain't no way she was ever gonna love me.

It's ironic that I went ahead and put Wendy in the same situation.

This phone call is late enough in the morning that she's out of bed but early enough that she isn't drunk. It's a fine line. Now I wish she was drunk so I could remember how much I hate her, for being such an evil bitch. For not loving me when she had the chance.

"You're such a wimp, Jack," her voice croaks back in. "Never say what ya mean, do ya? Listen to this, my favourite sound in the world, this is."

The clink of glass against bottle; it must be later than I thought. I hear the slug of drink in her throat, the catch of breath afterwards; picture the glaze settling over her eyes, the brief flush in her cheeks. A rush goes through my belly; my mind plays host to a vision of her lying on a bed beneath me, my hands pinning her to it by the wrists.

Stop it.

Fuck. The day I finally walked out on her I swore I'd get custody of Rebecca, the daughter who'd been given another man's surname.

I don't want to acknowledge that I wouldn't have taken Rebecca, because Wendy didn't want her, and by that time I wanted... needed, Wendy more.

I slam the phone down, as hard as I can.

Sixteen

Rebecca

SHE'S GAUNTER THAN ever. She's also wearing way too much makeup, like she's about to go on stage in a pantomime. My toes curl. I've got used to seeing Iris and Sarah's healthy skin, from all that fresh air. They're both nearly twenty years older than Mum, but you wouldn't guess it. Sarah, that's Connor's mum, by the way.

Mum's driven all the way to the airport to collect me. There's no smell of drink. Iris made me promise to ring Dad to come and fetch me if there was. I give Mum a careful hug, she feels so thin.

The walk to the car gives me a chance to adjust to being back in England. It was only this morning. . . shit; I'm going to cry like I did on the plane. No. Connor's a good friend, that's all. I told him I have to sort something out before I can think about having a boyfriend. And anyway, we live so far away from each other.

He finished with Deidre. He said it wasn't because of you but he did it, didn't he?

"You're quiet, jet-lagged are you?"

She must have noticed my red eyes.

"Sodding 'ell, Rebecca, you're not crying to go back there already are you? At least wait 'til you've managed to have a conversation with your mother."

"I'm just tired, Mum, been a busy couple of weeks. I'm looking forward to getting in my own bed and having a rest."

"Well I've sorted your stuff out as best I can; gave me something to do while you were off enjoying yourself. There was only room for your bed but you've got built-in storage all around the walls and some drawers underneath so you can't complain."

"Where's the rest of my furniture?"

"There's an old railway carriage on the land – most of your stuff's in there."

We reach Mum's car and she unlocks the boot.

"Thanks for coming to collect me."

No drink, but a whiff of sour breath; dehydration.

"Have you. . . "

She looks at me sharply. We get in the car.

"What?"

"Nothing, just wondering if you've been remembering to drink water, that's all."

She gives me a bitter look and lets her breath out with a harsh sound.

"Little Miss Meddle-bottom, as I live and breathe."

She starts the engine and I find myself checking the wing mirrors and craning over my shoulder.

"How are you getting on in your new job?"

. . . Everything I say sounds like I'm checking up on her.

"Did you put 'im up to it?"

I'm taken aback by her savage tone.

"What. . . "

"Your bloody father... Or was it really that bitch Iris's idea?"

"What? Mum, I don't know what you're talking about."

Pins and needles tingle through my hands. The air in the car shrinks. I can't breathe.

"Don't start your histrionics with me, young lady. There's a paper bag in the glove compartment if you're planning on doing that hyperventilating trick of yours."

You're so fucking mean! I take slow deep breaths, raise my chin.

"Dunno what you're talking about."

"Got a phone call from your father while you were away, didn't I?"

She doesn't even apologise for the false accusation.

"Said Iris wanted you to stay there in Ireland with her. You could've just fucking asked me yourself."

Iris wanted me to stay.

I wonder why she didn't ask me. But, now I know I have an escape route, it feels like oxygen's being released into my lungs. It gives me the strength to mentally pledge another year to Mum. I don't even let myself wonder what'll happen after that.

She hunches over the wheel, still hasn't once asked if I had a nice time.

The road surface rumbles through the tires into my brain. Connor's face floats beneath my drooping eyelids.

There's a sudden jolt in my head and there it is, another face superimposed over his behind my eyes. The skin's golden-coloured, straw-toned hair falls over the face as the lips come towards mine. I jump myself awake.

It's the ghost in my head, the boy I don't know, who comes between me and Connor.

"What's the matter with you?"

Mum glances across at me. I don't want her to see how shaken up I am.

The feelings for the boy are the same as the ones I have for Connor. I'm trapped in a dream.

Mum's obviously forgotten her momentary concern.

"I thought you might like me to take you to Burger King for lunch."

We enter Lincoln by Carholme Road.

"If you won't find that a bit mundane after all the adventures you've been having, of course."

I wish she wasn't so bitter. But at least she's making an effort.

"Burger King's fine."

She parks in the multi-story.

There's an ache so powerful inside me it makes my body heavy. I drag each foot up and place it on the ground again, one after the other, keeping myself trotting after Mum. She moves purposefully in the flow of Saturday people. The roar of incessant traffic on Broadgate hurts my ears. I don't want to be here, it's another world from the scenery of mountains I looked out at only this morning; when Gypsy was running around Iris's feet trying to herd the chickens. The goat kid was born only two days before. Iris got me up in the night to come and look.

Mum casts an appraising eye over the Gala Bingo place as we pass it. Two women in blue uniforms along with a couple of old ladies in wheelchairs are smoking in the entrance. Gala's one of the organisations who've given Mum the sack.

"That place used to be a cinema when I was a girl," she says. "I came over with my parents on a day trip from Nottingham once. We went to see Indiana Jones."

She rarely talks about her youth.

We turn in through the automatic doors of the Waterside Centre and get on the escalator to the next level up. Clusters of youths are visible in the town square through the big windows. I wonder if anyone standing in those groups'll become my friend when I start at my new college. It's only two days away.

"Where am I going to put my easel at the caravan, Mum?"

We're queuing for a Burger King. Mum's having a cheeseburger and I'm having a bean burger. I'm proud of her for not having a drink yet. Withdrawal could be the explanation for her particularly bad mood in the car. But it's all okay; I can do this. My world extends beyond the boundaries of Mum-and-me now.

"I've thought about that." She gives a satisfied smile. "I've asked Don over at the pub. There's an old conservatory round the back that's never used. He says you can set up your stuff and work there. No-one'll bother you, he reckons."

100

Home now, it's a sunny evening. My room is the tiniest in the world but at least it's my own bed I'm lying on. A finger of breeze whispers its way under the metal frame of the open window, strokes my cheek and neck and I have a memory of being touched that way before. By somebody I dreamed up when I was lonely and didn't have a life of my own. A time, I have the faintest memory of it, when I was ready to give up.

My starry net curtain covers the whole wall, the primrose wallpaper beneath giving the impression of dark orange through the violet. My purple furry blanket is over my feet the way I like it. I've got my lamp and mirror; the one I had to trek out to the old railway carriage to find.

I'm safe in the faintly purple light of my new private space. Drifting on a lake of dreams, movement and shadows, a rainbow of colours, a constant shifting of shapes, I feel an actual physical presence but can't see anyone through my half-open eyes. My hand creeps over my breasts in the loose t-shirt I put on after my shower. Circling and lightly touching there, pressing more firmly into my belly, finding its way into my soft cotton jogging pants, between my legs.

Yes. I retrieve the sensation of another hand on my thigh; a violent rocking motion, how the fingers of that other hand pressed against me, made me cry out.

I'm glad Mum's at work because I'm so desperate to get back to then that I find myself reaching for the blanket, bunching and stuffing it between my legs, riding it, crying in frustration until the flower I'm searching for explodes at my core and fizzles into the tips of all my extremities. I go limp and sink into the mattress, feeling him moving away from me then, the one who ought to be Connor, but isn't.

Seventeen

Bex

June 1990

EVELYN COMES INTO the small sitting room. She pauses to watch me counting the china animals in the glass-fronted corner cabinet, then turns to set a tray of tea on the table.

"We weren't expecting you both to get married this young, Rebecca."

She neatens the teaspoons on their saucers, replaces the spilt lump of sugar in its bowl.

"But I am certain you're the right wife for Sebastian."

Phew. I feel like Princess Diana, being approved for suitability. She comes over to stand beside me, gathers up a handful of my long hair. She feels she has the right to touch me, now I'm going to partly belong to her. She piles the hair on top of my head, turns me slightly to catch my reflection in the doors of the cupboard. Brown eyes flash in my pale complexion. Ivory, Evelyn calls it. She seems pleased. I'm surprised by the strong line of my neck, exposed by the lifting of my hair.

"Will you wear it up like this?"

"I might. See what my mum thinks."

Not that my mum takes much notice of anything. Shaking my head slightly under Evelyn's hand, she lets go of my hair. I don't want her to think she's in control of everything, just because she's the one with the money. It's not that I don't like her; I do and she's told me she already loves me like a daughter, but I wish my own family wanted to make some of the decisions.

"Sit down will you, Rebecca?"

Evelyn's gone over to the table and is pouring two cups of tea. I do as I'm told, still awkward with her though I've known her since I was a child. My palms prickle, the effort not to dig my fingernails into them causes me to rub them on my knees instead. It's because this is the first time we've been alone in a room together since Sebastian and I announced our engagement two weeks ago. She's going to be my mother-in-law, and even though I feel too young to have such a thing, I want to be Sebastian's wife so badly.

Evelyn passes me a cloth napkin, followed by the cup of tea on its saucer.

"Jonathan and I have been talking."

I nod politely. My grandparents have taught me good manners. *Don't interrupt, Rebecca, speak when you're spoken to.*

I dab at the corner of my mouth with my napkin, though I haven't yet taken a sip of tea. *Keep neat and tidy at all times.*

"We've made some enquiries with the vicar of All Saints." Evelyn pauses to smile. "We were wondering if you think September the twenty-fourth sounds like a good date for a wedding."

It's hard to speak, picturing the interior of All Saints and me walking up that blue carpet towards Sebastian, so soon.

But so what?

I've finished my A Levels. I'm eighteen-years old, a grown up.

"Oh Evelyn!"

It's weird that I don't have to call her 'Mrs Grey' anymore.

Delight bubbles up, despite me struggling to retain a composed attitude the way Grandma taught me. My hands disobey me and break out into a round of applause. Evelyn flushes.

"I haven't suggested it to Sebastian yet; I wanted to ask you first, my dear. Now you can tell him yourself when he gets in. They shouldn't be long."

Sebastian's been working for his father for the past year, choosing the family auctioneering firm over Cambridge University which is where he could have gone. It strikes me that I probably won't live in Nottingham again. I'll most likely stay with my grandparents for the coming months; there'll be wedding dress fittings, flower arrangements to choose. And a cake, of course. Sebastian and me, we've been dreaming of our wedding since we were fourteen- and fifteen-years old and I think Evelyn's always expected it to happen too.

"There's another thing."

Evelyn and I have finished our tea – the cups are so tiny – but she pours more. Afternoon light filters through the swathes of muslin at the window, giving Evelyn a silver crown of curls as she sits opposite me at the table. I put my hand up to the back of my head, flattening my palm against the silky length of my warm hair.

"Jonathan and I would like to put a deposit on a small house for you and Sebastian, if you don't mind. The one next to the tea shop, Rose Cottage. It's a darling house, perfect for the beginning of your married life. Of course, you are welcome to live with us here, but we thought you might prefer your privacy. What do you think, dear?"

Two reactions: first, joy at the thought of us having a home of our own. I know the house she means, have always loved it, and confess to a secret fantasy of owning it. I've often imagined pushing a pram across the road to the park once Sebastian and I are married. But there's also a sense of helplessness. Evelyn wants to orchestrate such control over us, albeit in the kindest way. Making sure we will stay in the village so she can keep in daily contact with her darling son. I don't know if I want to be that close for always.

I decide to show Evelyn only the joy.

"That's generous of you, but I'll have to ask Sebastian."

She gives a secret smile at that and I wonder if she's mentioned it to him already. Of course, it would make sense to stay in the village, what with Sebastian's work. I could go to university in either Leicester or Nottingham, with place offers at both.

I carry the tea things back into the kitchen while Evelyn settles into her silk chair with her feet up on the matching footstool. She always has a short nap when afternoon tea is over. I have my own smile because I know the routine of this home so well, glad that when I'm married, living in our own home, we'll develop routines of our own. I wash up, put the dried pots away. I know where everything goes in the kitchen. Mrs Evans comes in every day to clean, but I wipe everything down again anyway. At a quarter to five we'll put the oven on and the evening meal will be ready when the men come home at half past. Satisfaction bubbles up in me as I dry my hands on the spotless towel hanging from its special hook at the side of the sink: order and purpose, such a contrast to the life of my Mum and Dad.

I think about the moment Sebastian will walk into the front hallway. While Evelyn will slide Jonathan's summer jacket from his shoulders and offer the side of her face for a kiss, Sebastian will scoop me up in his arms, saying, "I missed you, Rebecca, I really missed you."

I can't wait to see him.

2010

I still can't believe he's gone. Every time I wake up from one of those dreams, I have to remake myself all over again. I'm not that nice girl, that carefully groomed and polished young woman destined to marry the boy from Greys Mount. Why do I still have those dreams? They've been regular, ever since I saw that bloody painting of Rebecca's. It's like some kind of portal has been opened up, dragging me back into my Great Grief.

I sit up in bed. I'll never get to sleep again now so I'm gonna have a drink. I need one, just a snifter. It's the only thing that'll get me through the rest of the night, brace me, stiffen my rubber bones and make me real.

I keep a bottle in the cupboard next to my bed so I don't have to scuttle about in the middle of the night. Every time I have a spare bit of cash I buy a bottle and put it somewhere so I never run out. I won't have to take money out of Rebecca's purse no more, never have to see that supercilious look on her face again.

Why can't I just have a few moments in Sebastian's arms every now and then? I'm always waiting to see him, but the dream ends before that happens. Stop all the clocks... But I never did. Not really. I just changed myself into someone else – gave everything I was or wanted to be a kick in the face, gave away the only thing that mattered after Sebastian was gone. And I kicked Evelyn and Jonathan in the face at the same time.

They lost me at the same time they lost him. And then they lost Rebecca as well. I wonder if they ever think of me now, after I let them down so many times.

1990

All Saints Church in Newtown Linford, the twenty-fourth of September.

That's where our wedding is... but it turns into Sebastian's funeral.

Evelyn asks me if I'm prepared to go through with it still and I say yes. It's as if she and I are locked together in our own universe that never got past four days ago.

I wear the wedding dress they had made for me and we keep the marquee and the cars, everything that's been booked for the wedding. The slot is free now after all.

Evelyn has a long meeting with the Vicar, a close family friend. She tells me he's been making a lot of phone calls, studying past cases, working out how to conduct the ceremony.

The flowers we have are white lilies and roses; some people say choosing them in the first place was a bad omen but Evelyn's chairperson of this thing called *The White Flower Society*. We chose them as a thank you to her.

Afterwards, I change my surname legally to Grey just like she asks me to. "You're Sebastian's wife now," she tells me, "I think of you as my daughter.

You two are so precious to Jonathan and me."

<hr />

I've never told Rebecca any of this and I never want to. My Great Grief's a private thing. Jack wasn't too pleased that I wouldn't give our daughter his name. He wanted to marry me. It was crazy the way he kept on believing in me.

The first time I ever saw him angry was when I insisted on giving Rebecca the surname of my deceased husband.

"At least will you allow her a double-barrelled surname if you don't want to give up the name Grey? Portman-Grey sounds all right, don't you think? She's my *daughter*, Bex."

I wasn't having it. Rebecca's surname would be Grey like mine and that's all there was to it. It was to make up for the terrible mistake I made in the heart of my Great Grief, something that could never really be put right, but I could try to cancel it out; start again.

My caravan window faces a sweep of fields. I can see forever. The morning's so pretty emerging above the edges of the world. I see this, but as ever, I'm detached from it. A black line defines the earth from the sky and as I stare at it, pinks and golds appear, with pale blue between them. I swallow another gulp from my green-bottle friend. It burns pleasantly inside me, but emotion wells painfully back up my gullet like a bubble. I want to stick a knife in it.

The drink's not helping. I should have died when Sebastian did.

Eighteen

Rebecca

IT'S TIME FOR my first one-to-one tutorial with my new tutor, Anne. She wanted to give me a week to settle in at college first and I have. I like it here. Dad was right; it seems a great place.

The bus service between North Scarte and Lincoln is rubbish though. What do they expect people without cars to do? Cycle three and a half miles to the railway station at Swinderby and catch the train into Lincoln, and then do the same in reverse later, is what. Uncle Rick lives on a farm down the road from us. He lent me a pushbike. He says he can get me a second-hand moped if I'd prefer that, but now Dad's offered to buy me one for my birthday instead and I'm booked in for a course of lessons starting next week. Once I'm mobile, I'll be able to get a job.

So far I've enjoyed my bike rides along the rural roads, especially in the mornings. It's nearly May, my most favourite time of year – probably because it's my birthday month. The weather is crisp and bright. Bluebells line up along the side of the road and cow parsley flourishes in the long grass at the edges of fields. It smells of nature. The centre of Skegness where I lived smelt mostly of fish and chips, even the sea which should be wild and natural seemed diminished by the arcades and casinos; they all masked the sea's true nature.

Cycling along, hedges and hawthorn flowers overhang either side of the road, and fields stretch away as far as I can see.

Pushing the pedals I sing at the top of my voice, constantly reliving the music night we had at the O'Toole's. In front of all those people Iris persuaded me to sing a song called *She Moved through the Fair.*

Connor and I've Skyped three times since I got back from Ireland, but he doesn't feel as real to me anymore.

"You have a very mature style for someone your age, Rebecca," says my tutor. "It seems expressionism..." she moves along my propped-up row of canvases, "... is your natural forte; the way you choose colour, the way you apply it, looks casual but I suspect is carefully premeditated. Your method demonstrates a deep understanding of your materials. I don't often see that in my students. I'm looking forward to your response to our current project."

The students have been working in 3D, which is something I haven't done yet.

"We're looking at figurative artists such as Antony Gormley, as well as some environmental art. I'd suggest researching Andy Goldsworthy to start off with though," she considers. "I think you'll enjoy the way he uses the colours and textures of nature in a similar way to a painter."

Anne takes a look through my sketchbook, discussing my views on the various schools of painting I've studied so far. A printout of *There is No Night* is pasted to one of the pages along with several other examples of Jack B. Yeats' work and some notes from my visit to the museum. The pages before those are crowded with melancholy figures by Dante Gabriel Rossetti and Edward Burne Jones along with my own copies of them, and before that the impressionists occupy about ten pages. Anne remarks on the subtlety of my soft pastel work.

During break, a girl with a nose-stud in the shape of a heart comes over to me.

"Hi, I'm Jade."

She has bright red hair, scarlet, in a loose knot at the back of her head with floppy strands spraying out of it. She's wear-

112

ing denim shorts over striped tights.

"You getting a coffee?"

My heart thuds. Does she want us to become friends?

"Okay, yeah, thanks. Hang on a minute; I'll just get my stuff."

We make our way down the wide curved staircase. Artwork hangs all over the walls and posters for gigs and activity clubs and house shares are stuck on with Blu-tack. It's like a giant three-dimensional sketchbook. We reach the bottom floor.

"I like that painting you're working on."

She's referring to my latest version of 'night'. To be honest I'm getting sick of the image; I've been trying to pervert it because I want it out of my head. I'm thinking of scratching that blond boy out of every version of the painting I've done. It's time to move on. Wherever the hell he came from, he's got to go.

Connor's the one who's real. I need to want Connor the way that imaginary boy makes me want him.

In the canteen we get a coffee and I wander over to the vending machine for a packet of mints. I offer Jade one. The college building is halfway up Steep Hill. The Cathedral looms over us. Steep Hill's an almost vertical cobbled street that looks like something out of Dickens. What with the daily cycling and my walk up here every morning I'm fitter than I've ever been in my life. Jade suggests we sit on the grass outside college since it's bathed in sunshine.

She leans back on her hands, eyes me sideways.

"You live in that caravan, don't you?"

I'm embarrassed that she might suppose I'm disadvantaged.

In the late April sunshine the Cathedral's ancient stones glow yellow. I think of all the hands that've touched those blocks of stone over hundreds of years and I have the feeling that if I closed my eyes for a minute, time would suck me backwards, enfold me in history. I pop a second mint in my mouth; offer another to Jade.

"Do you live in North Scarte too?"

"Yeah. I live in the house with the stables behind it, down the High Street?"

I don't know it, but that's because I've hardly been out in the village.

"I was wondering if you wanted to come and see my horses, maybe go for a ride at the weekend."

"Wow, you have your own horses!"

What a stupid thing to say. She pretends not to notice.

"Yeah, I've got two. Jonah's my old pony; he's a really quiet ride so you could have a go on him if you like? Tetra's my new black gelding; I've only had him about two months so I'm not letting anyone else ride him until he gets used to me."

I hear the crack as she bites her mint. I suck mine. My mind whirs. It's a good job I did some riding in Ireland, otherwise I'd be too nervous at the thought of getting on a horse.

"I've got a spare helmet you can borrow," she offers.

"Thanks, that'd be great. I'm really looking forward to it."

"No problem. Maybe you want to come over to the pub and play pool with us some time as well?"

I make a vague response. I know a lot of the village teenagers hang out at the White Hart, Mum told me, but I don't know if Jade knows my mum works there.

The train from Lincoln to Swinderby only takes twenty minutes. At Swinderby Station I unlock my bike and fasten my rucksack to the rack over the rear wheel. It's a warm afternoon, my jacket's thin and I roll up the sleeves. Air sweeps over my arms. I wonder if I'll enjoy this ride so much in the pouring rain and the freezing cold.

I push my bike into the storage carriage behind the caravan. Mum's not in. Milly lets out a tired cry, stretches her long back, jumps off the sofa on stiff legs.

She hasn't been eating properly.

"Here, see if I can tempt you with these..." I shake a few treats into her bowl but she's not interested. She brushes around my legs, staring at me. I don't know what she wants.

"What can I do? I don't know how to help you, old lady."

In the end she gives up and marches away, tail poker stiff with indignation.

"Sorry Mills."

I hardly give it a second thought.

My sketchbook's open, I have a handful of 2B pencils, which make black smudgy lines on the paper. I'm trying to draw a portrait of Connor. The table we used to have at the flat is pressed into a corner. I draw quickly with cramped movements, scratching impressions. Photos are spread out around my sketchbook but I hardly look at them; it's the Connor in my memory that I'm drawing.

His mother Sarah is small; she has blonde hair and very bright blue eyes. Her three sons are all much taller than her and they have dark hair like her husband Mark. Sarah says she has a nephew the same age as Connor who looks much more like her than any of her own children do. Oh yeah, and Sarah's brother is actually the novelist Callum Wilde. Get that. We did one of his books for GCSE English.

Connor told me their house was a ruin when Mark first got hold of it. He spent two years making it habitable before he proposed to Sarah and whisked her away from Yorkshire to Ireland. In the twenty years they've been there they've extended it to three times the size of the original.

The party I sang at was held in their barn at the back of the house. It's Sarah's studio and gallery. We sat on bales of straw and they put some pallets up to make a stage for The Shanbos; that was Mark and Iris's band. When I sang I was too shy to go up on stage so I hid at the side and someone handed me a microphone. Nobody could really see who was singing unless they knew to look out for me. At first my voice came out thin and wobbly but then this strange feeling overtook me and the voice that floated out over the crowd sounded haunting and powerful, even to me. It was Mum's singing voice.

I see a splotch on my sketchpad. Another appears. Idly I blend the water into the outlines of my drawing so that the dark, strong face looming out of the paper is partly created

115

from the drops. Connor looks back at me from the page, his lips seem intent on forming a word but I can't tell what it is. He seems to be staring at something over my shoulder but when I turn round, convinced by his gaze, there's nothing there.

For a minute I wonder if it was that girl, like a shadow at my shoulder that I sensed a few times after my illness. But it feels like a forewarning of something else.

I close the sketchbook, tuck it into the pocket on the inside of my folder; zip the folder closed. *Don't look at me like that.*

Nineteen

Bex

1977

I WAS FIVE the first summer I spent in Newtown Linford. My mother'd had stomach pains for months but the doctor said it was all psychosomatic. Stress, he said. It wouldn't have been surprising; the tea table at our house was a battle-zone every evening, words flying like missiles over the tops of our heads.

At home there was me, my brother Dave, and my cousin Rick who was fostered by my parents. I was the youngest.

I don't know what they were arguing about. Money, probably, politics with a small p, things she thought he should've done; what he called her airs and graces. Dad was a bricklayer. Mum always complained that he never got anything finished at home. He said that was because he had to work himself into the ground to support our family; she said he had no ambition and ought to have worked his way up to management by now.

Each night after the shouting match, Dad headed for the pub. Mum put on her waitress uniform and went to work. Dave or Rick had to put me to bed. I hated it when it was Rick's turn. Rick used to tickle me and lick my face with his big tongue. I don't think he ever touched me in the wrong way but the smell of his breath, the bulk of him leaning over me, the tang of his sweat in the back of my throat made me gag.

It turned out that Mum had gallstones, undiagnosed for a long time. She went into hospital for an operation and my brother had to take me on the train to Leicester where we were met by our grandma. From there it was a bus journey through lush wooded countryside to the picturesque village of Newtown Linford, where my grandparents lived. Dave stayed with us for a few days and then went home.

I hadn't had much to do with my grandparents before but they liked me. They decided I should stay with them for the whole summer. After that I went for more time every year.

Mum had married Dad against their wishes but I became the olive branch, or maybe a second chance, for Grandma to create the kind of female descendent she wanted. Grandma said it would be good for me to experience an alternative environment and Mum would get better quicker without having to worry about me.

Mum recovered from the operation but she was never strong again. She and Dad didn't argue as often either, but on the other hand they didn't really speak anymore. Progressively, over the next few years, I started to live as much in Newtown Linford as I did in Nottingham.

1978

Sebastian and me play in our secret room. It's dark in there; it has no window so you have to put the light on before you go in. I might have been scared about being shut in the dark on my own, but I knew Sebastian would never do that to me.

The room is like a stage that we can make into whatever we want. There are so many rooms in Sebastian's house it doesn't matter that we've claimed this one. We have toy animals all over the carpet and there's an army of soldiers as well, but I won't let Sebastian's soldiers kill the animals like he wants them to. They have to catch them for a circus instead.

Sebastian's well-mannered, my grandma says. But I think of him as delicate, a word Grandma uses about the lace covers she crochets. It means you have to be careful not to damage them and I feel the same about Sebastian. When my grandma and his mum first introduced us he was too shy to speak so we just looked at books together. This summer we've invented a secret language that we only use in this room and he lets me tell him how the game should go. I like him much better than the boys at my school in Nottingham. All they want to play is cowboys and Indians and football, and they don't like girls playing with them.

Mrs Grey calls us into the sitting room for our afternoon tea. We sit up at the table, legs dangling. We eat white bread with sandwich spread; crunch on celery sticks. We drink glasses of milk with strawberry powder magically mixed in to turn the milk pink. Mrs Grey uses this special long-handled spoon.

I'm nearly seven but Sebastian's eight and he's grown lots since last summer. He used to be smaller than me but now he's taller. I didn't know anyone could grow that quick. After tea we're going out to ride the ponies. Mrs Grey said my grandma should buy me a pony of my own, which I can keep in their stables. I heard my grandma say to Granddad that it will be good for me to learn to ride and play tennis so I can move in the right circles, but that made me sad because I want to go all different ways not just in circles.

1989

I stand with my arms folded on a stall door. There's a sweet, pungent smell of straw and manure, the restless stomp of hooves on concrete. The stall on my left is empty, piled high with fresh straw, hay in the net and water already in the shiny bucket, ready for a new occupant.

Tara, my black mare with a white star on her face, shifts from one side to the other; she nods her head at me, kicking the door with her front hoof, startling me out of my reverie.

I step back. I'm wearing a yellow shirt and fawn jodhpurs, with glossy brown riding boots which reach to just below my kneecaps. Beside me is a saddle on a stand. A slice of sunlight coming through the narrow window cuts it in half with a white stripe. I run my hand over the warm leather, breathe in the smell. Tara's impatient; waiting for me to take her out while I've been standing here daydreaming. She nuzzles my arm, lets out a whicker. Then she starts nibbling at the end of my plait where it hangs over my shoulder.

She makes me laugh: a horse with a sense of humour. I flick the braid behind my back then lift her bridle from its hook. She pushes her nose into it for me.

"Good girl."

She snorts gently. I saddle her up and place my foot into the stirrup.

"Hold on, Tara, impatient girl."

We clop out into the yard. It's 4 o'clock, so only a couple of hours until Sebastian's home. And soon after that a horse-box will drive into the yard, bringing Sebastian his birthday present, a beautiful white stallion coming to live in the stall next to Tara.

<hr>

2010

Rebecca's alarm makes a funny noise. Wait, no, it's the cat. Oh, shit. The little bastard's spewing up on my bed, digging her claws into my feet through the quilt.

"'Ere, Milly!" Too late, there are puddles of sick everywhere. It's all I can do not to vomit myself.

"Milly. . . "

The cat keeps retching. I'm furious at being woken from a dream, sure I was going to see Sebastian. But now I'm frozen in the bed, calling Rebecca. I bang on the tin wall between us, shouting.

"Hurry up!"

She blunders in, rubbing her eyes.

"Oh no, Milly!"

She leaves again - what? But then she pushes back into the room, twisting her old baby blanket in her hands. Formerly pink but now grey. She wraps the shivering cat in it.

"I think this is it, Mum."

Milly's all bones. She hasn't eaten properly for weeks so I don't know what the hell she's still throwing up.

"What're you gonna do with her?"

Rebecca drags in a shuddering breath.

"I think there's a box. . . that box Uncle Rick brought the vegetables in from the farm, I'll put her in it."

She's whispering sweet nothings to the cat. I'm scared to move for fear of disturbing the sick.

"What about this?"

I hold my nose. But she makes a tutting noise.

"I'm gonna look after the cat, Mum, you sort the sick. Pull the quilt carefully out of the cover and. . . Oh, I don't know."

Her voice shakes.

"Throw the cover away or something. Or soak it in that plastic laundry tub; it's just outside – use the hose to fill it with water. Do whatever you want. I'm not thinking about sick tonight."

Alright, I had an accident two nights ago after a lock-in at the pub. Rebecca woke up while I was being sick. I'd managed to get the key in the lock; it wasn't my fault I tripped on the step into the caravan. I banged my head on the corner of the sink. She said I'd been unconscious but I wouldn't let her call an ambulance. A&E's full of drunks and thugs on a Saturday night, not the place for a mother and daughter. I've got a whopper of a bruise on the side of my head now though, not a pretty sight.

Payback time I guess. I get rubber gloves from under the sink, drag the cover off the quilt; stuff it in a bin bag. Bizarre that I can hear Rebecca singing in the other room, low and breathy. It makes a shiver run up my back.

Clutching my stinking bundle I glance in the living area to see that she's singing lullabies in front of the gas fire, hunched over, her face close to the box. When I've finished my disgusting job I come back in and see the cat lift its head for a few seconds. It stares at Rebecca, drops its head back onto the blanket.

Rebecca says, "Mum, I think Milly's dead."

I feel dirty from the sick. She gives me a pleading expression. But I can't touch her until I've washed my hands, despite the rubber gloves I wore.

"Back in a minute love, I need to clean up."

Ducking into the shower cubicle I realise I forgot my towel so I have to slink out again. The bedroom smells bad. I push open the window. Sick's soaked through the cover into the quilt. I can't sleep under that quilt again. I feed it through the window until I hear it collapse on the ground outside. Ripping the sheet off I do the same with that. There's still a faint damp patch on the mattress so now I have to go and get the disinfectant. I'm only wrapped in a towel.

When I peep back in at Rebecca she's sitting on the settee. Her face is blank. She holds the dead cat like a baby. I swallow the lump in my throat. *Fuck.* But it's only a cat. Wait until she has to suffer real grief like I have.

I go for my shower.

Rick's pretty good actually, has been since I moved here. He digs a hole behind the caravan and we put Milly in it, still wrapped in Rebecca's blanket. Rebecca didn't want a funeral. She just wants to stand here in silence for a few minutes.

She's crying again.

Turning away, she hesitates at the edge of the land, and then moves off across the road. She goes down Chapel Lane towards the High Street. A weight lifts off my shoulders. She'll be all right when she's had some time to herself.

Rick pats the soil with the back of the spade.

"Heard from our Dave?"

"Not since he arrived in Santiago. We got a postcard when we were still in Skeggy; you?"

"Nah, I was just wonderin', your mum said she was expecting him home."

Dave's been doing this thing with a Spanish name which means 'The way of St James.' He saw a film about it. A kind of pilgrimage, where you don't have to be religious to do it. Dave thought the long trek would help him get over his divorce. He was married for nearly sixteen years, our Dave.

"Settling in all right then? How's the job going?"

We're walking back to the caravan. I'll offer Rick a drink but I hope he'll leave when he's had it. I could do with an afternoon nap before work. Rick's no good at realising when he's overstayed his welcome.

"Yeah it's okay."

I don't tell him I got a warning from Don.

"The punters love ya, Bex, but you're not pulling your weight, ducky," he'd said. "Clarice is complaining and I can't say as I blame 'er. It's these funny turns you 'ave, standing around for ages doing nothin'. Now you've gotta do sommats about it. I'm sorry duck, but you're goin' to 'ave to take this as a warning, much as I love ya, ya understand."

Trouble is I never remember anything about the funny turns, just the fact that minutes have passed – half an hour once. They're a blank space in my head, or sometimes they're filled with memories. And I come to with everybody making jokes about the walking dead and stuff like that. I don't know what I can do about it.

Twenty

Jack

REBECCA SEEMS HAPPY at her new college. At least she's made a friend in that village Bex dragged her to, she's always talking about Jade this and Jade that. It's probably to do with the horses Jade has. All girls like horses, don't they? Wendy told me she also went through the pony-mad phase as a teenager. Not quite sure what she was getting at when she made the comment about having crushes on other girls at boarding school though.

I'm trying extra hard to be good to Wendy. Can't help thinking that to some extent it's an unspoken condition of her making an effort to get to know Rebecca, but anyway it seems to be working. "What about the Eagle Hotel?" (Wendy: suggesting the venue for Rebecca's 18th birthday party). The Eagle's a listed building, a four-star establishment. Wendy's done cupcake demonstrations there for corporate events. It'll be bloody expensive. But I want to make her happy, both of them.

"Okay," I say, "I'll make some enquiries."

"Oh no, it's all right, I've already spoken to the events manager. They have a free slot on the evening of June 5th."

"But that's two weeks after her birthday."

"That doesn't matter. It's the perfect place for a party."

"It does matter, Wendy," I say. "Rebecca will want her party closer to her birthday. We need to at least discuss it with her.

But it was wonderful of you to take such an interest, darling, thank you."

I can see her clenching her jaw. I step in hurriedly with, "Are there any other places you can think of?"

She looks pissed off.

"I still need your input," I say. "Really, I'm useless at organising stuff like that."

She seems mollified.

"Okay then, I'll have another think."

She's brushing her hair at the dressing table. I'm standing behind her. Both the images I can see of her are pleasing, the one in the mirror and the one from my viewpoint over her shoulder. Her cotton gown's coming undone and one large breast is visible, helped by a strategic shift of her bottom on the stool. She meets my eyes in the mirror, her eyelashes heavy with mascara. Her expression is an invitation, which is unusual after she's already put on her makeup. I know what she's doing, re-establishing her claim on me, but, mmm. She looks as delicious as one of her cupcakes. I can't resist.

On my tightrope walk between Wendy and Rebecca it's necessary to take Rebecca's side when it comes to her birthday. Which means acquiescing to Bex's wishes, which in turn involves a lot more soothing of Wendy's ruffled feathers.

"Why do you have to kowtow to her?" Wendy demands.

"I'm not kowtowing to Bex," I say, "I'm just trying to make my daughter's birthday a happy one. You must remember your eighteenth, how important it was to you?"

"Well, yes. I suppose."

"It does make sense for her to have the party near her home, doesn't it?"

"I suppose so." Wendy bites her lip. It looks like we're okay. Then she starts up again. "But in that scruffy pub? I wouldn't normally be seen dead in it."

That's because you're a snob, comes to mind.

"It's not actually in the pub," I remind her. "It's in a function room upstairs."

Bex is paying for the use of the room. We're paying for the DJ, the lights and the catering, and for a minibus to pick up kids from Skegness and Lincoln.

Wendy wanted to make the cake but Bex said she knew someone who could do it. Wendy's making a cake anyway and is insisting on bringing it to the party. It'll be perfect, the cake Wendy makes, a professional masterpiece. The one Bex provides probably won't be; not perfect by a long chalk. That won't bother Rebecca, but it might bother Wendy when Rebecca prefers her mother's offering.

Now that Wendy's finally decided to launch herself into step-motherhood, the touchy subject of my daughter has become even trickier. Wendy's now competing directly with Bex, a battle she can't possibly win, though she's clearly much, much better at the job of mother. But she wasn't the one who gave birth to Rebecca and that's what really counts, it seems.

⸺◦◦◦⸺

The first time Rebecca met Wendy was years ago when the social workers were involved. They wanted to know whether she could live with Wendy and me. I wanted to have her... of course I did. But Wendy and I had just got married and she was pregnant with the baby we later lost. She needed a lot of bed rest. It wouldn't have been practical.

Six years old, Rebecca was. She was sent to live with a family called the Martens while Bex was in rehabilitation. Don't get me wrong, I hated myself for not taking my little girl in.

Sometime later, Rebecca went home to her mother for a while but returned to the care of the Martens when Bex had a relapse. Wendy was desperately trying to get pregnant again and she was distraught when I suggested us taking on my resentful nine-year-old.

Bex had poisoned Rebecca's mind to me and she refused to see me or reply to my letters for the next few years. At twelve she was deemed capable of making an informed decision to go back and live with her alcoholic parent.

⸺◦⸺

After Rebecca's illness I decided to get firm with Wendy, I told her she had to get over her aversion to my first instance of fatherhood.

Rebecca came along with me to a production of Bugsy Malone by Joshua's drama group. Wendy and she sized each other up. I saw my daughter watching Wendy with the boys. We all had a drink after the show and although my wife and my daughter barely spoke to each other Rebecca surprised me.

"You did the right thing marrying her, Dad," she said when I dropped her off at home. I wanted to say sorry for the mess I'd made of being her father, but it wouldn't have been the right time. Instead I kissed her glossy dark head.

"You remind me of a seal," I told her.

She laughed.

"Is it my eyes?"

She widened them and gave me an intense look.

"I say the same thing to Mum. She has seal eyes too."

Then she went quiet and got out the car.

"See ya, then."

"Yeah, see you soon."

I rolled down the window as she started walking away. She turned to wave at me.

"It's your hair," I called out. "It's the way it gives your head that smooth shape, that's what reminded me of a seal."

Not your eyes. Not Bex's eyes.

I paid special attention to Wendy when I got home, nuzzling her neck where it disappeared into her Angora sweater.

"You're a wonderful mother."

128

"And you're a good father, to all your children. Rebecca's a lucky girl to have you watching over her."

"Come 'ere, you." I buried myself further in her. I guess she got three out of three that night.

Once Rebecca moved into the caravan, we had her to stay with us at the house. She was tickled pink by the spare bedroom with its ensuite.

"It's like a hotel."

After dinner she helped Wendy box up some cupcake orders for the next day. She read the boys their bedtime story.

"I could get used to having a step-daughter," Wendy remarked.

<hr />

"Dad."

Rebecca and I are having a quick coffee in Lincoln. I had to come in to discuss a new commission with a guy who's setting up a hydrotherapy centre for rehabilitating accident victims and I had a spare hour.

It's an exciting commission, the guy needs us to design a pool with a floor that can be raised or lowered to make getting in and out easier and so the therapists can choose what depth they want the pool to be. It plays on my mind as I talk to Rebecca.

"Yeah?"

"Have you ever had a lucid moment?"

Bex on the dance floor that first time flashes into my mind. The way that moment was honed to a perfect point.

I think that's what she means.

"Er, maybe... why?"

"Oh. I had one when I was riding across a field with Jade the other day."

My gaze has fixed itself to the door-closer on the staff-only door, which is nestled in the gap between two sets of shelves

129

near the till. A member of staff taps the code on a keypad and pulls the door open towards her. After she's gone through, it closes with a jagged motion that sets my teeth on edge. I wonder who has their door contract; I assume all the shops in the chain, countrywide, use the same firm. It would be a massive contract, hmm. . .

Rebecca's staring at me. I try to remember what she's just said, ah, yes.

"What makes you describe it as lucid?"

"I don't really know how to explain it."

Rebecca screws up her face to think and I suddenly remember her doing that when she was a small girl. She looks just like she did then.

"It was like it had happened before," she says, "but not exactly the same."

She twists a strand of hair falling over her forehead around a finger.

"I'd been on a horse before but it wasn't the horse I was on then. The lucid moment, was like a memory from a dream, super-real, kind of."

"Hmm."

I take a bite of my scone.

"You have been on a horse before though, a few times."

"Yes, but it wasn't a real thing I was kind of re-experiencing when I was on Jade's horse. I told you. It was a super-real experience I've had that I can't quite remember." She blows out through her lips.

"It keeps bugging me. There's a place, a person, someone I keep feeling around me. I mean feeling as if someone's there who isn't – they may not actually exist. Oh. You wouldn't understand."

She's lost me. I study her, a memory dawns.

"When you were this big," I say, holding my hand level at the height of the table, "you used to see people. That's right. Nobody else could see them. It used to freak us out but it never bothered you. You used to talk to them."

"What, you mean like invisible friends?"

130

"No," I think back. "I think it was more than that. Erm, ghosts, if that doesn't sound too frightening?"

Rebecca laughs.

"Not at all." She sounds proud. "You mean you think I'm psychic, ha ha. Yeah, that's great. I like that."

She bites into her scone.

She tells me she does her painting in Jade's studio, a converted stable. This is rather than in the conservatory 'that old perv' at the pub offered her.

"Jade likes having someone to talk to while she works. Her canvases are huge. They're figurative, but in a very abstract way, if you get me."

I don't. But I do enjoy hearing her talk.

"What do they look like?"

She pauses, wipes the edge of her finger along the plate where a blob of butter has fallen off her scone. She licks her finger.

"They could be horses or they could be humans, it's difficult to tell. She likes my 'Night' paintings so much because of the abstract horse and human in them. I'm trying to wean myself away from that image though. I don't want to paint it any more. But it keeps coming back to me. Dad, I think that's what that lucid experience was."

Uh-oh, she's left me behind again.

"You think it was. . . ?"

"The painting I keep doing, I think it's because of some weird experience I had when I was ill, in hospital, before I had the fit."

She stares at me. I stare back.

She looks disappointed.

I pat her hand.

Then she continues talking about art.

"Jade does these thick black charcoal drawings, made with huge sweeping strokes. She brushes over them with turpentine and lets it drip everywhere. I usually spend more time watching her than doing my own work 'coz to be honest I work better in private. I can't talk when I'm making art."

Gazing off into the corner of the bookshop, she seems to lose herself.

"Drippy bit," I prompt.

"After she's done the drippy bit with the turpentine she lets it dry and then she adds solid colour with paint, or she might not. She glues tissue paper and all sorts of stuff on her paintings; bits of collage or 3D materials, she doesn't care as long as it gives the effect she's looking for."

"Sounds fascinating," I say.

She stares at me, takes a slurp of coffee. I begin inspecting the hinges on the faultily-closing door; check what type they use, wonder if Doorphenalia could improve on the complete product and calculate costs in my head for a single door, a shop-full of doors, enough doors for every shop in the chain, my head reeling.

"Another thing she does," Rebecca's saying. "Dad, are you interested?"

"I am interested, of course."

"Well then."

Rebecca coughs. "I'm learning a lot from watching her work, you know. It's important. Anyway, she scrapes away at her painting with a knife. You can see the raw canvas beneath all that stuff she puts on. Sometimes she throws bleach at the canvas. It's amazing."

"It sounds it," I agree.

Saturday 22nd May

Music throbs in the fabric of the walls and the floor. Whoa, it wasn't this loud in my day. A guy at Rebecca's college recommended the DJ; but... they actually enjoy this racket?

Apparently the students do.

I can't believe she's eighteen.

There's a row of vodka-and-cokes lined up along the edge of the table where the sandwiches are, all drinks her friends have bought her.

I keep an eye on Bex across the room. God, she looks so thin. We haven't spoken yet and Wendy's keeping a firm grasp on my hand.

I remember Rebecca just after she was born, and the way Bex cried and cried. What was that all about? She could hardly look at her.

"Come on, Rebecca!" A bunch of girls drags my astonishingly grown-up daughter onto the dance floor.

I think it's a song by Lady Gaga they're dancing to, but I wouldn't swear on it. I watch Rebecca getting into the groove – if they still call it that.

Purple, orange and lime-green lights glow on the faces of the young, on Bex and Wendy and presumably on me as well. A couple of girls give me a thumbs-up sign.

Huh, why're they making that gesture at me?

"Rebecca's dad," one girl laughs to another.

She can't possibly be flirting with me, can she? Wendy pulls me out of the way, into a dim corner. I'm standing beside the appallingly-fitted door into the toilets; it's got completely the wrong kind of hinges which are splitting the wood of the frame apart. Not only that but the handle's the wrong kind, a knob you have to turn, when it ought to be a streamlined push-down lever to minimise the necessity of hand contact. Maybe I should have a word with the landlord, see about doing him some kind of deal. . .

"Jack!"

Wendy gives me a shove.

Rebecca's dancing with her friend Jade, but a boy is muscling in between them, he starts throwing his body around my daughter. Rebecca dances harder, facing him.

Oh dear, I hope the surprise I planned for her isn't a mistake.

There's a break in the music.

Rebecca goes over to the table where her drinks are. Nobody's eating the sandwiches, the edges curling as the bread dries. The music starts up again and bloody hell it's *'One day I'll fly away'*. I recognise Bex's favourite song.

Shit, there she is, microphone in hand, swaying slightly on the circular podium. She drains her glass and passes it to the DJ. The DJ turns the music down as Bex begins to speak.

Wendy makes a disgusted face.

"Why does she have to ruin it for her?"

Bex's voice crackles over the microphone.

"My darling Rebecca. . . "

Rebecca's staring at her, eyes stretched wide.

"My. . . my only daughter. . . " Bex's voice breaks. She starts coughing.

Or is she crying? It's excruciating to watch.

Feet shuffle all around the room.

Bex straightens; neck long beneath piled-up hair. She moves her head from side to side. Then, mercifully, she finishes quickly, not making much of a speech after all.

"Happy Birthday, Rebecca, come and have this dance with yer old Mum." There's a scattered round of applause, a communal outlet of breath.

Rebecca looks as if she hasn't breathed for a long time.

Rise and fly from dream to dream. Bex mouths along to the words. She had such a lovely singing voice on her. Shit, shit, shit. Why did she have to ruin tonight for me, bring back so many memories?

Rebecca dances with her Mum. My head buzzes.

"Let's get some food, shall we?" Wendy moves her body in a stiff way, leading me across the room.

Towards the end of the mother and daughter song the music somehow transmutes into 'Happy Birthday to you' and everybody joins in. Wendy and I are standing with plates of food. Bex is standing behind Rebecca with her hands on her shoulders.

A woman with birds-nest hair and vivid lipstick carries in a cake.

"But I thought. . . " says Wendy in my ear.

The cake she made, a pink, three-tiered amazement, stands on a small table by itself under which Rebecca's gifts have been stacked. Bex flashes one look over to Wendy as her daughter blows out the candles on the normal-looking birthday cake with a plastic '18' propped up in the centre.

I'm disorientated for a moment as people around us shift to both sides. A hand presses my arm.

"We made it, little bro," booms a voice.

Wiry curls brush my face and it's Iris, kissing me on the cheek. I haven't seen her for such a long time. Just behind her stands a tall, good-looking lad who must be the Connor Rebecca's apparently sweet on. I check to make sure she isn't still dancing with that other boy.

Twenty-One

Bex

REBECCA'S AT HER dad's for a week.

She's making a mistake, getting involved with that Irish boy. She'll end up with a Great Grief just like mine, but she won't listen.

I've received a letter, makes me nervous; a scribbled-over envelope, our Skegness address and then this one. Posh paper it looks like. I can feel in my bones, it's something earth-shattering.

A quick bracer, that's what I need. Raise the temperature of the ice my hands and feet seem to be plunged in: ease the nagging pain in my side that's worse than ever.

Hmm. Miss that cat. Miss Milly-Tilly-Willy. Head stuck in memories, bogged in possibilities, can't get out.

Hasn't sunk in yet, what that letter says. Ohmygod. How can this be happening? It's addressed to Mrs Rebecca Grey and Miss Rebecca Grey. But which Rebecca is it really meant to be for? It'll all come out in the wash.

The Past, can't remember the date.

When Rebecca is two months old we go back to Greys Mount, travelling by train. I've got pins and needles in my arm where she lies on it but I don't want to wake her up.

I have to push each breath in and out of my lungs, as if a machine inside me's broken.

They've been writing to me, Sebastian's parents, begging to see the baby.

It's the first time I've been back.

On the last day before I left I helped Evelyn pack away my wedding dress in layers of tissue paper, running silk and pearls through our fingers the way we had done so many times during the fittings.

"I'll save it," says Evelyn. "Your daughter will wear it one day. It can be altered."

She looks at me, lets her gaze fall down my body.

To be fair, she's never said: "What were you thinking of, Rebecca?"

She hasn't blamed me for Sebastian's death.

I don't say anything. I've hardly spoken since he died.

---

24 September 1990

My wedding day is now the day of Sebastian's funeral.

I walk down the aisle of All Saints Church in my cleverly-cut wedding gown. I cling onto Jonathan's arm. My parents and Rick refused to attend, saying it's a 'sick' idea. Granddad feels the same, waiting outside the church until the funeral part of the ceremony begins. He was fond of Sebastian.

"A good lad you had there, Rebecca."

He wants to pay his respects but not have any part in what he calls the grotesque fallacy we're about to enact.

Grandma and Dave are in the church, sitting in the front pew on the left side. Sebastian's parents, together with an old aunt or two, sit on the right. Mr Grahams who does the garden is on that side as well. The remaining pews are packed with villagers, family friends, and Sebastian's school and work friends. There's a whole other crowd standing outside as well, as close to the church as they can get, it's all they can do. The church is too small for them all.

The coffin is already there at the front between the choir stalls, attended by Sebastian's best man Joe. He'll be standing in as proxy during the marriage, saying "I did" instead of "I do". A choir of boys from Leicester Cathedral sing *Pie Jesu.*

My beautiful Sebastian lies in the casket wearing his wedding suit, a carved form in porcelain, his wedding ring already on his finger.

Evelyn and the vicar decided it wouldn't be appropriate for me to attempt to put it on him during the service. I'm just to lay my hand over his. And I'm glad because my hands shake uncontrollably.

Sebastian's have been placed over his chest, I know because I was brought in here before all this began, Grandma holding me on one side and Evelyn on the other so I could look at him, understand what I was about to do, so it wouldn't be too much of a shock when it was time to lean over the coffin and give him my last ever kiss.

Mrs Evans, who cleans house for the Greys, plays the Bridal Chorus on the church organ as I tremble my way down the aisle. Jonathan, a mannequin figure colourless with shock, does his best to support me.

The smell of white lilies is overpowering, as is the cold, biting smell of the unheated church.

I walk on a blue carpet, gazing ahead at the stained glass window behind the altar. There's been no sunshine today. I'm not really here. It's the ghost of me walking down this aisle; I know it because I can't feel anything, can hardly hear the music, only the raucous sobs of the organist; the sound of shuffling feet and a hundred noses being blown. This is the day Sebastian and I have talked about since we were children, but it's turned out so differently from what we planned that it can't be real.

Unspecified date

It hurts so much coming back. In the back of the taxi, driven through Newtown Linford, I keep a hand on my sleeping baby. I thought I'd stopped feeling anything as strong as this; blocked it all out, but I've never put it to the test before, didn't want to risk it by returning. Evelyn's been kind and patient in the letters she sends me regularly.

"I know you will both come back to us, Rebecca dear."

Evelyn and Jonathan are waiting at the front door. The taxi driver comes round to the boot and lifts out the wheels while I lean back into the car for the neat grey carrycot. Then Sebastian's parents move at the same time, hurrying forward, tripping over themselves.

Jonathan pays the driver and reaches for my bags, Evelyn trembles.

"Oh please, may I? May I hold her, Rebecca dear?"

When Rebecca's in her arms she breathes in the baby smell.

"Oh look, Jonathan, do look."

I don't say anything. I can't. On the way past Rose Cottage opposite the park gates, I swear my heart stopped beating. There's fog in my head, so thick I can hardly see.

We move through to the sitting room with the green striped wallpaper. Rebecca turns her head as she lies in Evelyn's arms, looking around with her big brown eyes. She hates being held in that position, preferring to be upright. But Evelyn keeps tucking the blanket more tightly round her.

Jonathan moves across the room towards his wife, everything silent and in slow motion. Why is there such a fog?

He puts his arms out for the baby.

She rests her head happily on his shoulder as he parades the room with her. A look of peace settles over Evelyn's face as she watches them together. Sound bursts back into life.

"He was just like that with Sebastian; he could always keep him calm."

I still haven't said much, hunched miserably in my armchair by the fire.

"Are you all right, Rebecca dear?" Evelyn's putting on a look of concern but I get the feeling she's irritated by me.

"My name's Bex nowadays."

Evelyn's shocked, I can tell. She pushes herself off the sofa, brushing her gnarled fingers delicately over the front of her woollen skirt. Her arthritis looks a lot worse.

"I'll see how Linda's getting on with that tea."

Jonathan comes over and perches in front of me on the padded footstool, holding Rebecca against his chest.

"Mrs Evans works for us full-time now. Evelyn fell into a terrible depression after everything." He says it gently but the words make a raw gash in my heart.

"I'm suffering my own Great Grief," is all I can offer.

I've recently come up with this term, liking the guttural sound of it, an appropriate grating, scraping, Grr-ate Grr-ief. Rebecca clutches Jonathan's finger with her surprisingly strong grip.

"I know you are," he says." I can't imagine your pain, Re-becca."

I twist my wedding ring.

"Bex," I croak, "my name's Bex now."

Why does it hurt to tell him this?

Jonathan withdraws his head, or that's how it strikes me; like a tortoise into its shell. But after a minute he makes an-other attempt at connection. He rubs the baby's back with his big hand. She burps softly. It makes me want to cry.

"We've all been through a terrible pain. . . but we're so grate-ful to you for bringing Rebecca to us. She's the one thing that can bring Evelyn alive again, and I'm sure she's done the same for you."

I feel like I've been stung. How can he think that? Nothing can ever, ever bring me alive again.

I feel myself curling up inside like a snail, looking at Rebecca nestled against him. I wonder if she'd be better off staying with them. It's the first time it occurs to me, and also that it might be what they want.

My childhood here was the making of me and now I'm broken, unmade. I can never be put back together.

"I can see how unhappy you are. Let us help you, Rebecca – Bex. Come back to us. We can give you and baby Rebecca everything you both need."

Now

I come back to myself as if I've been away a long time. The light's changed in the caravan. Big hand's moved round the circle twice. The letter in my hands tells more of a story than it knows.

How the eff am I going to sort this out?

Twenty-Two

Rebecca

Wednesday, 26th May

CONNOR'S STAYING IN the campervan in Dad's front drive. It's hooked up to electricity via the garage, and it even has its own shower and flushing toilet.

Iris and I are sharing the spare bedroom in the house, me on what Wendy calls a z-bed.

On the night of my birthday party Iris slept in my room in the caravan while Connor and I sat up all night holding hands, staring into the gas fire.

Mum had collapsed in the pub and we had to carry her home. Jade was there too and I was so embarrassed, even though she assured me her dad had been exactly the same, before he died of alcohol poisoning.

I leave Dad's house for the day on Wednesday and go into Lincoln for my college tutorial. Connor's going home on Sunday.

We haven't kissed yet. The tension's unbearable.

I'm chatting to Jade, slinging my bag onto my shoulder and suddenly he's there, hands in his pockets, right hip pushed forward in that way he has. He's so sexy, even Jade does a double-take.

Then she has the nerve to ring her mum and tell her she doesn't need a lift home because she's getting on the train with me and she'll walk, yes walk, huh? She'll walk home from Swinderby.

It just so happens that the Nottingham train Connor and I take also stops at Swinderby. All she really wants is to sit and stare at Connor throughout her ten-minute journey. She flirts with him disgustingly.

Cow.

But it's my hand he slides his fingers into even as he laughs at her jokes.

I can hardly look at him; every time I do I go red, have to catch my breath, shift around on the train seat; Jade laughs.

"Ants in ya pants, Rebecca?"

I go even redder, wish the train would hurry up and get to Swinderby; discharge her.

Connor gives me a grin.

"Lucky ants, is all I can say."

Jade puts two fingers in her mouth, makes a retching sound. She's sliding out of her seat, gathering her stuff. Thank god.

The train slows, creaking towards her stop.

"Have a great rest of the week then. I'll see you at the weekend, yeah? Fancy a ride on Sunday evening?"

She knows Connor's leaving then. She leans forward and gives me a peck on the cheek.

"I've got to walk bloody miles with this lot now! What a crazy idea, why didn't you stop me? Oh well, I might see if I've got enough money for a taxi."

She's still muttering as she makes towards the door.

"You have one hot boyfriend, Rebecca Grey; good on you, girl!"

We lapse into silence as the train judders into motion again. Finally I turn my head and look at Connor; we both know this is the moment, if we don't kiss now we never will. He pulls me against him, my head in the curve of his shoulder, his hand cupped around the side of my neck. His fingers move on my face, trailing my cheek and under my ear; back up into my hair.

This has happened before. No, it hasn't.

"I love your hair."

His lips against my ear, I smell his clean sweat, the scent of deodorant lightly covering it. His touch seems so familiar, as if I've known it my whole life.

Familiar. . . but not what you're thinking of.

My face turns up to meet his, skimming his lips for an infinite moment before some instinctive signal welds us together like barnacles to rocks. Connor cups the back of my head in his hand as he kisses my mouth, my tongue tugging at his.

The noise of the train becomes the rumbling of hooves on hard earth. I begin to tremble.

To break the intensity I pull away from him then slide an arm behind him, lay my other hand lightly on his stomach. His chin digs gently into my shoulder. I wriggle until my head rests on his chest and I can hear his heart. Makes me want to cry, it's the nicest feeling ever. It's all woozy and impossible to think beyond this moment. His hand strokes my arm, his voice in my ear.

"I missed you so much. . . "

I have an overwhelming feeling of lucidity. Nothing has ever been this real.

. . . Except, it has; oh God.

I jolt like I've flicked an electric switch with a wet hand, a hallucinatory reality jarring against my safety in Connor's warm arms. I'm crippled by the strongest sense of déjà vu I ever had in my life. What happens next?

I can't bear to find out; I just know it's bad. Something goes wrong.

I pull away, retreat across the seat, the plastic armrest digging into my back. The people opposite stare. Connor's eyes flash. I fight nausea.

The train pulls into Newark.

The couple opposite get out. More people get on. A whistle blows, doors slam shut, the train starts up again with a high pitched whine, a deafening rumbling, hooves galloping faster and faster and I wish they could take me away from this unexplained terror.

But they can't because it's inside me. This has all happened before, *somehow*, but in an essential way different.

It wasn't you, Connor. It wasn't him.

We stare at each other. I can't blink or move. Connor's got no idea what's going on.

"What have I done, Rebecca? I didn't mean to upset you, I'm sorry."

I try to flatten the panic. Slowly my hand snakes out across the seat towards his. My fingers open, waiting. I won't blame him if he hates me now, if the first thing he does when he gets away from me is ring directory enquiries and find out Jade's number. She'd never mess him about like I do. And she's all hot, not hot and cold like me.

The train's rocking steadily on its tracks; the high-pitched whine like a horse's neigh has abated. I feel calmer, lulled by the motion. But I have a dead spot inside me – like skin that's healed over with a scar, and you can't feel anything when you touch it. Connor's fingers curl into mine, his eyes still questioning, but I don't have an explanation. I feel too young for him, so inexperienced.

"It's not your fault," is all I can offer, "I just felt this horrible panic suddenly, I don't know why... I can't explain. I'm so sorry."

In a way it's a relief; it'll be all over now. At least I won't have to go through the kind of Great Grief that ruined Mum's life. She's warned me ever since she found out about Connor.

"Don't make the same mistake as me," is what she told me. But it's impossible to avoid making that mistake if I don't know what it is. Maybe the mistake she made is acting like I just did. How can I know?

We hold hands for the rest of the journey but we're hardly talking. Connor tells me he isn't angry. I lean against him as the train rocks but there's tension in his body; he holds himself aloof.

I go out to the campervan after the evening meal, take Connor the drawing I did of him weeks ago.

He's been lying on his back on the bed, one knee up, but now he raises himself to a sitting position and swivels so that his back is against the window. He pats the space beside him, saying nothing. I sit next to him on the narrow bed, our feet braced against the cupboard opposite. The rolled-up drawing feels unimportant for now and I put it to one side. Our breathing synchronises and we still don't talk but I have the feeling I want to get closer to him. I can tell he's still unsure of me; it was awkward during dinner, maybe he thinks I'm going to fly into a panic again. I wait to see if that feeling will return but it doesn't, I feel deeply calm. Right now his breath close to my ear seems a good substitute for words.

The smell of sun-warmed grass carries through the open window on air just starting to cool. Connor's fingers move on the blanket between us, curling in and then opening out again like a starfish. He glances sideways at me, clears his throat.

"Do you want to go for a walk?"

No.

I'm lightheaded, almost pushed out of myself by the strength of my feelings. I slide my hand over his and close my fingers around it, aware of his breath catching in his throat as I trace the veins on the back of his hand with the tip of my finger. I make him meet my eyes; his are full of water, which amazes me.

I nod slowly.

His hand starts to move of its own accord, transmitting heat deep inside my skin; now cupping my breast under my top, fingers sliding into my bra. I lean in closer and an electric tingle in my nipple echoes in my groin. We breathe in tandem, synchronise all our movements.

I'm under the covers with him now, my clothes a messy pile on the floor. I lift my hips to help him push into me. It only hurts a tiny bit.

I open my eyes after I hear him groan and let out some whimpers like a hurt animal, and he comes to a shuddering stop on top of me. But - and oh this is so weird - he's not Connor anymore. He's that boy with blond hair from my vision

147

or dream, smiling at me with his light blue eyes, long hair falling over his face.

Twenty-Three

Bex

YESTERDAY I GOT the letter. Today a strange man sits in my caravan, squeezed into the corner by the TV. I was going to ring Rebecca and tell her she has to come home, but no. I've decided I need to deal with this on my own.

Mr Johnson, the man is. Says the Greys never forgot about me or Rebecca. But... he means my Rebecca, Sebastian's. Not Jack's. Not our Rebecca.

He's giving me a funny look, Mr Johnson is.

"Are you sure you're all right, Mrs Grey, can I get you a drink of water at all?"

It's those black shapes crowding around me; pinpricks at my hairline, an army of ants rushing up my scalp. My vision decreases to a narrow tunnel, blackness filled with tiny stars all around the edge, colourful, quite pretty really. Like a kaleidoscope. It opens out slowly and I focus my eyes on him, Mr Johnson.

It will be all right.

Get up, Bex.

I push myself to stand. I should have got dressed before he arrived but he got here early. I wish people would stick to the times they arrange. That pain in my side, the ache and drag, eating me from the inside.

If I offer him a cup of tea I can pour myself a quick stiffener, sort us both out. He looks like he could do with a drink.

"Are you sure you're okay Mrs Grey? This must all be a bit of a shock for you."

He rises from his chair. This space is too small for the both of us.

"Sit down, sit down, Mr Johnson. . . "

"Call me Adam."

"Adam then, sit yourself down and I'll put the kettle on, eh?"

I pull my dressing gown around me. There are times I snap back into my head and wonder where the hell I've been, people giving me funny looks like now. Each time I turn my head it takes a moment for my vision to realise it's moved on to another view, catching up ever so slowly.

"If you're sure you're okay?"

He won't let up, will he?

"Fine, fine, just a bit tired that's all."

Funny how conscious I am of having to put my lips together in the right shapes to form the words.

"I'll make us a coffee. Would you mind if I pop in my bedroom and get some proper clothes on while the kettle's boiling?"

He looks relieved.

"Not at all; I'll just sort through these papers and make sure they're all ready for you to sign. If you could just fetch your driving licence for me and er, your Deed Poll documentation and any official paperwork with your address on. Oh, and your daughter's birth certificate. I'll need to see some kind of government letter to do with the two of you as well, Tax Credits or some such."

He starts scribbling in a notebook on his lap. Next to him on the coffee table is a folder of papers he keeps flicking through. I take the few steps to the bedroom, my hands doing that funny thing; pins and needles when the fingers and thumbs clench together and it's hard to separate them. It makes getting dressed difficult. Before I fasten my bra I have a sniff of my armpits, add an extra squirt of deodorant.

Every movement of my arms feels like lifting a heavy weight and despite what Mr Johnson's just informed me, yep, I'm certain my time is running out.

It's because of all these dreams about Sebastian; dreams of waiting for him but he's never there.

Not yet. I would've given anything to follow when he died – I didn't want to go on living but they made me. Evelyn, she took over everything, insisting I went ahead with the marriage, took Sebastian's name, continued living in his stead. She wanted me to have a baby. It was her who wanted the baby, not me. Not after Sebastian was gone.

September, 1990

I can't seem to feel the ground under the soles of my feet as I walk; however hard I stamp on the paving stones. I've been in this suspended state since I sat there with Sebastian's bleeding head wedged in my lap.

I wiggle my fingers: can't feel anything, pinch my thigh hard through my jeans and it has no effect at all, although I know there'll be a bruise there later because I'm covered in them, all over my arms and legs. I laugh out loud, into sunshine that I can't feel on my skin. How dare it be sunny now? As if it doesn't matter that Sebastian's body was put in the ground.

I want him back. Even though he's dead, broken, I want to see him again. I just want him back.

I'm not ready for this. *Stop it! Stop all the clocks.*

Evelyn takes my arm firmly and marches me along.

"Watch the traffic," she says. "You've got to look after yourself. It's not just you."

She's not being unkind, just handling me the way she's learned to over the past week. I wouldn't do anything otherwise; wouldn't move or speak or eat or sleep. I'd just be nothing. But it seems if she puppets me I can give the impression of being alive.

We're taking my birth certificate to the Register Office in Leicester to get my name changed by Deed Poll. Spattered rain dries up on the now sunlit streets; I try to step around the patterned drops on the pavement, pulling Evelyn with me.

I'm sure if I look hard enough, I will see him, his flash of gold hair in the sun. My shadow's there on the grey stones – all that's really left of me.

I break away from Evelyn, spinning at the edge of the road, my hair flowing after me like a banner on the shadow picture that's realer than the real me.

"Mind the traffic, Rebecca."

It's not just you.

Evelyn grasps me more firmly.

In the waiting room it's gloomy and dark, no sun reaches our sombre bodies sitting on the hard chairs. I came to this place only last week with my mother-in-law to register the death.

That was after I'd married him, but we have no certificate to show for that, which is unfair because if I was in France I could apply to the President for a special dispensation to legally marry my deceased fiancé. It makes me feel better knowing that. There are other girls like me, all over the world, who became widows the minute they said 'I do'.

I twist the ring on my finger, exactly the same as the one on Sebastian's under the ground. Evelyn and I chose a double plot so I can be buried beside him, in a beautiful place on the outskirts of Leicester because the churchyard in Newtown Linford is full up. We'll be visiting Sebastian on our way home.

Evelyn's face is grey in the darkness; I can see the skull beneath the skin of her face, something that's been happening a lot. Mrs Evans; Jonathan; the vicar; my grandparents: all of them are nothing but walking skeletons to me.

I'm not even that. I'm a ghost already; less solid even than my darling Sebastian.

Now

Gawd, how long have I been out? It's hot in here, like living in a baking dish. There's a man in my living room. He asked me about Rebecca. Well. *A rose by any other name...*

Our Rebecca's determined to head for her own Great Grief whatever I say. I warned her Sunday morning after her party, before she went off with her bloody father.

She was with that Connor boy.

He had the effrontery to put out his hand as if he thought I'd actually shake it.

I wondered how I'd got home, couldn't remember a thing. Then Rebecca went to the trouble of spelling it out for me.

I felt hemmed in, in that tiny space with the two of them, vibrant and alive looking like they were joined at the hip. The smile she had for him full of a million promises. I'd seen it on my own face once.

A clump of my hair comes out on the brush as I run it through, that can't be right. I pull the rest of it up into a ponytail; tie a short scarf around it to give myself some volume and colour. Bit of eyeliner, bit of lippy. *That, my dear, will have to do.*

Squeezing back around the bed, I reach into the cupboard above the headboard, all my papers and important stuff is in there. The biscuit tin with a scratched picture of a thatched cottage on it is dusty already; despite we've only been here a couple of months, or maybe its Skegness dust I've brought with me.

Rebecca's birth certificate – did he say that? Wonder if I can get away with not... oh, but here – the original one.

My driving licence, yeah. The Deed Poll I'm looking for. What else did he say, couple of letters? They'll be in the sideboard drawer in the living room.

Here it is, the Deed Poll that made me officially Mrs Rebecca Grey.

"Are you all right in there, Mrs Grey?"

I come to with a shudder. The papers have slid off my lap onto the floor. I've been off somewhere again. I press my hand into my side, wish the pain would abate.

Quick, get the lid off the bottle, another stiffener should keep it at bay.

Ah.

Adam's actually pushing the bedroom door open and peering inside – the cheek of it. . .

"Excuse me!"

The door bumps into my knees, "I could've been doing anything in here!"

"I'm so sorry but I was beginning to worry about you, you've been such a long time and you didn't answer when I called several times."

He bends to fish around my feet for the papers, there's not enough room for both of us in here. I can't open the door because he's in the way.

He's quite good-looking, a bit polished for me though. I need to get out. I go hot again, prickle and tingle. I just need a minute to catch my breath. Somehow we wrangle ourselves out of the tiny space and shuffle back into the living room.

"I've made us a coffee, I hope you don't mind."

He's apologetic, but it's still a bloody cheek.

I want to stamp my feet on the caravan floor, shake this tin box from side to side just to feel real.

I slip off to the kitchen on the excuse of finding him a piece of cake, left over from Rebecca's birthday. Mustn't tell him that, though, gotta be careful what I say.

Try not to let the glass clink, oops. Slide the bottle behind the tea tin.

"Thanks very much."

He takes a fastidious bite of cake, lays the plate to one side.

He studies Rebecca's birth certificate, looks at me, then back at it. Looks at the letters I've given him out of the drawer. Tax Credits and all that. I clench my hands. He gives me a long stare.

"She's with you then?" he says. "I thought. . ."

"She's with me, still in education, she is."

He thinks she's older than she is, except the letters I've given him say otherwise.

He makes a 'hmm' sound.

"Kept her name, did she?"

Brain starts to disintegrate.

"She. . . er, yeah, family line and all that. . . "

My hands fidget wildly with the ends of the scarf at my hips. He stares at them. I can see him lingering on the bit of stomach that shows above my jeans.

"I'll need to borrow these for photocopying; you'll get them back in the post. I'll look after them for you."

He gives me another intense look.

"They can so easily get lost, can't they?"

I don't know what the hell he's on about. Or has he spotted my dilemma? Wonder what he wants in return for helping me.

"Right, that seems to be everything in order then."

It will all be found out. He knows it and so do I. He spreads his hands over the paperwork. Stands up, looks bulky in the small space crammed with oversized furniture. He tucks his leather folder under one arm and takes up his shiny black briefcase with the same hand. He puts his right hand out to be shaken by me, leaves it in mine overlong. There's a twinkle in his eyes now.

"I hope to see you again very soon."

His eyes slide down to my hipbones. He clears his throat.

"I left all the relevant copies for your daughter to sign. I look forward to seeing her at our next meeting. If you have any questions at all you can contact me on this number."

I turn his card over in my hand.

"Feel free to ring, any time."

When I've watched him step carefully out of the caravan and pick his way over the land to his car, I fetch my glass and bottle. Something's rumbling inside me, the beginnings of a storm. My scalp screams, the hairs on my arms stand upright. It'll all come out in the wash.

Twenty-Four

Rebecca

ON THURSDAY DAD takes the day off work and Wendy takes the boys out of school for the afternoon. All of us are visiting Nottingham Castle.

We go in the underground caves; the dungeons the twins call them. They're really excited. Connor tells them all sorts of stories involving skeletons and ghosts; he knows just when to stop before getting them too terrified, but they're at such a high level of excitement anything could set them off now into fits of hysterical giggles or screams.

"Shh, boys," Wendy keeps telling them. "You're annoying all the other people with your noise."

But the other visitors on our tour seem entranced by the two cherubic faces surrounded by crowns of golden hair. I'm proud they're my brothers.

Connor holds my hand as we go up and down the hundreds of steps in the carved-out tunnels. My cheeks are hot but not in an embarrassed way, I'm just so happy. I'm a woman now, conscious of my breasts straining against the inside of my bra, the slight swells of my stomach and hips against my jeans

I'm Connor's proper girlfriend now.

Only the risk of me being pregnant has worried us. Connor says he'll never forgive himself if what he did has caused that to happen without us planning it.

"I'm sure it won't have; darlin'," he says. "We'll be more careful in future, I promise."

This morning we took a tram into the town centre and went to a big, impersonal Boots where Connor bought a large box of condoms. We'll never get through them all before he has to go back to Ireland but I'm not going to let him take them with him. I'm wildly jealous of the red-haired, far more experienced than me Deidre, even though he says he hasn't seen her since I was in Ireland.

I nestle my hands into the holes in the sandstone tunnel walls where, over the centuries, birds have made their homes. Everything at the moment reminds me of sex with Connor. I can't wait to get back to the campervan and experiment with our new condoms...

"Rebecca, are you listening?"

Dad's tone makes me jump back, guiltily, to the moment.

"Huh?"

He exchanges a raised-eyebrows glance with Wendy; they both smile and turn away for a moment, then Dad continues with his question.

"I said do you and Connor want to go and have a look in the Long Gallery at the Fine Art collection? Wendy and I will take the boys to the military display, unless you'd prefer to join us in there, Connor?"

"Ah, no thanks Mr Portman, I'll do whatever Rebecca's doing, thanks."

He turns to his godmother. "What about you, Iris?"

"There's also the 'Threads' Gallery," Wendy says. "I quite fancy having a look at clothes through the ages. Iris, what d'you think? Rebecca, would you prefer fashion?"

She turns back to my dad. "You can take the boys to look at the guns by yourself." She winks at me and it's slightly uncomfortable.

I can't decide: clothes or art. We're just coming up the last few steps out of the tunnel into daylight.

We walk back around to the reception area where the toilets are. Dad's been distracted by the swinging shut of a door behind him. Wendy and I notice his fanatical gleam at the same moment, and Wendy rolls her eyes. I giggle as Dad moves closer to the door, running his hand across the wall to one side of it, making a measuring gesture.

"Jack, stop it at once. You've taken the day off work, remember? Anyway, I'm sure they have their own perfectly good door-suppliers."

"Sorry," says Dad, laying his hand on Wendy's shoulder. "It's just, they'd be better off with a pocket-door there."

Wendy pulls him away, directs him towards the twins.

"You take the boys to look at the guns, then; I'll do whatever Rebecca and Connor are doing."

"Well, I'm off for a ciggy," Iris announces. She tousles the hair of one of the twins. "Never do what nasty old Auntie Iris is doing boys, killing herself with cigarettes."

Sensitive Joshua starts crying. "Is Auntie Iris going to die, Mummy?"

"Oh dear no," says Wendy, "not for a long time anyway."

She gives Iris a hard look. Connor and I laugh.

Iris stands chastened like a naughty schoolgirl.

Iris has brought her accordion from Ireland.

"Cost me a bloody fortune on the plane. Rebecca, can you remember the notes you learned at mine?"

I watch her teaching Bobby a few simple tunes. Then the flashback hits me. I was small like Bobby and I sat in the curve of her arm just he is, her fingers over mine on the buttons and keys, her patient voice saying; "that's right Rebecca, F, C, G, and D; well done."

Then Mum singing She Moved through the Fair, the one I sang at the O'Toole party. I see Dad looking far away as well. We glance at each other. Iris notices.

She gives Connor a wink.

"Jack must have a guitar somewhere around, lad, get him to fetch it and we can have us a big old sing-song. Rebecca can do her party-piece."

"Oh yes," says Wendy to her twins, "we know a few songs, don't we boys?"

Connor tunes the guitar and plays an Eric Clapton song that he knows I have on my iPod, picking out the notes while Iris experiments with the chords on her accordion.

"Come on," goes Connor, nodding at me as he repeats the intro.

"Yes, come on, girl." Iris isn't asking, she's telling.

I decide to stop being coy, closing my eyes while the voice comes out of me that sounds like Mum's.

"It's late in the evening. . . "

A deep male voice joins in half-way through. Connor.

"My darling, I feel wonderful tonight."

I do.

After the song I have a memory of mum standing up in the audience at a school concert, tears streaming down her cheeks and everybody looking at her.

Here no-one makes a fuss and I feel content to sink back into the sofa cushions and listen to Iris belting out an upbeat version of *The Tennessee Waltz.*

Dad kisses his sister on the side of her face. She swats him away like a bothersome fly.

"You should visit more often, Scruff," he says, making the twins scream. "Daddy called Auntie Iris scruff."

"It's because she used to be one of the great unwashed," he explains gravely, which does nothing to abate their glee.

Next we all sing *Wheels on the Bus* and *Jamaica Farewell* topped off with *The Bare Necessities* and after that the boys fall asleep in Dad's and Wendy's arms.

"I'll just go out with Connor and say goodnight."

"Goodnight then," Wendy offers her cheek, arms full of sleeping child. I brush the air beside her cheek with closed lips.

"Goodnight Love," Dad says. He stretches over the other sleeping twin to give the top of my head a kiss.

"Goodnight niece, I won't bother to wait up for you then will I?"

Iris envelopes me in one of her suffocating bear-hugs.

"Come on, you."

Connor pulls me, carrying the guitar in his other hand, into the hall and out the front door where we stand staring at the quarter moon. Good job his arm is tucked around me, otherwise I might have floated away.

Twenty-Five

Jack

1991

"JUST FOR A few days," she'd said that first night. "Until I get myself sorted out."

A couple of weeks after she moved in she was sitting on the bed one evening, naked, facing away from me. Her arms were wrapped around her knees, her chin resting on them. The knobbles of her spine reminded me of coral, their thin covering of flesh rippling when she moved, like underwater sand. She was allowing me to brush her long hair. I manoeuvred carefully through the thick locks that seemed to have a life of their own, wrapping themselves around the brush's handle and my wrist.

"Do it harder, Jack," she said, half-turning her head towards me.

I disentangled the brush from her hair.

"I'm worried about hurting you, these bristles are sharp."

She put her hand over mine, digging the nails in. She stared into my eyes.

"You can't bloody hurt me. Don't you get that yet?"

I winced, pulled my hand away; examined the small scratch. She could hurt *me* all right.

I wanted to enfold her in my arms, feel the silk of her hair against my chest. But I'd learned to first offer physical affection, then wait and see if she'd accept it. Sometimes she did.

I opened my arms but she shook her head with a frustrated look. She let her chin sink back onto her knees, joined her fingers together across the front of her ankles. An ache burgeoned under my ribcage.

"You're going to end up being incredibly disappointed in me, Jack," she mumbled into her knees. "I'm not what you think I am. Not just some damaged girl who can be healed. I'm really not. My whole life already happened before I met you. Full stop. This. . ." she loosened a hand and made a dismissive circular gesture. "This isn't real. None of it is."

She told me that repeatedly yet at the same time we acted like a normal couple. We went to the cinema together regularly and once back to the nightclub in which we'd met. In there I spotted the Bex who'd first intoxicated me, dancing with abandon. That time we did have sex in the alley afterwards. I'd never done anything like it before, but was more excited than I'd ever been, pushing her up against the cold wall.

"Harder, Jack," she'd cried out. "You can't hurt me, I told you. I want it harder. "My knuckles were raw afterwards from protecting her head from the rough bricks.

Most weekends we ate Sunday dinner at my parents' house. Bex showed impeccable manners, discussed Mum's household routines with her and helped with the washing-up.

"Nice lass you've got there, lad," Dad remarked. "I can see why you stood your mum and me up that day she turned up at the stall."

I felt helpless to explain how complicated our relationship really was. What could I say?

None of it is real, apparently, Dad.

It *seemed* real when I lost myself inside her though, when she wept against my shoulder in the dark. Night after night she cried harder when she thought I'd gone to sleep, pushing her face into her pillow. I felt the bed shake with her sobs but I knew her enough not to interfere with her private grief. Our nights followed a pattern: sex, feigned sleep for me, out-letting for her of her deep well of sorrow.

I was entranced by her body, wanted to know every inch of it. Her stomach was surprisingly soft despite that she was quite thin.

"What's this odd scar you have here?" I asked this one night when we'd made love with the lights on – and it did feel like love that night – not just sex.

"It's like an 'X' above your belly button."

The skin there was silver.

But I'd gone and ruined the mood. She recoiled like a spring from my hand resting on her belly. She curled away from me and flicked off the light.

"You want to possess me, Jack, that's your trouble. You want to know everything about me and I don't want you to know. Why can't you just accept that my past is locked out to you, to me even? I won't be able to stay with you if you keep doing this."

I felt cold all over. It was late summer; she'd been with me a few months, much longer than she'd ever agreed. I was hoping she was going to stay for good, almost believed it most days.

Like my mum did for my dad, Bex kept the house clean and cooked a basic meal in the evenings and to be honest that suited me. My days on the stall were long. I don't know what Bex did all the rest of the hours and I didn't really want to. She was my sleeping beauty. I liked to think of her in the flat, only really awakening when I came home.

But by October there was less and less evidence of Bex having done anything during the day. It was unusually cold for the time of year and I was fed up of the darkening evenings, standing at the stall doling out the same screws and batteries and cleaning products as always. I'd begun to take Bex for granted maybe, convinced she'd stay with me now. Where else was she going to go? She didn't have any friends. Not that I'd met anyway.

So when I came in one evening and discovered again that the flat was a mess and she hadn't cooked any dinner, I forgot that she wasn't living with me on some kind of contract, I forgot how much I'd wanted her to be my princess in the tower.

That day she seemed tediously human; worse, a good-for-nothing housewife. It was only for a few moments when I first walked in, tired and disappointed that she hadn't noticed me. But shit. In those moments I messed-up big time.

Something about the way she finally looked at me when I plucked some dirty clothes off a chair and dropped them on the floor triggered the release of my poisoned barb.

"What the fuck do you do all day anyway, Bex? Look at this place; it's a shit-hole."

She regarded me from her position in repose on the sofa, her hands linked loosely over her stomach. It seemed ages before she spoke.

"If you feel like that," she said, "I'll go. I wasn't meant to be staying as long as I have anyway." Her voice was so disinterested it was chilling. She stared at me without any emotion. "I'll get my stuff together just as soon as I can summon the energy to get off this couch."

She meant it as well. She wasn't trying to give me a shock or play some kind of game. One thing Bex wasn't was a game-player. No, she was absolutely serious. I'd made the fatal mistake of taking her for granted. My fantasy bubble had burst, stupid fucking idiot. I felt all the hopes and expectations drain out of me.

I felt stunned, not knowing what to do. She was still lying there, head tilted sideways and face pushed into the back of the sofa. Eventually I managed to speak.

"Bex, I'm sorry. I didn't mean that. I'm just tired, that's all."

"Oh, you meant it," said Bex, pushing herself into a sitting position.

Glass clinked under the sofa when she brought her feet to the floor.

"You're finally getting it, Jack. At last you're beginning to understand what I've been telling you all along. I don't exist, I'm not real; this is never going to be what you hoped for."

She stood up shakily.

"Don't get me wrong," she said, swaying slightly.

The lamp on a table at her side threw her shadow up on the white wall, thin as a branch. She'd lost weight. Her jumper hung off her.

"Don't get me wrong," she said again. "You're a nice bloke. It was good of you to, y'know, take me in. Good on you, Jack. My hero, so to speak. But it was under false pretences really, wasn't it? Admit it."

Her words slurred.

"Go on," she said. "Admit it, Jack. You were hoping I'd fall in love with you. No real woman could resist your charms, eh?"

She stood swaying above me, a raw look in her dark eyes. It was true and I saw what a fool I was.

I'd known she didn't love me but I'd convinced myself she needed me; hoped she wanted me.

I put my head in my hands, tugged at my hair. I heard her go into the bathroom. At first there was quiet and then I heard the sound of retching. It soon changed to violent vomiting.

I wanted to go to her but was sure she'd only push me away. I guessed it was the alcohol she must have spent her day consuming. Dave's warnings seeped into my brain.

She don't need no more complications in her life right now mate.

We'd never got round to talking about what she'd been through. I'd only wanted to keep her with me from day to day, hoping maybe I'd become her addiction instead of the drink. It killed me to think I'd got her into an even worse state than she'd been in when I first met her.

I lurched into the kitchen, knocking my shoulder against the doorframe. Pull yourself together. Maybe she'd be able to eat something once she'd emptied herself out. I'd do something simple: scrambled eggs, a couple of slices of toast. My hopes began to rise. By the time she came out of the bathroom she'd be feeling weak and in need of comfort. She'd have forgotten she was planning to leave. It'd be okay. It would. She did need me. I'd prove it to her.

167

She didn't leave that night. I heard the shower running and she eventually came out wrapped in one of the big, soft towels I'd bought for her (wholesale, we sold the rest of them on the stall.) Her long hair hung like wet ropes over her shoulders. She looked pale.

"If you don't mind," she mumbled, "I'll stay one more night. Need to get something a bit more permanent sorted out."

"That's fine," I said, keeping my voice level. "Here, try and eat something." I placed a plate of eggs on the sofa beside her together with a knife and fork.

For the next couple of weeks we slept in the same bed but I didn't touch her. Nevertheless, she'd cleaned the flat and prepared a simple meal by the time I came home each evening. We ate mostly in silence but the tension had gone. We moved comfortably around each other but without any intimacy. Her leaving wasn't mentioned again. I could only pray that she'd come to want me again the way I'd believed she was beginning to before I fucked everything up. As far as I was concerned, this was Purgatory. I remembered being taught about it as a child.

Even being kept in limbo forever was better than her leaving.

It was a Friday at the end of October when we sat down to a plate of macaroni cheese and she gave me a small smile. I noticed that she had a bit of colour in her cheeks.

I cleared my throat, scooped up a forkful of pasta, began to chew.

"We haven't been to your parents' Sunday lunch for a while," Bex said. "Do you want to call them and say we'll be there this Sunday?"

I looked up, surprised. A curl of macaroni fell off my fork.

Bex looked at her plate.

"Just a thought, we don't have to if you don't want."

I loved the sound of the word 'we' when she said it, Bex and me.

"No, yeah, definitely, Mum'll be thrilled. She's been asking why. . . "

I didn't want to push it by digging over recent difficulties.

"Okay then."

"Thanks," I said.

Thanks, thanks, thanks.

Bex had been with me for five months by then. Every day she stayed, I let myself believe it would turn into forever.

On the Sunday I noticed she took more care over her appearance. I was dressed and laid back on the bed, arms crossed behind my head, admiring the view. She brushed her hair thoroughly and twisted it into some kind of plait that swung against her back. She even put lipstick on. I watched her button a shirt over a long-sleeved cotton top.

There was something different about her.

She's put weight on, I thought, *necessary weight.*

I realised that I'd been taking fewer bottles to the recycling bank lately. We were eating decent meals in the evenings.

Maybe she was getting better. My *softly, softly* approach was working. And now she'd proposed joining my parents for lunch. It felt like she was making our relationship official.

"Wow, you look gorgeous," I said as she turned towards me from the mirror, earrings swinging against her neck.

"Hmm."

She was bending to collect her handbag from the bottom of the bed and she paused, mid-movement, pressed a hand to her stomach.

Without saying anything she left the handbag where it was and walked quickly out of the bedroom. I heard her push the bathroom door open and then the sound of retching.

The toilet flushed. Taps were run. She came back into the bedroom and picked up the handbag. She stared at me. There was a drop of moisture on her upper lip and her lipstick had been rubbed off.

"You ready then?"

I swung my legs off the bed.

169

"You sure you're okay?"

She started to breathe quickly. The quick breaths became angry punctuations of air. She was clutching her handbag in both hands, staring at me.

"Am I fucking okay?"

"Yeah, hey, calm down bab. . . " She hated it when I called her baby. "I didn't mean to upset you."

Eggshells were everywhere; I tried to avoid stepping on them.

"It's just. . . I heard you in the bathroom, sounded like you were being sick. I was just worried about you, that's all."

"Oh, you've finally noticed have you, Jack? This has been happening for weeks and you've finally noticed. Well done, you." She threw the handbag onto the bed, visibly trembling. "Well say something, you wimp. What have you got to say about what you've gone and done to me? Bet it was what you wanted all along, wasn't it?"

Wanted all along? What? She was saying it was my fault. Maybe it was. If I'd left her to work her grief out of her system she might have gone back home, decided to go to university after all, started a new life. Instead I'd made her feel so trapped she was killing herself with alcohol poisoning.

I edged around her, reaching out to her but afraid of getting burnt. I pressed my hands flat against my sides, holding myself together when it should have been her I was holding.

Even I could see why she had no faith in me.

"Look," I said. "I'm sorry." I took a step closer. "I'll help you get better, I promise I will. We'll do it together. I'll go to all your doctor's appointments with you and everything."

I loosened my arms from my own body, desperate to reach out for her, but I still didn't. I was sure sparks would fly if I put my hands on her.

Bex stared at me, narrowing her eyes.

"Help me get better? This is never going to get better, Jack. Why won't you listen to me?" Her hair started to unravel from its plait as she threw herself onto the bed, pummelled her hands on the quilt, fists balled like rocks. "This is not what I wanted. Oh God, not after. . . "

She was sobbing loudly now.

"I did the hardest thing I ever had to do, giving up. . . "

Snot tracked the grey and blue quilt cover like a slug-trail. She moved onto her side, glistening eyes fixing on me like a dying animal.

"What've you done to me, Jack? Got me locked in your tower good and proper now, haven't you? I never wanted another. . . "

She took a sobbing breath, fumbling in her bag for a handful of tissues.

"I never wanted a baby. But it's too late now." She rolled back over and pushed herself up off the bed.

Meanwhile my heart had dropped into my stomach. I fought for breath. Bex blew her nose hard. She unravelled the messed-up braid completely, brushed out her long hair all over again. Every scrap of emotion drained from her expression.

I was still struggling to breathe properly. She looked at me, amazingly calm despite blotched skin and red eyes.

"What's done is done," she said. "Give me a minute while I get my face washed and put on some more lipstick. Then we'd better go and tell your parents."

Twenty-Six

Rebecca

WE'RE IN DAD and Wendy's front room looking out the bay window at the black tarmac of their drive, slick with rain. Iris is sitting on the sofa; Connor and I are standing in the middle of the room, doing nothing. Our bags are stacked up in the hall ready for loading. Dad's on the phone in the kitchen, Wendy and the twins have already said goodbye; she's taken them to visit their Granny in Beeston for the day.

Dad returns, throwing his arms wide and smiling as if it's all a bit of fun.

"Are we ready then? Any last toilet visits or drinks of water needed before we set off?"

I try not to roll my eyes; does he think we're the twins?

Iris sits next to Dad in the front of the car and I'm in the back with Connor. Iris's wiry curls bunch through the gap in the headrest in front of me, like a small brown animal. The car smells of its recent valeting but my nose is blocked up, stupid tears keep coming out my eyes. My head aches.

Why did I have to get involved with Connor? It's too painful; I don't want to feel this much. Maybe Mum was right; it's not worth it.

Connor kisses the top of my head and I can't believe that miles and miles will soon be between us.

"All right in the back there?"

I scrub my eyes; look up to see Dad peering in the wing-mirror. Iris gives him a poke with her elbow.

"What d'you think, eejit?"

"Hmm. Sorry guys."

In the airport I stand on spaghetti legs. Lead balls roll in my stomach. I don't want to go back to Mum. She seems pathetic rather than tragic now, not the fairy-tale heroine she made me believe in. She's gotta face it: the prince in her story is never coming back.

"Rebecca. . . " Connor's eyes are red. "Come over here me darlin'."

I drag my feet as if it's all a bit of a pain. It'll be easier to walk away if I don't let it hurt too much when we say goodbye.

But I let him kiss me, run his hand up the back of my neck, his fingers on my scalp. I pull away, trail my hands down his arms. I curl my fingers loosely into his, study the dark hairs on the backs of his wrists, then give him a gentle push away.

"Okay, you got everything?"

"Sure."

He searches my eyes, then slings his bag up onto his shoulder. Iris charges over, barrelling Connor out of the way.

"I'll see you in the summer holidays then, niece. It's not very long 'til then at all. Maybe we could get you a job at the art shop in Carrick. . . Connor's mam knows the owner – you could come over for the whole summer then?"

My heart jumps painfully. But of course I couldn't.

I fold my arms.

"I'll definitely be over for a couple of weeks, anyway."

A heavy hand descends on my shoulder. Dad.

"Come on then, Pet, no point hanging around any longer. You okay? Stupid question, I know."

He drops me off at the edge of our bit of land.

"Are you all right with your case?"

"Of course."

"Okay then. I'll see you in a couple of weeks."

"Bye for now and, you know, thanks for everything."

I bite my lip.

"Hey, Rebecca," Dad calls softly over the top of the car, "Connor's a great lad. I really like him."

"Yeah, I know, Dad. Thanks. Bye."

Mum opens the caravan door.

"I was expecting you back earlier." Her skin's slightly yellow, the same tint in the whites of her eyes. I never noticed that before. It makes my breath come out hard, as if I've been punched in the stomach. She gives me an accusing look as I climb the steps and squeeze past her.

"Sorry. I went with Dad to take Iris and Connor to the airport."

"Uhm. Gone then, has he?"

"Yep."

That's what you wanted isn't it?

She sniffs hard. She wants to say something, I can tell. My skin tingles with our forced proximity, bunched together in the tiny kitchen.

I breathe in her alcoholic breath and it reminds me of when I was little. In those days I was so sure of her I would fall asleep in her arms. But she scares me now.

She lifts a bony hand to her face, runs a finger under her eye. My heart pounds. Her fingers, long and yellow from all the ciggies she holds in them, creep up my arm. I have a vision of the witch in Hansel and Gretel, pinching Hansel's arm with her bony finger and thumb, half-expecting her to ask me to check the oven. There's a shift in the air between us.

"What're you staring at then? Come on; put that case out the way. We'll be tripping up if you leave it in here."

She sways when she takes her hand off the doorframe and moves aside for me to pass. Nobody but me would be able to guess how much she must have had to drink for it to actually show.

I close the door to my room and unpack my case on the bed. There isn't room to do it on the floor. When I've sorted everything into 'put away' and 'put in the washing machine' I stash the case underneath the bed. After a minute's thought

I crumple up the pair of blood stained knickers, mentally perceiving myself as a figure in a painting with a bitten apple in my hand, Pre-Raphaelite style, me wearing green velvet robes. My hair long and rippling.

I wrap the knickers in a plastic bag and stuff them in the bin.

I need to get back into painting; it was always enough for me before. Anything to mask the misery of the dragging months until I see Connor again.

So long, it will be so long.

The kettle's whistling and I hear the clatter of mugs. God I hope she doesn't want me to watch one of her Casualty DVDs with her.

I play for time, taking my hair-slide out and combing my hair. Mum and me used to love it when it was just the two of us, like back in Skegness when the funfair closed and it was just us on the beach.

Yet now I can hardly bear being in the same room as her.

She's got a mug of tea ready for me on the coffee table, patting the settee beside her. I go over and sit.

"Come on, closer."

She doesn't like me having a life of my own. It suited her when she was my whole world. But I'm a woman now. I've had sex. Whatever happens between Connor and me, I'm glad he was my first.

"You've gone off into one of those trances again, duck."

Mum pats my knee.

"You're getting as bad as your old mum. 'Ere, drink your tea."

I hold the mug in both hands, steam blossoming into my face.

"I've got something to tell you, ducky."

A smell of sweat comes off her clothes. I don't want a heart-to-heart talk, not now. None of her 'you know I love you ducky don't you?' nonsense.

"What is it?"

176

"You'll have to take the day off college on Wednesday; we've got to go somewhere."

We never go anywhere. What does she mean?

Anyway, Wednesday's my tutorial day. I don't want to take the day off.

"Where?"

Mum puts her mug down, folds her arms. She shuffles herself into a more important-looking position.

"We're going to see your grandma."

"Nana?"

Bloody hell, what's the point of going to see Nana? She wouldn't even know we were there.

"No, not Nana. Your other grandma. She lives in a place called Newtown Linford."

"But Dad's mum. . . "

"Not your dad's mum either. You're right; she died when you were six."

"Well. . . what do you mean, who is it then?"

"She's kind of my adopted mum, your adopted grandma. She was good friends with my grandma."

Mum coughs against her sleeve, deliberately avoids my searching gaze.

"Why haven't I met her before?"

"We fell out. It's a long story. But we have to go and see her."

I can't take it in. "What did you fall out about?"

"I told you," Mum snaps, "It's a long story. Too long for now. I'm tired; can't you see I'm not feeling well?"

It's true that her right hand's doing that trembling thing. She grasps her wrist firmly in her lap. The hand keeps shaking. I look away.

"Why have we got to. . . ?"

"Oh it doesn't matter now. We're going to see her on Wednesday. She's in a care home; she's quite poorly apparently. I'll explain it all later."

Twenty-Seven

Bex

THIS IS GOING to be tricky, managing both Rebecca and Evelyn.

At first Rebecca kept asking questions but she seems to have given up now. But she's coming with me; curiosity got the better of her after all.

Oh yeah, and I've still got to deal with the rest of those papers yet.

Seeing Adam Johnson again on Thursday. With Rebecca there this time, but at least she'll know what's going on by then.

Fucking hands, they keep on trembling. What with the blurred vision and the bloody nagging pain in my side the whole drive to Newtown Linford's a nightmare. Doesn't help having Miss Poker-Face gripping the sides of her seat like she's on a white-knuckle ride.

Its dead close in the car, sticky. My hands are clammy but cold. It's pouring with rain; the windscreen wipers don't work very well; squeal horribly, a tidal wave washing back and forth across the glass.

Rebecca's staring fixedly ahead.

"Get the map, duck."

"What?"

"Get the map off the back seat. We're on the A46 and we've just passed Syston. We're going to Newtown Linford, keep a look-out will you, ducky?"

It was a good plan. She puts on her imperious voice.

"Er, you have to turn onto the A5630; it should say Beaumont Leys or maybe Anstey... yeah that's right, round here." The map-reading keeps her occupied and makes her talk to me. "The next thing we're looking for," she says, "is a roundabout. We need to take the fourth exit onto Leicester Road."

I can hardly see through this wall of rain, my head hunched forward to help make anything out. But I'd rather be here in the car, much as I hate it, than sitting in a high-backed chair facing Evelyn in the old people's home where we're going to be in about twenty minutes. The thought of it sends me cold. What am I going to say to her?

"Now at this roundabout," Rebecca sounds like a teacher. "We need to take the first exit onto Bradgate Road. That will take us into Newtown Linford. Do you know where we want to be when we get there?"

I concentrate on the roundabout; change into first before I stop. My foot slips off the clutch too quickly and the car stalls. A line of cars builds up behind me. Slippery hands on the wheel. Every single time I drive this car I get in a state. That's why I hardly drive anymore, and I won't be doing for a long time after this.

"Keep calm, Mum. Getting upset won't help, will it?"

Rebecca ought to practice what she preaches, gripping the bloody seat again.

I get the car started and we head into Newtown Linford on Bradgate road. It's narrow and tricky and the traffic calming measures don't work on humans. Especially in this torrential rain. It's not my fault I don't see the red car and the driver who holds his hand on the horn when I fail to stop at a Give Way sign. It makes me stall a second time.

But the worse thing is the way the pain in my side flares up like I've put whisky in the frying pan. It hurts to breathe and I fear I might be sick. Rebecca's too busy rubbing her sleeve on the steamed-up window to notice.

Everything has a wavering outline. On the footpath by the park I swear I see Sebastian, with the young me.

When I manage to breathe enough to speak I tell Rebecca, "We're looking for an old people's home called 'The Beeches'."

She gives me a sideways look.

I don't point out the old brick house up a wide drive on a rise, looking down its nose at us as we come into the village; no. I keep my eyes fixed on the road in front of me. Rebecca searches. On the left is the lych gate to All Saints church.

I should never have come back. It marks the end of me as surely as the gravestones do of Sebastian's ancestors in that churchyard.

The Beeches. It's not far past the church. Rebecca spots it first. The house belonged to the Horrobin family when I was a teenager, the one house in the village bigger than Greys Mount. I've already driven past it so I have to keep going now. The car slips on the wet road as I crane my neck to look back at the place Evelyn's ended up.

"Carefu. . ." Rebecca clips the word off, snapping her lips shut.

Irritation prickles the back of my neck.

I pull in at Bradgate Park. If it wasn't raining so hard we might be able to see the ruins of Lady Jane Grey's childhood home in the distance.

Make a show of turning off the engine. Anything to put off the moment.

"The trees in that park had their tops lopped off in sympathy with Queen Jane's execution," I say. "You know, the nine-day queen. She used to live here when she was a child."

Rebecca actually looks interested.

"We'll go there and have a look at them one day, eh? They all grew back in funny, twisted shapes afterwards, those trees."

Like me

We used to go for picnics up there when we were children. Sebastian explained how he was descended from royalty, from the sister of King Henry the eighth.

I start the engine again, drive round the car park in a big sweep. A crowd of people with husky dogs straining on leads appears, making for the park entrance.

"Funny thing to see, so many huskies at once, and on such a rainy day."

Rebecca looks as tense as I feel, but at least she's attempting conversation.

I make sure to look both ways before I drive out into the road.

Cars splash past; rain sluices the windscreen faster than the wipers can shift it.

Over there's the house Sebastian and me were going to live in, Rose Cottage. It's just to the left of where I swing out onto the road, but I'm not going to look at it, not today anyway.

It feels too soon that I'm indicating right and pulling into the driveway of The Beeches. We both get out of the car and stand in the rain a second; I look at Rebecca and she looks at me, still uncertain of the reason for our visit. I lock the car with a shaking hand, snapping that we should get inside.

I wear my freshly coloured hair in a loose knot at the back of my neck. I'm dressed in a pale purple top and my best pair of jeans.

Rebecca's in a short stretchy skirt with patterned tights and a dark blue top with tiny daisies on it. She smells of vanilla and looks bloody young.

I wonder what Evelyn'll make of us both. Is it wrong to deceive her the way I'm about to, or is it okay because it'll make a sick old woman happy?

I have a nervous sniff of my armpit but can't smell anything. We stop and look at each other as we stand in the amber-lit lobby between the entrance hall and the sitting room of The Beeches. After what seems a long time Rebecca tells me:

"You look nice, Mum, really you do."

I would reply, but I'm suddenly in a vacuum, all the sound sucked out of my head. I can feel my kneecaps rattling. One of my hands is on Rebecca's shoulder as if to guide her forward but it's really to keep me steady as I take the first step into the primrose room with armchairs and settees dotted all around. It's occupied by old people in diminishing stages of animation, the odd relative sitting to attention, turning their heads to look at us with interest as we enter the room.

Our old lady's in an armchair by a big bay window, intent it seems on the view of a wide stretch of lawn, parts of it flooded by the rain. Evelyn's silver hair is clipped with what I bet are real pearls. She's looking out at a square rose garden beyond the lawn. A stone path curves through it, and at one side a huge magnolia tree drops the last of its petals, waterfalls of rain cascading off its branches. I spot a low stone wall behind that.

A big black cloud hangs over the woods at the back.

Evelyn had such a passion for white flowers. I look around frantically; I need to find some before I face her. It would be wrong for her to be in a place with no white flowers.

Ah, now I can see some between the tulips – some kind of oversized daisies. And May Blossom is in white abundance along the hedge over the other side. I drag in a breath; feel my fingers curl more tightly into Rebecca's shoulder. She turns and gives me a surprised look.

Evelyn's got much thinner since I last saw her, bony shoulders poking through the back of her pale green cardigan. But then I expect she'll think the same about me. She turns her head back into the room just as we approach, perfectly timed manners as usual. I'm slightly behind Rebecca and it's her Evelyn sees first. I see her eyes widen, a smile come into them,

"Rebecca dear, how lovely to. . . you've cut your. . . "

And then she spots me standing behind. Her eyes drape me; her voice seems to pull into itself: curl up is how I imagine it, like a hedgehog presenting its prickles, protecting its soft underpart.

Shock registers on her face, quickly reined in.

She forces her now narrowed eyes away from my face, back to my daughter. Warmth floods her eyes.

Very slowly, she pushes herself up out of the chair; one of her hands on the arm of it, her other using a walking stick as leverage. Rebecca moves forward hesitantly, but the old woman, now upright, wafts a hand at her.

"I'm fine dear, thank you." She stands in front of Rebecca, rheumy eyes swimming with moisture. "You've grown up into a beautiful young woman. For a moment there, I thought you were your mother. You wouldn't believe how quickly the years have passed."

She hasn't remarked on how young Rebecca looks for her age. The age Evelyn thinks she is. She shifts her glance back to me.

"Oh my dear, you don't look well at all."

Some kind of retort springs to the back of my throat, like, 'Thanks for the compliment,' something like that, but I swallow it down. She's bloody right, so what's the point of being smart-arsed? I killed myself, the real me, when Sebastian died, and she knows it.

"Shall we all sit down?"

Evelyn summons a blue-uniformed staff member to help pull two other armchairs over to the window.

"We'll have some afternoon tea." She tips her head towards us.

We share an uncomfortable silence; I stare at the gold-patterned carpet.

A flock of sparrows swoops onto the lawn outside, squabbling for a few seconds over something unidentifiable, ascending again in a chattering cloud. They scatter raindrops as they disappear into a jasmine hedge off to one side of the lawn, and I wish I was with them.

We all watch as if Rebecca and I have come here especially for the bird show.

The tea comes fairly quickly. At Evelyn's command a table is inserted between us. She hasn't lost her impeccable organisational skills.

"I'm sorry about Jonathan." I feel guilty for not saying this on arrival. "I only found out when the solicitor came."

184

Rebecca's head shoots up when I say that.

Evelyn dips hers again on its stringy neck, reminding me of a bird. The skin on her chest puckers when she moves her body in the deep chair.

"Well, I tried to write to you, dear. But as you know, you managed to disappear without trace."

There's only a tiny pause for bitterness. She regains her composure quickly.

"I could have found you... I know that. But I decided there was no point forcing you: you were so determined to run. However, extreme measures had to be taken to get in touch with you on this occasion. I was always certain I'd see you again one day."

She looks me in the eyes, then at Rebecca.

"You know how much this dear child means to me."

Rebecca chews her fingernail. She stares first at Evelyn and then at me.

"Jonathan's death," says Evelyn, "was very sudden, mercifully."

Two personalities struggle inside me.

Rebecca wants to come back, the one I was. She's trying to push Bex out the way. And Bex doesn't belong here in posh Newtown Linford: she should never have come.

Evelyn pours tea with a quivering hand, her ritualistic movements evoking those pre-wedding afternoons we spent in her sitting room. Rebecca and I both lean forward, perched on the edges of our seats.

I steal a glance at my girl, shocked to see she's pale as a ghost, like when she was sick. Her illness seems like a thing from another lifetime. The Rebecca my daughter used to be has gone now as surely as the one who used to take afternoon tea with Evelyn.

"I'm very sorry that things turned out so badly between us, Rebe... Bex," says Evelyn. "Circumstances beyond our control, we could say."

I don't understand how she can be so forgiving. I took away the only grandchild she would ever have. Rebecca gives me an accusing stare. I feel cold from her marbled expression, scared it's going to get inside my heart, freeze me from the inside out. I want a drink so badly I think I'm gonna cry.

"Rebecca. Has your mother told you why I've asked to see you both?" Evelyn's addressing my ice-princess daughter.

"No. She doesn't tell me anything."

Good, I think, watching her sullen face, you're acting like a normal teenage girl. It strikes me that she's always been older than her years.

A sudden gust of wind sends a squall of rain against the window. Branches screech against the roof of a garden shed at the side of the house.

The desire for a bracer of gin and tonic is a craving I don't think I can fight much longer. I pick at the skin around my fingernails.

"I thought it would be better if we explained it together."

I'm not looking forward to telling Rebecca she's got to move home again.

Twenty-Eight

Rebecca

I'VE GONE ALL dizzy, like when I was ill. I don't seem to have any control over my own life, or have a clue about my background. I don't understand anything.

Mum looked like someone had snipped all her muscles and her face had fallen apart.

"I forgive you, Bex."

That's what the woman, Evelyn, said.

"I forgive you and I want you to know I still think of you as my daughter."

Mum - yeah, my mum - burst into tears.

I'm pretty certain she hasn't had a drink today.

Something oppressing creeps over us, like the bunching storm clouds outside. It's not lessened by this nice home; the kind lady giving us tea.

I want to scream, but instead I go to the visitor toilet and stand before the mirror. I see violet patches beneath my eyes and remember Mum saying something about me being the most beautiful girl in the world. It was only a few months ago. I surprise myself by not crying.

Hot eyes stare back at me. If I don't make a stand now and decide what happens in my own life I'll be trapped behind a wall of brambles, growing so thick and fast nobody will be able to reach me.

I bite my lip so hard I taste blood. Then I have a pee, wash my hands and go back to the huge room with yellow walls.

The other relatives seem to have gone, old people shuffling off with their walking frames or pushed in wheelchairs by blue-shirted staff, making their way down the thick carpet of a wide corridor leading off from an archway out of the lounge. It's like an exodus of the chorus in a show. It leaves the stage clear for Mum and Evelyn, standing by the bay window with their backs to me.

As I approach I get another shock. Mum's talking in a totally different voice from usual; sounding her aitches, giving her words a round tone, all la-di-da. She sounds more like Wendy than Mum.

I hesitate.

"We're retiring to my quarters, dear."

The old lady looks strained. She leans heavily on her stick and manoeuvres herself in a circle on the carpet.

"Let me help you, Evelyn," offers the woman with a straight back and poised chin who came in here clinging to my shoulder like a child. Is the ground still under my feet? I'm beginning to think when I left this room to go to the toilet I ended up in a time machine. It's a different Mum standing here now, a younger woman.

She helps Evelyn along the corridor, slow progress while I take small steps behind, like a child suddenly, not the woman I recently became.

Evelyn's room is large, pale pink with a deep rose-coloured sofa and two armchairs, arranged around a patterned rug and a polished coffee table. On the table is a big glass vase full of white lilies.

"Oh."

Mum gives the old woman a meaningful look.

"From my old greenhouse," Evelyn gestures towards the flowers. "Grahams is still in charge of it you know. Still, you will be familiar with all that soon enough, Rebecca."

She's looking at me but I have no idea what she's on about.

"Are there any horses in the stables?"

188

Mum's still talking in that plummy voice. I've only ever heard it once or twice before when she answered the phone. We used to joke it was her telephone voice but now I'm beginning to think it was her real one all along and she's been playing some kind of weird game my whole life. I give her a pointed look but she doesn't notice.

"No, I'm afraid there aren't anymore."

Evelyn sounds regretful, lowering herself stiffly into one of the armchairs as we move to sit on the settee. She heaves a sigh of relief once she's settled among the cushions. Tiny beads of sweat cling to her brow and her breath sounds laboured. I find myself watching her the way I've spent the last few years watching Mum.

"One of the Thompson girls, well, Charlotte's a woman now with a child of her own of course, used to come and ride Captain for us, he was the last horse we had, but we felt there was no point getting any others after him."

Mum's eyes have roved over to a small sideboard supporting a tray of bottles and glasses. Oh God, don't let her. She's got to drive us home.

Evelyn sees it too, making a distraction with a wave of her bony hand.

"Rebecca dear," this time she's talking to Mum, and Mum doesn't correct her on the name like she has every other person who's called her by it.

I'm gritting my teeth. That's my name, how dare she steal it? We've always been Bex and Rebecca, the two of us *more like sisters than mother and daughter.*

"It's time we gave Rebecca the good news, I think."

Evelyn places the same hand that she just waved at Mum over mine, resting on the arm of the sofa. I look at it and for a minute I can only see the hand of a skeleton, like an X-Ray or one of those plastic models they had in Science at school. When a gust of wind blows rain against the window I shudder, looking into Evelyn's watery eyes; a depth of understanding in there that scares me.

"I'm leaving the house to you and your mother."

189

She continues looking into my eyes while tightening her grip on my hand. I hold my breath, let it go again. Flicking Mum a glance I find the unfamiliarity of her held-up head disturbing; she's looking at me in a funny way too. I bury my gaze in the patterned red and gold rug.

"What house?"

"Grey's Mount. Your mother would have inherited it anyway, eventually."

"What. . . I don't really know what you're talking about. Mum's never. . . I don't understand how we're connected to you."

Evelyn's voice rolls over me like a stone, grey and old.

"Your mother was engaged to my son Sebastian; he died in a terrible accident."

All these years later her lip trembles, water escaping from her eyes into the runnels of her face. She suddenly gasps, as if she'd stopped breathing.

"Married," she corrects, "they were married."

I wonder why she didn't just say married in the first place.

"Rebecca, your mother is my daughter-in-law. You're my grandchild. I haven't seen you since you were a tiny baby."

This sets off a further waterfall of tears. Her free hand wavers towards me like a leaf barely clinging to a tree. She's so old, the skin on her face looks like paper.

"Rebecca, darling child," she says in her gravelly voice. "I've left everything to both of you in my will."

She sinks back in the chair, visibly depleted, her hand slipping off mine. With an effort she pulls it back towards her own body. It falls limply into her lap, fingers curving inwards as if of their own accord. Her eyes drift, not quite closed but almost.

I can't take it in. Her grandchild, what does she mean? She's an old lady, sick as well by the looks of things. Confused.

She mentioned stables and gardeners. I think of the caravan we live in at the moment, how can this be?

"I'm sorry, I need a drink." Mum jumps up, knocking her shin on the side of Evelyn's chair. That same bony hand of

190

Evelyn's grasps Mum's wrist as she tries to pass. Her eyes force themselves fully open.

"Just one, dear. We'll have a toast to your future. I'll have a small brandy."

Her head drops back against the brocaded chair.

"Rebecca?"

Mum's hand is shaky as she pours the brandy for Evelyn. Her eyes covet the green bottle of gin, her hunger for it palpable. I think of the caravan jerking when she falls up the step into the kitchen at nights, how I'll be frightened to get in the car with her for the drive home today. A cold wave swills in me and I curl my toes in their soft leather boots.

I won't get in the car. I'll get a taxi to the nearest train station instead. I crane my neck to see what's on the tray.

"Just a lemonade please."

She gives me a nasty look. If we were at home she'd call me 'Miss Prissy-pants' or something like that. I don't care; I'm a grown-up and I can do what I want. That's the thought I try to hold in my mind but I slide around in a sludge of conflicting emotions.

Sebastian, Evelyn's son. Mum was married to him?

I suppose I always associated the wedding ring on her finger with my dad.

Mum's fairy tales mingled with her own 'Great Grief' in my mind. There were princesses trapped in towers, a spell cast on a prince, rendering him forever inaccessible. Redemption came in the death of a witch, releasing the prince from the spell so he could rescue the princess.

If I asked Mum a question about her life she always managed to twist it into a tale, her head close to mine on the pink pillowcases of childhood. She leans over me with a glass of lemonade, gin already drying on her lips. Evelyn is sunken in the high backed armchair. She looks grey.

"Mum."

It frightens me: age, fragility. I don't want to see death but I fear it might be close by. Mum looks at the old lady.

"Evelyn," she murmurs low, holds the brandy under the old woman's nose. Evelyn stirs and moves her head to one side, raising it with an effort.

"Sorry, dear, I must have dozed off for a minute."

Mum and I exchange a look.

"It's been lovely to see you again, Evelyn, but you seem to need your rest. We'd better go. Thank you so much for everything you've done for us, and I'm so sorry about. . . "

"No need for apologies," Evelyn interrupts. "I am tired, as you can see. You've signed all the papers, have you?"

Mum's hair, fastened back in a low bun, has escaped at one side, falling over her face as she leans over the old woman. She looks so young, something I haven't thought for a long time. She nods her head.

"I have, I can't. . . "

"Don't say anything else then."

Evelyn sounds so tired, in the overheated stuffiness of the room I could drift along with her into a muffled sleep, not have to do battle with all my tangled thoughts.

"Get up, Rebecca."

I stand wearily, trying to assess Mum's competence to drive at the same time as wanting to say something to the old lady, ask an important question I haven't been able to form.

"Come here, dear."

Her voice croaks in her throat. With a surprisingly firm grasp she takes my hand and pulls at me and I find myself kneeling on the thick rug in front of her.

"You are such a precious child to me. You brought hope back into my life when I found it hard to think of anything to live for. It doesn't matter now that we haven't seen much of each other; the important thing is that we've come together again before I die."

The brandy glass quivers when she struggles to lift it, sighing on an outward breath after she takes a sip. Another gust of wind hits rain against the window, stirring my concern about the drive home. But I want to get out of here; it's stuffy, oppressive. Too much emotion that I don't rightfully feel a part of hangs in the stale air.

This is between Mum and Evelyn, not me, despite what this woman who thinks of me as her grandchild has said.

"I hope you enjoy living in Greys Mount," Evelyn gives my hand a frail tug, indicating I should get up now. Mum's making gestures at me like I should lean and give Evelyn a kiss so I do, pressing the side of my cheek against the powdery slackness of hers, feeling the dry lips brush mine as I pull away, trying not to shudder.

When I get some space between us I put my hand up to my face, pressing the tip of my finger with relief into the tight, bouncy skin of my cheek. Mum goes next, sliding her arm carefully around Evelyn's bony shoulders.

"I've never forgotten him, Evelyn, just so you know. I was always his."

It's a whisper but I hear it, shivering.

This is so new.

Then Evelyn says the strangest thing, just as we're about to pull the door closed behind us. She meets my eyes and her voice becomes clearer.

"Your father lives on in you, Rebecca. Never forget it."

And then her eyelids have dropped closed and look like they'll never open again.

At reception Mum goes up to the desk.

"Mrs Grey," she says to the receptionist, still talking in that la-di-dah manner, "I'm concerned about her. She seems very weak, is she all right?"

The receptionist takes off her black-framed glasses, giving them a wipe with a small piece of silky cloth. She purses her lips for a moment.

"We're managing okay with her at the moment. She really doesn't want to go into the hospice so we're doing our best to keep her here."

"Oh my God." Mum looks genuinely shocked. "I didn't re-alise it was that bad."

In the car park we stand letting rain soak our clothes, it's a relief after the stuffiness and bottled-up emotion I've just nearly drowned in. My legs are weak and I'm scared my illness is coming back. I try to bring Connor into my mind but it's like the door's locked and he couldn't get in if he wanted to. I feel so far away from everything, just when I had a place in the world.

"We'll go and see the house," Mum says.

The house.

What, now? I'm not ready.

Despite the still plummy quality, she sounds more like herself than she did inside the home. I look at her standing there in her quilted jacket from Primark, skinny legs, hair escaping from the bun. The lady of the manor, it's a joke. I'm not sure if what's bubbling up inside me is laughter or vomit.

"It's only just up the road, well, a bit of a walk but I could do with it, I don't know about you."

I let the rain wash me; it's the only thing that seems real. Mum hooks her arm into the crook of mine but it feels like a parody of how we used to be together. I have the sense of having been lied to my whole life; I don't know this chameleon of a woman walking beside me.

Twenty-Nine

Jack

2010

REBECCA RINGS ME in a state. She says something like:

"*Ohmygod-dad-I've-got-to-move-house-again.*"

"Huh? Slow down pet, I can't understand a word you're saying."

"Just when I was getting really settled here and I'm enjoying college and I've made friends with Jade and I get to go riding and everything, now I have to move again." Her breath catches.

"Slow down," I breathe calmly down the phone at her. "Explain everything, one thing at a time."

"Oh yeah, and that's not the worst of it. You'll never guess what?"

There's a pause.

"No, I won't. What?"

"Did you know I have another grandma?"

My poor mum died just a couple of years after my dad. She can only mean Bex's mum.

"Yeah, of course; Nana."

"No Dad. Not Nana. Yeah I know Nana's my grandmother too but there's this other one. Mum took me to see her in this place called Newtown Linford today. The lady's name is Evelyn and d'you know what she said?"

My heart thumps.

Oh shit.

I take a sip of the gin and tonic Wendy made me when I came in just a few minutes ago.

"No, what did she say?"

"She said, 'your father lives on in you, Rebecca.' What does she mean, Dad?"

I exhale slowly. Rebecca's started talking again but I've stopped hearing.

———◁▷———

1992

Bex was extraordinarily quiet during the labour.

"Is she one of those birth without violence people?" one of the midwives whispered to me after confirming that Bex was fully dilated and ready to give birth.

"I don't think so," I answered, but had to admit to feeling disturbed by her silence. I'd been led to believe women yelled and swore at you during labour.

Her face was stretched with pain but she seemed to have disappeared inside her own head. She didn't answer when I spoke to her.

"That's quite normal," said the other midwife. "She's mustering her strength, aren't you, pet? Here, rub the small of her back gently like this."

Bex was on all fours.

There was something primeval about the way her body tightened with each contraction. Her face lengthened and went puce, her fingers splayed as if they were being dislocated from her hands. Her spine curved like a cat's.

"Let it go," said the midwife. "Let it all go, pet."

She lifted the long t-shirt Bex wore up over her bottom.

"Come round here, Dad," she said to me.

Then I saw an incredible thing

"Oh God," I said. "Dear God, it's a baby."

"I should fucking hope so."

Bex had found her voice at last. She screamed: a long, drawn-out note. The baby, arms crossed over its chest, swivelled round and split its mother open as it dropped out onto the sheet between her spread knees. It trailed a thick, waxy rope behind it through which I could see blue and red veins. Blood and water gushed out onto the sheet in the baby's wake.

"Come on now, pick baby up, Mum," said the first midwife, Elena.

She helped Bex straighten her body into a more upright position. Louise, the other midwife, was examining the baby where it – she, I could see her miniature femininity – lay on the sheet.

Louise nodded at Elena.

"Come on, Mum," Elena repeated.

Bex let out a low groan.

"Let him," she said.

"Dad?"

"I can't, I don't know if. . . "

Blood was still flowing into the baby from Bex; I could see it pulsing through the cord quite clearly.

"Aren't you going to cut that?"

"In a minute," Louise said. "Pick baby up and give her to Mum."

I touched my daughter for the first time.

"Mind her head now," said Elena. "Slide your hands under her like this."

She popped a towel around the baby as I lifted her up from the sheet. The baby looked straight at me with her dark eyes. I handed her to Bex, who took her without looking. But I could see the baby gazing fixedly at her mother.

"What're you going to call her?" Louise asked.

"We haven't decided. . . " I began.

"Rebecca," said Bex. "Rebecca Jane Grey."

It was strange having a daughter called Rebecca. It was the name I'd always called Bex in my head. But it wasn't that name I minded. I minded that Bex insisted on giving our baby the surname of her dead husband, fiancé, whatever he was. The name she refused to give up herself, though I'd begged her to marry me.

"I promised," was all she'd say in explanation. "I promised I would keep the family name going. It's something I have to do. I can't explain why."

"You still can, just double-barrel it. Give her the surname Portman-Grey if you must. At least then she'd have my name as well."

"Sorry Jack. You don't get to decide on this one. I've put your name on the birth certificate. That confirms she's yours."

She wouldn't give in on the matter.

She cried a lot at first. Bex did, not the baby. She would never tell me what made her so sad. But she looked after Rebecca all right, picked her up and cuddled her, breastfed her for a few weeks. But she looked exhausted.

"Why don't you put her on the bottle, love?" asked my mum one Sunday when we were round for lunch. "I'll pop out and get some formula and some bottles now, if you like?"

"Mum, are you sure that's the right thing to do?"

"Oh, you don't want to worry about all this 'breast is best' nonsense. I bottle-fed you and Iris and you've both turned out all right, haven't you?"

She tutted.

"Look at the state of Bex. She could do with a break, that's all I'm saying."

I looked over at Bex. She was holding Rebecca at her breast. You could hear the sound of the baby sucking contentedly. I don't think Mum liked Bex being the sole provider of Rebecca's food.

A tear rolled slowly down one of Bex's cheeks and compassion pulled in my chest. Anger burned at Mum. How could she be so insensitive? She was still muttering about how much easier it'd be for everyone if Rebecca was bottle-fed.

I went over to Bex on the sofa.

"What do you think?" I asked. "Is it the breastfeeding that's tiring you out?" Bex didn't answer. She wasn't crying as such but there were still tears wetting her cheeks. She kept her eyes on the baby. I watched Rebecca's fist opening and closing on the folds of Bex's t-shirt. Would she be as contented drinking milk from a bottle?

"She feeds all the time," Bex said eventually.

She pushed her hair behind her ear with her free hand.

"I'm just so tired."

I knew she was awake half the night feeding Rebecca while I fell back to sleep every time Bex lifted her out of the carrycot and settled back against the pillows with her. It didn't seem fair.

Mum could be right; maybe I should be doing some of the night feeds.

Mum sensed my vacillations. She jumped into the gulf with: "Well that settles it, then. Jim, you put the kettle on while I pop to that 7-day-a-week shop on the corner. We'll have that baby on the bottle in no time and then you can start getting some proper rest, Bex."

Bex stiffened beside me but said nothing.

It was impossible to know how she really felt. I hoped I wasn't betraying her by going along with Mum's plans. Dad went into the kitchen to put the kettle on and Mum unfolded her canvas shopping bag in the porch, talking to herself about bottles, sterilizers and formula milk.

I watched Rebecca's rhythmical jaw. She associated feeding with the smell of her mother. Feeding her from a bottle would mean one degree of separation from Bex. I got a bad feeling about it, picturing the stash of alcohol bottles I'd used to have to collect up for the bottle bank every week. But I didn't want to have to tell Mum about that.

When Rebecca was a few months old Mum organised a shopping trip for Bex and the baby. Rebecca was growing out of her initial supply of clothes and Mum wanted to treat Bex to some new outfits as well. Bex hadn't been out the house much and was still looking pale and peaky. Mum had decided it was time to start building her up and giving her confidence as a mother.

Bex protested at first but my mum was hard to resist once she set her mind to something. The pair of them were similar in that respect. Mum's car arrived outside our flat bright and early that Saturday morning. Bex was installed beside her in the passenger seat and Rebecca strapped securely into her car seat in the back. Dad had given me the day off so I could do some decorating in the box-room (not much more than a cupboard). We planned to put Rebecca's brand-new cot in there.

"A million love songs I've made up," I belted out along with the stereo.

A splodge of paint dripped off the brush onto my shoulder.

It took a few rings before I noticed the doorbell. I stopped the cd and went to answer it, picturing Bex entreating me to rescue her from my mother.

A tall man with dark grey hair and a much shorter woman with silver curls stood in the lobby outside my flat. They were a well-dressed couple; you could almost smell the money on them. My skin prickled.

The man put out his hand. "Hello. Is it Jack?"

I hesitated, wiped my hands on my jeans and checked them for paint before accepting his handshake.

"Yep, that's me."

The man smiled but there was something wrong with the way his lips lifted at the corners. The woman looked nervous. The man said:

"I'm Jonathan Grey. This is my wife, Evelyn."

The pair of them looked at me expectantly.

"Hi," I said. "Yeah, I'm Jack. Jack Portman."

The woman broke in with:

"We're Rebe. . . Bex's parents-in-law."

I registered the name Grey.

Shit.

I drew back, kept my body in front of the doorway. Jonathan Grey sniffed the air.

"Painting, are you?"

Evelyn Grey was craning to peer past me into the flat.

"So this is where she's living," she said. "Are you sure it's big enough for a child?"

How dare you bloody criticize how I provide for my family?

I ignored her and answered the man.

"Yes. Yep. Painting the baby's room actually."

Why am I talking like this? I was thinking, 'Yes. Yep.' Yes Sirree.

Go away, Greys. You're not part of my life. I don't want you here. I tapped my foot.

Evelyn struggled even harder to see in. I kept my body where it was, blocking the doorway.

"Little Rebecca. How is she? We haven't even had a photograph, you know. Are they both in?"

All sorts of questions were circling like vultures in my brain. Why would they have had a photograph of my baby?

"No, sorry, they're out for the day. Hence me taking the opportunity to decorate."

Hence. There I went again. These people gave me a sense of foreboding, made me speak in unaccustomed ways. They were both staring at me. I shifted my weight from one leg to the other. They showed no indication of moving.

"Sorry, but I really need to get on."

One fucking day off, that's all I had.

"But couldn't we. . . ?"

The man put his hand on his wife's shoulder.

"Evelyn dear. Can't you see that Jack here's busy? I tell you what, young man. I'll give you my card with the telephone number of the hotel we're staying in. We're here for the whole weekend. Get Rebe. . . Bex to give us a ring. We're in room 47. We'd like to take you all out for lunch tomorrow."

"But Jonathan. . . "

"I know you're disappointed, dear. She's been very much looking forward to seeing our girls again," he said to me.

Our girls. Huh?

Then he said something even more sinister. "We've been very patient. But it's time we saw our granddaughter again.

Thanks for looking after them, old chap. We realised Bex wouldn't stay on her own forever."

I stood in front of them, both hands still on the doorframe.

He said *our granddaughter.* He said *again.* These people were mad. I coughed.

"You will get her to ring, won't you?"

The woman made a kind of praying gesture with her hands. Her husband put his arm round her shoulder and began to lead her away, but she kept her eyes trained on my face.

"Yes," I said. "Er, would you mind telling me how you know my name?"

And how you know Bex lives here.

"We got in touch with her mother. She doesn't seem well, by the way. Said she hasn't seen Bex for ages either. Couldn't make much sense of what she told us except that Bex has been living with you for a while. It's been too long since we heard from Bex, you see. We wanted to give her some space but we were afraid we'd lose touch completely if we waited any longer."

I had this buzzing feeling in my head. Bex's past was coming back to claim her. I couldn't believe she'd stayed with me, had my baby. Now... it was coming apart. I needed to sit down, try and work out what to do.

"I see. Well, if you don't mind, I must be getting on."

"Of course, of course," Jonathan said. "Thanks for your time. Tell Bex we look forward to hearing from her later."

"And seeing our beautiful granddaughter tomorrow." Evelyn's eyes lit up like sparklers.

"I can't wait," I heard her saying to Jonathan as I closed the door.

She must be a mad woman, deranged by grief at the loss of her son. *Oh shit.* I had such a bad feeling about it all. Why did they keep calling Rebecca their granddaughter?

Bex had some colour in her cheeks when she came in, Rebecca against her chest. The baby twisted her head around and gave me a gummy grin. She buried her face in her mother's shoulder, peek-a-boo.

My heart clenched. My family was my own personal miracle. Mum followed Bex in, laden with bags.

"You have to look at all the sweet clothes we got for Rebecca."

She plonked the bags on the sofa and grabbed an outfit from the top of one of them.

"Proper little girl she's going to look in her summer dresses. We got some clothes in the next size up for autumn as well. Won't be long now 'til the nights start drawing in."

"That's great Mum," I said. "Thanks ever so much for all this."

"Yeah, thanks Beryl."

Mum's cheeks flushed with colour when Bex leaned over and gave her a peck on one of them.

"I really appreciate it, honest I do. You're right; I need to get out more. Maybe I'll take Rebecca to one of those mother and baby groups like you said."

Bex had been wrong when she told me our relationship wasn't real. I watched her carry Rebecca into our bedroom. She'd come round to accepting there was life after Sebastian, and it was all because of Rebecca. But I couldn't shake the feeling that she'd somehow sold her soul to that couple. They acted like they had a claim on Bex. Worse still, on Rebecca. What had Bex promised them?

"Let's have a look at your handiwork then," said Mum.

She bustled past the stepladder in the doorway of the box room.

"Lovely. Once you've put up a few shelves it'll be perfect. Now, how about I make you a quick dinner? I think Bex'll need a bit of a lie-down, she's not a hardened shopper like me."

I ushered her out of the freshly painted room.

"That's really kind of you Mum, but I'm ordering a takeaway tonight. I'm sure Dad's waiting for his dinner at home." I desperately wanted to talk to Bex alone.

Mum gave me a quizzical look. She licked her thumb and rubbed at my cheekbone, just under my left eye.

"Paint. Primrose yellow doesn't suit you son. Okeydokey. I'd best get off home; your father'll think he's been abandoned, poor man. I won't disturb Bex again."

Our bedroom door was closed. Mum hesitated.

"Say ta-ta to my little cutie for me, won't you. Bye bye now."

When she'd gone I put the chain on the door and moved into the bedroom. Bex was lying on the bed. Rebecca slept in the crook of her arm, dressed in a sleep suit.

"D'you want me to heat up a bottle?"

"Nah, it's all right. She had a feed about an hour ago."

Bex slid herself carefully out from under our daughter.

"Put her in her Moses basket, will you? While I nip to the loo."

"Okay, and Bex?"

"Yeah?"

"I need to talk to you. It's important."

I told her about the Greys. She pressed herself as deep into the cushions of the sofa as she could. The mug in her hand shook. I leaned over and took it off her, placed it on the coffee table.

"How did they find me?"

"They said they'd spoken to your mum."

She was so white-faced she looked almost blue. She held herself still but her eyes roved restlessly and she breathed quickly.

"We have to get out of here, tonight. They're coming back again tomorrow, you say? No. I can't let them see Rebecca. I need to leave now."

"Bex."

My sense of foreboding had been justified.

"Why is it so bad? They're your ex-parents-in-law. I guess it makes sense them wanting to see you, even if your life's moved on. Theirs probably haven't."

But there was also the weirdness of them calling Rebecca their granddaughter.

Bex was leaning forward now. She squeezed her hands into fists, splayed them back open.

"Oh God, oh God. I can't let them see Rebecca."

"Why do they. . . ? What's their interest in her?"

Even as I said it a door closed inside me. I didn't want to know. Since Bex got pregnant I'd wanted only the life ahead of us. Like her I saw her past as a dead country. Maybe I knew my fairy-tale world would collapse if she came out of the tower we'd constructed between us.

"They. . . I promised Evelyn when Sebastian died I'd carry on the family name. They think. . . They, they understand Rebecca to be their granddaughter. But I did something, Jack."

She took her fists away from her cheeks where she'd pressed them and there were two red imprints on the pale skin. She lifted her face to me and her hair fell back. Her brown eyes stared at me. I wasn't going to let her down. I loved her more than ever.

"I did something bad. Evelyn would never forgive me if she found out. I can't let her see Rebecca."

I didn't ask why. I had to keep on believing in Bex. My job was to protect my family; that was all.

I paced the confined living room.

"They're expecting you to ring them tonight. They're planning to take us for lunch tomorrow."

I fumbled in the pocket of my jeans, pulled out the card with the number of the hotel scribbled on the back.

"Ask for room 47. Speak to them and ask where they want us to meet them for lunch. Or they can come here if they want to pick us up."

She started to pull at my arms then, pleading with her eyes.

"No Jack, I can't. I've told you, they can't see Rebecca. She's not what they. . . "

"Shh," I interrupted. "You need to make the phone call otherwise they might turn up here again tonight. It doesn't matter what they do tomorrow because we won't be here anymore. I've got a plan. And I'm sorry Bex, but we're not going to be able to tell your family where we're going because that man and woman might manage to get it out of them. Are you with me?"

She stared at me. Her face relaxed and her hands started moving on my arms.

"Fuck me, Jack, if it isn't Mr Masterful."

She stood up, draped her arms around my neck. We hadn't had sex since Rebecca was born but now her stomach pressed into mine and I felt myself harden. She moved against me.

"Hold on, big boy. Get me the phone and when I've made that call we'll celebrate, eh?"

I've cracked it, I thought. She'll really love me now I'd managed to open the lock on that tower of hers.

Thirty

Rebecca

A part of me detaches itself, floats away in a daydream.

Mum blows her nose noisily into a bunched-up strip of toilet roll. She removes it to say to me:

"You can't bring that dog in here, Rebecca."

Her eyes are red, mascara streaking her face. She's genuinely upset about Evelyn.

So I have to leave poor Dusty howling in the luggage compartment of that huge car in his metal crate, when all I want to do is hold him in my arms and let him lick my face.

Jade gave me this darling puppy as a late birthday present, the runt of her auntie's litter. He's a Labrador/Cocker Spaniel cross, all floppy ears and big feet.

"He won't let you forget me."

That was what Jade said when I opened the box containing my future best friend.

"Dunno who I'm gonna hang out with now you're leaving."

The driver Mum hired to bring us here stays with the dog in the car, watching football on a screen in the back seat. He wears earphones to drown out the sound of Dusty's whining.

I don't understand what I'm supposed to feel about Evelyn, so I'm kind of feeling nothing except awkwardness. We're being taken to view the body. Although I don't know why anyone would want to do something like that.

I seem to separate into two halves, one dragging her feet down the corridor behind Mum, the other noticing a girl about my age standing by the window of the lounge we were in before. Her clothes are fancy dress. Green velvet like I imagined myself wearing in the painting with the bitten apple.

Maybe she's come to do a performance of some kind.

She doesn't speak and I take a closer look at her, all the while aware of my 'other' self behind my mother, accompanied by a care assistant and the manager of the nursing home.

And with that I'm snapped back to the corridor outside Evelyn's room, a wave of panic rising in my chest. Mum's nose is red and her mascara still smudged; but she looks exasperated at me as I try to pull air into my lungs, thinking I'm going to faint.

All the months of being better from my illness seem distant now. Art College, Dad and the boys, Iris and Connor, all are sucked away from me in the doorway of Evelyn's room. She's dead inside there and I don't want to go in.

I'm not ready to see an empty body.

"After you, ladies."

'Mrs Gretchen Malham' is printed on the manager's name badge. In her olive tweed skirt and smart jacket pulled in at the waist to try and make her look slimmer, she steps aside and I have no choice but to follow Mum in. We walk past Evelyn's sofa and coffee table, the vase on it filled with white lilies and roses. For some reason Mum starts sobbing when she sees them.

Reluctance turns my feet to lead, and it's hard to lift them and keep placing one in front of the other across the carpet. I see Mum's gaze pulled towards the sideboard with the tray of drinks on.

She's bloody imagining what the staff of the home will do with all the left over bottles of drink, I know she is. She'll suppose that since she and I are Evelyn's legal heirs, they belong to us now and that we can take them away with us when we go to Greys Mount.

I'm ready to knock her hand away but she restrains herself from grabbing the green bottle, forces her hand into her handbag to search for another tissue instead. She folds it around her nose, the handbag hooked securely on her arm.

I can't catch my breath.

I'm about to look at a dead body.

When we go through the archway into the bedroom part of Evelyn's suite it's very dim because of the heavy velvet curtains. Evelyn doesn't seem dead at all. She lies in her bed, looking asleep. The care assistant and the manager stand respectfully to one side while my mum goes over to the bed.

"She left us less than an hour ago," murmurs Mrs Malham.

There's nothing for me to do apart from stand slightly behind Mum with my hands folded together at the base of my stomach. The care home staff stand behind me and I worry I might accidentally start laughing even though it's not funny. It's just that it feels like some kind of performance.

Evelyn made everything clear. There's an envelope for us with a welcome letter and some instructions, and most important, as Mrs Gretchen Malham pointed out, the keys.

Two key rings full, in fact.

The uses of them all are in the instructions. The other thing Evelyn has done is set up a joint bank account for Mum and me at the family's branch in Coalville. In her letter to us Evelyn suggested we telephone the bank and activate our online account so we can order shopping to be delivered to the house. She says we have broadband installed and the passwords are written on a piece of paper in an envelope under the router.

A woman called Mrs Evans will be coming in to clean the house every day. As if it needs cleaning every day, for crying out loud. A standing order to pay her is set up on our account. It's amazing that despite her illness Evelyn had time to think of all that, and her thoughtfulness makes me wish she were still here so I could get to know her. It would have felt right then. She's the sort of person Mum would have listened to.

Mum doesn't seem interested in any of this, but I need to understand how we're going to live here. I want to know who our electricity supplier is and how much the water rates cost every month. So while Mum trails round the house touching things, I'm reading the instructions for everything and tapping notes into my phone so I'll know what to do in emergencies.

"Are you not going up to look at your room, Rebecca?"

She can't understand how I'm not gobsmacked by all the stuff they have here. *We have here.*

"Your bed's already up. I got the removers to drag that beautiful antique one into the orange room since you insisted on keeping your crappy old one. It's a bit crowded in the orange room with two beds, but that'll make a good guest room."

Who does she think she is? Orange room, guest room, as if. As far as I can tell she never did anything to deserve Evelyn leaving her all this. Why are we here?

It's something to do with that old fairy tale Mum's been trapped in since her Great Grief. Will the Prince come back to life now?

"I need to read this, Mum. I'll look at my room later."

One of us has got to be responsible. She's pouring her third gin from the bottle she nabbed from the care home. I doubt it'll be her last drink of the night; it's only seven o'clock.

We're in a small sitting room off a dining room. This in turn leads off the kitchen. But I need the loo. I can't remember where it is.

I don't even remember where my room is. There are two staircases in this house.

These are the things I miss: the caravan, cycling to the station at Swinderby, making a sofa out of hay bales in Jade's stables. I miss horses blowing their warm breath on us while we sketch them. I've been cut adrift in yet another direction. I don't want to have to make new friends all over a-bloody-gain.

We have a big garden but apparently it's all taken care of by a gardener so it doesn't feel like ours. None of this feels like ours; no reason it should really, 'coz it isn't. This is like living in a hotel. I would never have chosen the stuff in here;

it's from someone else's life. Gingerly, I run my hand over the polished top of a fancy sideboard. My fingerprint remains and I use the edge of my sleeve to wipe it off.

Maybe it would have been easier if Evelyn hadn't died. We could have brought her here in a wheelchair from the home; she could've shown me things, explained why she's given it all to me and Mum.

I still don't get it.

If you walk across the back garden you come to a row of stables. The one thing that does make me think I could get used to living here is getting my own horse. But it still feels wrong. We're not the kind of people that have this kind of money. I didn't even know Evelyn; I shouldn't be getting all this stuff. I'm losing the 'me' I was just beginning to discover, and I don't recognise Mum at all.

Dusty stares at me in the empty stables. There's a hopeful look in his bright eyes. He should be tired; we've just got back from a walk around the outskirts of a large paddock that also belongs to us.

It's getting dark. I feel the rippling muscles under my dog's silky fur as he backs into me. He makes a satisfied grunting sound, gives my face a quick lick. I imagine my potential horse snorting, clopping on the hard floor of the stall behind me. At first I picture a bay gelding with a white star on his forehead and then I decide I'd rather have a dappled grey mare. I know when I meet my horse it won't matter what colour it is. Mum said we should probably get a second one to keep it company. She told me to put up adverts in the local shops or in the paper to find someone to help look after them and go out riding with me; she showed a surprising amount of knowledge about what I'll need.

I wonder who's riding with Jade now.

A line of trees looms up in the dark behind the house, outlined in silver. The stars in the purple sky remind me of my net curtain, brought with me from one home to another since I lived at the Martens' when I was six.

211

Out here in the dark nobody but Dusty can hear me. Crying doesn't bother him. He's used to the taste of tears.

Thirty-One

Bex

I HAVE TO accept Sebastian into my life again instead of trying to be dead like him. It'll all work itself out. It's got to. Gotta make sense of all this. I must be good now. Evelyn's given me another chance. At least she never had to find out about--.

"This room used to have green striped wallpaper."

It's rosy pink now, warm and cosy. I count the animals along the windowsill, the ones that used to be in that glass-fronted cabinet.

"Evelyn had it redecorated after Jonathan died. We had his hospital bed in here, you see."

Mrs Evans has finally started talking to me. She told me when we first came that she'd only stayed on 'coz Evelyn begged her to. She was still furious at me for doing what I did to them, but she doesn't know the half of it.

Gawd; it's gonna come out sometime, the minute one of them realises when Rebecca's birthday is. Yet it's Rebecca that's charmed them, Mrs Evans and Grahams.

I'm hot, burning up. Yet my hands are cold. Mrs Evans brings me a hot toddy; whisky, my second-favourite drink. I can't read the newspaper cause I can't see properly, not that I'd want to. My whole world's inside this house. But everything's gone blurry.

"You mustn't worry about anything."

Mrs Evans knows I'm fretting about the funeral. "It's all arranged, dear."

Ah, she's accepted me again, I feel safe in her care. She brings me an extra blanket.

"Come on now, don't throw it off, it'll help you sweat out the fever."

She's got to be in her seventies now but she don't look it. She dresses like a much younger woman. But I suppose she won't last forever.

"Evelyn's to be buried next to Jonathan and Sebastian of course, at Saffron Hill Cemetery."

My own plot's waiting beside theirs. It's a comforting thought. I often dream about that green, green grass. Home. Back with him.

"What about... who...?"

My brain's spinning like one of them merry-go-rounds. Mrs Evans shushes me.

"The Beeches have informed anyone who needs to know, mostly elderly relatives, dear. You will have met most of them at your engagement party."

And at Sebastian's funeral.

"Now you try and sleep."

I get the feeling Evelyn deliberately waited until just before she died to get me to make my peace with her. Probably so there would be no chance of things kicking off again. I feel bad about misleading her the way I did, but it's too late to change what happened now.

My bedroom's been redecorated as well. It's the room I was going to share with Sebastian before we were to move into Rose Cottage. It now has white wallpaper with a fine mint stripe, a varnished wood floor with a thick cream rug covering most of it.

Rebecca's room's around the corner from mine. It was Sebastian's when he was a teenager, but I haven't told her that. There aren't any traces of him in it. There are no photographs of him around the house: I got Mr Johnson, Adam, to make sure of that before we moved in. He was to tell Mrs Evans it would upset Rebecca too much.

"Evelyn wanted her to sleep in her father's room," Mrs Evans tells me. Thank Gawd she hasn't said that to Rebecca.

Evelyn left instructions for the decorators to bring colour charts and fabric for her to choose from. It was all painted in one day. She's got it done out in pale blue, the floor painted white with a blue rag rug on it. She chose a custom-made patchwork quilt for the bed. Lovely, it is. But she still insisted on having that tatty net curtain with the stars on it up at the window, and her raggedy purple blanket. Bloody stubborn kid, she is.

"You could have had that lovely antique bed," I told her, "instead you want your cheap one from the flat-pack shop. It really spoils the look of the orange room, having two beds crammed in there."

"Stop harping on about the bloody orange room, Mum. It's not as if anybody's ever going to be sleeping in there is it? And anyway, we have two other spare bedrooms besides that one."

Rebecca also insisted on keeping her grotty old mirror. I remember Jonathan being very excited about the geometric sunburst pattern on the frame of the Art Deco one that was in the room before she moved in. He picked it up from a house clearance in Wollaton. I was about seventeen at the time. But Rebecca seems to have no appreciation of these things.

I have all Evelyn's photo albums in here, but I carry my favourite around with me; full of pictures of our last year together – mine and Sebastian's. There's just one photo of me and my Rebecca. I take it out and slip it under the tissue paper that lines my top drawer. Such a tiny thing she was, and I a girl demented by grief when she was ripped out of me. I can't stop thinking about her now.

My baby, my baby.

In the front row at the funeral I stand next to Rebecca. The church walls swell and recede around me, the stained glass window behind the choir tilts precariously. The colours blind me.

Mrs Evans is on my other side. She's wearing a clinging black velvet dress. I want to tell her to tuck a handkerchief into the low neckline of it; a cleavage of that age isn't a pretty sight. She keeps glancing resentfully towards the organist at the front. Mrs Evans' fingers are too twisted by arthritis to play anymore.

Grahams stands beside Rebecca. It's a blazing June day, the air thick with summer, annoying flies buzzing around our heads. We walked here; the four of us behind the funeral car decorated with white lilies and roses the same as at Sebastian's.

It's warm even inside the church; crowded with people in the pews behind us. There are friends of the family from the village and Evelyn's few remaining relatives from Hertfordshire.

I'm strangely emotionless. Mrs Evans suddenly starts making a terrible fuss beside me and I have to practically hold her up. Maybe there's no room for my own emotions, or maybe I've cried them out every night in my bedroom instead.

Rebecca has to come and stand on the other side of Mrs Evans and help support her.

In the chief mourners' car on the way to the cemetery is when the shaking begins. I'm still not crying. But now I can't stop trembling. I panic; my heart's going to break out of my chest.

There's only one thing that'll help and it's a good job I slipped a miniature bottle of it into my jacket pocket before I left the house. I only had one glass up in my bedroom before that, just to help calm my nerves for the funeral. Or it might have been two or three, I can't remember.

"Mum," Rebecca looks worried. "You're scaring me. Are you all right?"

Do I look it?

Even Mrs Evans stops sobbing into her handkerchief.

"Mum!"

The driver gives us a funny look in his rear view mirror, but he manages to keep his funeral face on. Grahams turns in his seat and stares at me. My hand hesitates for a few seconds at my jacket pocket.

The jacket is dark grey silk, from the boutique in the village, exactly the kind of thing Evelyn would have liked to see me wear.

I don't care what the others think. My hand continues downwards and I plunge and grab, tip the contents of the magic green bottle into my mouth. I hold my breath as the car swings round a roundabout on the road into Leicester.

I'm composed until we reach the graveside. But it all comes back then, so close to the grave of my darling. There I stood in my wedding dress on a cold September day nearly twenty years ago.

I see them looking at me, Evelyn's crone-like relatives in their extravagant black-feathered hats and glossy black furs pulled up around their leathery necks despite the June heat. Their black-bead eyes watch to see what I'll do, waiting for a drama, they are. They look like ravens. They were here that day too, when I sobbed in my wedding dress as Sebastian was put in the ground.

They fix their eyes on me, swivel them over to the grave of the perfect boy I buried in his wedding suit. I wonder how much of the expensive fabric of that suit is left now - or is it in tatters, a gourmet meal for the worms?

Rebecca knows nothing of this and I won't tell her. She's got my looks and the name that was never rightfully hers, but I guard the love of my life, my Great Grief, carefully. I move to block her view of his headstone should her eyes wander. I pat my pockets but there are no more bottles to be felt. So I endure what I have to and pray for it to be over soon.

Thirty-Two

Rebecca

"YES I AM. I am sure; he's definitely the one I want!"

I lean forward; slip off the horse's back, slightly giddy as I make contact with the ground. I put my arms around his neck and breathe in his strong horse scent. I laugh when his exploring lips feel their way into the pocket of my shirt. He knows I've got mints in there because he saw where I got the one I gave him just before I rode him round the field. Walk, trot, canter; he responded to my commands effortlessly.

Just like the horse I imagined owning, Topaz is a bay gelding with a streak of white on his face. He's almost fifteen hands high: nine years old, a Connemara with some Welsh cob in his bloodline.

"Ohmygod, this is so exciting, Mr Grahams, I can't believe I'm getting my own horses."

He grins.

"Aye Rebecca, it'll be good to have horses in them old stables again. I'm looking forward to it myself."

Mr Grahams is like having a grandfather, something I don't know much about since Granddad Portman died when I was really little and my Mum's dad died when I was seven. Mr Grahams wanted me to call him Bob but I don't feel comfortable doing that so he said I could just call him 'Grahams' instead, like Evelyn used to and Mum does now. But I'm not comfortable with that either, so in the end he's agreed to respond to 'Mr'.

They're leading the other one out now. Her name's Bo, a 14.2hh sturdy New Forest pony, golden chestnut with a pale mane. She's twelve years old. She and Topaz have been here five years and the family that owns them are moving to London, unable to take the horses. They're glad they may be able to find a home for both of them together.

How can I refuse Bo? She blinks at me with her dark brown eyes, taking the mint from my palm with the softest lips.

"You are such a beautiful girl," I tell her. "Mr Grahams, what do you think?"

He comes forward, casting an expert eye over her as he has already with Topaz, running his hands down the sides of her face, inspecting her teeth, stroking her neck, probing her hindquarters with his fingers. He stands looking in her eyes for a minute and then he examines her legs and checks each hoof.

"Up you get then."

He takes hold of her bridle while I mount, waiting until I'm settled in the saddle with my feet in the stirrups.

"Ready?"

I nod; the signal for him to give her a gentle pat on the rump and she moves across the yard towards the field with me on board. I gather in the reins and adjust my seat. She seems lazier than Topaz, slower in her trot and canter, reminding me of riding Jonah back in North Scarte; I was always behind Jade as she rode the powerful Tetra.

I'm proud of myself for searching out these horses. I used the internet to find them, and Mr Grahams agreed to come with me to look at them because he used to help look after the ones that lived in our stables before.

His granddaughter Sophie's about my age. She'll be loaning one of the horses. She can have Bo, I decide, as I ride her a second time around the field.

We've agreed she'll pay a nominal fee of ten pounds a week – it's not as if I need the money but Mr Grahams says she needs to learn that she can't have something for nothing and she'll have to pay it out of her Saturday job wages, and anyway she's had to pay more than that for her weekly riding lessons. Then I feel guilty for having been given so much without earning it. I decide to donate the ten pounds a week from Sophie to a charity that takes underprivileged children on riding holidays.

I'm scared of having excess money, afraid I'll forget how to be self-sufficient. What if something goes wrong and this all turns out to be a huge mistake?

Sophie lives about half a mile from me. Mr Grahams brought her to meet me last weekend; she seems OK.

We can take it in turns feeding and mucking out the horses; turning them out and bringing them back in again, go on rides together. Mum made me promise I wouldn't ride off the property on my own.

"People can die from coming off a horse."

Her hands were clenched into fists. I was shocked at the glint in her eyes. She's been so quiet lately, ominously calm. I waited for her to elaborate but as soon as I made the promise she clamped her lips shut again.

"I think we should take them both," I tell Mr Grahams. "But should we go and look at some other horses first?"

It seems too easy. My legs are shaking now I've slid to the ground a second time. I'm nervous about actually doing the buying.

"Can you think of anything these two don't have that you were looking for?"

Mr Grahams is still checking out the two horses. They stand patiently, Bo nodding her head, Topaz nuzzling my shoulder. I love them already.

"Nothing, it just seems a bit too good to be true, finding them so easily."

"Fate," Mr Grahams makes the pronouncement.

He scratches his ear. His thick white hair curls into his collar at the back. His alert green eyes make me trust him.

"You were meant to have those horses. Tell you what lass, you go and help turn them back out while I go through the paperwork with Mr Norton. You sure now?"

"I'm sure."

Mum didn't want me to do that by myself. She said her solic-itor 'friend' Adam Johnson could do all the work, ask people who know people to just deliver a couple of horses to our sta-bles.

She doesn't even acknowledge what's been going on between her and him. She acted genuinely offended when I enquired whether she would prefer to ask him in for supper rather than have him wait in his car at the gate until I went up to bed.

"You've got a disgusting mind, Rebecca."

Wonder where I get it from.

Looking back I think I've known for a long time about her random sexual conquests: but this Adam concerns me; soft and stupid, I think he actually likes her. She doesn't even re-member what she's done the next morning.

I got the impression Evelyn put her trust in Mum. I think she believed that offering her the opportunity to live at Greys Mount would finally turn her life around. But I don't think it's made any difference. Mum's eyes are always focussed so far away. She doesn't live in the present at all.

"Eat a proper lunch, Mum. Try not to have a drink until teatime at least."

My words are lost on her. She just looks at me as if I've asked her to climb Mount Everest.

I set up a weekly shopping order from the supermarket, which gets delivered to the house. Mrs Evans is usually there to help put it all away and I saw the way she sucked in her bright pink lips when the crate with the bottles was brought in to the kitchen. Her silver roots visible, she ducked her head in disapproval.

It wasn't me who ordered it, the booze. Mum's perfectly capable of lifting a finger when it comes to the 'add to basket' button.

It was stupid of me to use Dusty as the password, I realise that now.

Dusty's been left out in the stables on his own all day, paddling in his own wee. I can tell by the mucus under his eyes that he's been seriously distressed, although of course he's bouncing around joyfully now.

Mum doesn't give a shit. She promised to get out the house for once; take him for a walk in the paddock. It looks to me like she's been sitting in her favourite armchair with a bloody glass in her hand all afternoon.

She gazes at me blankly when I bang my way in. Her eyes wander off to one side; one hand clutches her photograph album.

I don't know where she keeps those albums but I can never find them when I search. I want to see the pictures of her past, that mysterious Sebastian of hers.

"I don't suppose you feel like cleaning up Dusty's crap, do you Mum?"

I wasn't expecting her to answer. Her vacant eyes never stray off the album. She takes care to keep it angled away from me. I shiver.

She's ill, can't you see?

She's an alcoholic. It's an impossible illness. I've tried, but there's nothing I can do.

I go and change my shirt, which has horse slobber all over it, and then stride into the hallway to grab Dusty's lead, get a bottle of water from the fridge. I slam the back door as I leave.

Dusty's learning to sit nicely outside the village shop, a low building with black beams criss-crossing its white front. I go in and get myself an ice cream.

"How're you getting on with the puppy training?"

The girl who works in there always comes out to stroke Dusty's floppy ears and get a lick from his long pink tongue in exchange.

223

"Good," I say. But the conversation doesn't go much further than that.

We cross the road and go through the gates of Bradgate Park. It's not like any of the parks I've ever known before.

The landscape is huge. There are bridleways I'll be able to ride along when Sophie and I get our horses. Maybe she'll be the friend I've been missing since I moved here. I've explored a lot of the park with Dusty so far but there are still parts of it I haven't been right into yet, uncultivated, covered in huge boulders, carpeted in bracken.

On the ranging slopes of the wilder parts you can find countless hollowed-out trees, appearing normal from one side but when you go around the other you find their innards are blackened, scooped-out. A place to shelter but with a spooky twist. A shudder ripples through me; they remind me of Mum.

I let Dusty off the lead and hope he won't chase the deer. They come right up to you, especially if they know you've got something to eat. Dusty jumps towards a creamy-coloured animal. It jerks up its head, backs off and moves on to investigate the more promising prospect of a young couple sitting on a blanket with a picnic.

Dusty has a paddle in the brook while I finish my ice cream, then I wash my hands in the cool water.

Everything seems unreal, the sun on the blindingly green grass, the sparkle of the stream, those funny twisted trees spreading long shadows before me. It's lovely but I'm disconnected, wondering what I'm doing here, how my life can have changed so much, so suddenly.

I climb back up from the water's edge to the roadway that runs through the park. Maybe I can walk this feeling off. Occasionally a vehicle crawls past and I tense, call out to Dusty who runs after the car, barking. A steep bank rises up on my left, topped by those weirdly shaped trees and looming boulders, ancient and all-seeing. I'm out of breath by the time we get to the ruins of Lady Jane Grey's birthplace; broken remains of an impressive red-brick Tudor building planted on the hill above. I sit with my back against the warm walls. Dusty flops onto my lap, panting.

"You want some water?"

I take a swig from the bottle first and then attempt to drip some onto his tongue. He doesn't seem to be imbibing much and I get more on my bare legs than in his mouth, so I try letting him lap from the bowl of my cupped palm. I daydream about my horses, to be transported to Greys Mount as soon as the payment is authorised.

Before long Dusty falls asleep in the cradle of my crossed legs. I stroke him for a while and then take out my mobile and scan through my contacts, hovering over Connor's name. I have a constant dull ache in my chest about him, I've been trying to cover it with distracting activities like getting my room organised, setting up a painting studio under the skylight in the stables, planning for the arrival of my horses. But things seem to have gone horribly wrong between us.

It was my fault. It all started with the cold shoulder I gave him at the airport when he left.

I remember how irritated he got by Deirdre's texts, picture the same look on his face if he receives one from me, and halt my hovering thumb over the screen of my phone. It's no good. If he wanted to talk to me he could ring or text.

Connor seems like a distant dream now. Was he even real?

Dusty wakes up briefly to give me a puzzled glance. I wipe my eyes. There. Then he lowers his head again in slow motion to rest his nose back on his paws. I lay my head back, eyes half closed against the lowering sun. I think I hear a voice but it must have been in my head.

"I've missed you, Rebecca."

I doze off, feeling warm and safe.

My first love, I remember now.

There's a rustling noise and a slight thud in the grass beside me, a shadow across the sun. Something soft brushes against my thigh followed by the furious wagging of Dusty's tail.

It's the girl I saw at The Beeches. She's not sitting too close to me but there's so much of her odd green velvet dress that

225

she takes up a ridiculous amount of space. I squint at her silhouetted face, not sure whether I'm awake or asleep. She gazes back at me calmly, her small white hands folded neatly around a little book.

Dusty clambers off my lap and sits to attention in front of her. There's something quite weird about her, but I can't pinpoint what it is, apart from her costume.

"Are you here for a performance?"

I wonder if it's one of those evening shows they have in parks and the grounds of castles, where people bring camping chairs and a picnic.

"You have given ear to those who at the time appeared to be wise and now have manifested themselves to the contrary," she replies, pulling up blades of grass and scattering them to the breeze.

Her face is turned half away from me and her voice sounds sad. Dusty takes off in chase of the fluttering stalks, a happy bark punctuating his bouncing gait.

"It was your own lack of prudence...although the error imputed to you has not been altogether caused by yourself."

A shock jolts through me.

"What do you mean?"

The way she uses language is weird. In fact, I'm wondering if she's practicing lines for her play. But she just looks at me hard, giving me an uncomfortable feeling.

A terrible melancholy seems to bubble under her surface; it's in the way she moves, the slow pace of her speech.

"I might have taken upon me that of which I was not worthy, yet no one can ever say either that I sought it.... or that I was pleased with it."

The fake jewels in the headpiece she's wearing glint like real ones in the reddish light of the sun as she struggles to her feet.

With the effort of taming the fabric of her dress, she loses her grip on her book and it slips onto the grass. I hand it back to her, unable to read the faded title but it looks and feels like a very old Bible. I get to my own feet and stand there for a moment, dissatisfied by the confusing content of

226

our conversation, if it could be called that. But I don't know what to say in return.

She gives me the smallest of smiles before she turns her back, her hair under its headdress lifting in a flurry of wind. She walks away and disappears around the corner of the ruined wall.

I scan the surrounding landscape for Dusty and see that he's being petted by a family with three small children working their way up the slope towards the ruins. When I look back I can't see the pale girl with red hair anymore.

Thirty-Three

I SHAKE DUSTY'S food into his bowl.

"Sit... stay... get it then... good boy!"

I can't help but laugh at the sight of his paws scrabbling on the kitchen tiles.

My own footsteps unnerve me as I move across the bare wooden floor of the dining room, trailing my hand over the unused table. I switch the lights on.

Mum lives here like a ghost in the near-dark.

She's still in her chair in the smaller sitting room, snapping the book of photos shut on her lap. I'll get hold of it next time she lets down her guard, determined to see pictures of the past she safeguards so jealously. I want to know who my mother is, because I've sure as hell lost her recently. Cold tightens up my muscles. I pinch myself to feel real.

Those albums are the only thing she's bothered about. Her eyes are vacant. Why can't she at least enjoy what we've been given? The whole thing is pointless otherwise: I was happy before. It was her who wanted this.

As she sits back in the chair I notice that she's thickened around her middle. It's not as if she eats, not that you would notice, and please God she's not pregnant! It must be simply that she gets no exercise at all.

Or she's ill, really ill.

She's an alcoholic; it's an impossible illness.

It's not just the drink anymore. It's something deeper than that, she's retreating into a chasm inside herself. Sometimes I

229

just wish it would be over, because I do know something bad is going to happen.

But hey, we're forced to keep on acting out our parts, and I've been playing mine well for years now.

"You want anything to eat? I'm about to make a sandwich."

She runs the tip of her tongue over dry lips, puts a hand up to her head for a moment, lowers and pushes it into her right side as if she can't decide which hurts more.

"Are you okay, Mum?"

Of course she's not.

The low energy bulb in the overhead light is warming up now and I can see how grey she looks. I shiver, thinking I'll speak to Mrs Evans tomorrow about trying to get Mum to see a doctor. She shifts to one side in her chair, pushing the photo album between the seat cushion and the chair arm. Eventually her voice comes out.

"We got any of that ham left?"

I remember when I used to make her a ham sandwich to take to work. All those years I spent looking after her. It's no different now, even though she's sitting slumped in an expensive chair in her expensive new clothes.

She actually had the staff from that boutique in the village bring them over for her to choose from, too lazy – or was she unable? – to walk down the road herself. I never thought of that. I can hardly look at her.

Still, I continue to recite my lines.

"Yeah, I'll make you a ham sandwich. Drink of squash, or coke?"

"A coke'll be nice, duck."

Her voice is croaky. Her hand fumbles under the cushion at her back and I guess she's got a bottle hidden there. She must think I'm stupid. Secrets and lies. I don't think she knows where I went this morning, and she doesn't care where I've been all afternoon. I don't think she even knows I've started at my new college.

I want to beat my head against the wall, convince myself I'm real. But Dusty does it for me, jumping up at my bare legs, scratching my identity back with a sharp pain.

"Ouch! Dusty, bad boy!" I rub at my leg. "Get on your bed!"

He slinks to his basket, posture low to the ground, sending me mournful looks over his shoulder. I feel like crying for all sorts of reasons. But I go in the kitchen, take a deep breath and let it out slowly, and then I pour a tall glass of coke for Mum, juice for me. I come back in, try to be normal. Have a conversation with her.

"I met this really weird girl at the park."

She clears her throat; takes a long drink from the glass. Croaks: "What kind of weird?"

"Well, she was dressed in like, a Tudor costume. Green velvet. Must have been hot in this weather."

Her eyes track down my body to the brown legs in their denim shorts.

Yes Mum, it is summertime out there, not that you'd know it.

I dig my toes into the deep pile of the rug.

"She spoke really weird as well. She said something about how I listened to people who pretended to be wise, but who've now proved otherwise. Or words to that effect."

She takes another sip from the glass, nods knowingly. "Well, that'll be your father, won't it?"

I'm disappointed. Somehow I was hoping she might give it some consideration. But she never really thinks about anything. She's always quick to take an opportunity to blame someone else. Dad. I decide to ignore what she just said and try again.

"But don't you think it's weird, that a total stranger should say something like that to me? She doesn't know me."

I pause.

"Although I saw her at The Beeches. Maybe she knows about Evelyn leaving us this house and thinks I was wrong to accept."

I really want to know what Mum's opinion is. About us accepting all this money, moving here, because it really bothers

231

me. Has Mum even considered it might have been a huge mistake?

"The Beeches?"

"Yeah, she was there the day Evelyn – you know. I think she was there for a play or something. Maybe the same one is on at Bradgate Park this evening."

"Mmm." She lets herself relax in the chair, loosening her hand which has been pressed into her side all this time. Beads of sweat sit on her forehead, she feels behind the cushion and I hear the slight slosh of the bottle. She's planning to tip some in her coke the minute I walk out of the room. She cocks her head on one side. God, I hate it when she gives me that faux innocent look.

"Did you say we do have some ham?"

I get off the arm of the sofa, resigned to the fact we aren't about to have any kind of useful conversation.

"Yeah. I'll bring the sandwiches in here. You don't want to go in the dining room to eat, do you?"

As if we might sit at the table together like a proper mother and daughter. My chest tightens. The hate shocks me.

I know this is wrong but I actually offer to pour her some gin, pretending I don't know she's got a bottle hidden behind her back.

"Just one won't hurt, will it?"

I make it a large one. I want her out so I can get hold of the album hidden in her chair. Or sneak into her room and see if I can find the other albums. What kind of mother doesn't want to let her daughter see photos of her when she was young?

Some colour comes into her cheeks as she painstakingly finishes most of the sandwich. The drink was no trouble.

"Aww, you wouldn't pour me another, would you, duck? One more won't hurt now. I'll get an early night then I think."

I pour it silently. If she falls asleep I'll just cover her up with a blanket. I can't be bothered with trying to lug her about. I settle myself with my feet up on the sofa. It's cosy in here; I like it much better than the big sitting room across the hallway. But I wish I could learn to love this place like Mum does. Two of the walls are filled with bookshelves and I've found a book about Bradgate Park with beautiful photographs, and etchings from when the house was built. It tells the story of the Grey family.

"Mum?"

She stirs out of her semi-sleep, the glass angled dangerously in her hand on the arm of her chair.

"Eh?"

"The name Grey, our name. It's the same as Lady Jane Grey, who lived at Bradgate Park when she was a girl. Was Evelyn – no, I mean Evelyn's husband, descended from that family?"

She takes a sip of her drink.

"Err, yeah. I thought I'd told you about that. Jonathan was a direct descendent. There's a family tree thing somewhere."

Her speech is slurred and her head tips sleepily to one side after she's made the effort to push out all those words. I know it doesn't have an effect on my own lineage because I'm adopted into the family rather than born into it, but it gives me a shiver of excitement that I have a connection to Lady Jane Grey, the nine-day Queen.

That's when I realise what gave me such a strange feeling about that girl in the park. She looks exactly like the portraits in the book.

Maybe she's an actress playing the part in a production. But I suspect she isn't.

It's me. Sometimes I'm scared of the power of my own imagination. Having a lucid visualisation of Rossetti's wife Lizzie Siddal while she rocked the empty cradle of her dead baby was one thing – but actually seeing Jane Grey in the flesh, having a conversation with her, is another. Maybe it's me who needs to see a doctor!

I can't help being haunted by empathy for the young Jane Grey; forced to marry a boy she hardly knew when all she really wanted was to read and study and learn. To make her own choices. She was younger than me when she got beheaded. How life ran away with her, from her. Her words – I must have read them in a book sometime, come back to me, resonating with my own situation.

"I might have taken upon me that of which I was not worthy, yet no one can ever say either that I sought it.... or that I was pleased with it."

It's late, but I light the fire anyway. Mum's snoring in her chair and Dusty's making a similar noise in his basket and I feel intolerably lonely. Once I've managed to get flames licking at the small pieces of wood in the grate I brush my hands off on the bum of my shorts and sit fingering my phone. I hold it, willing it to ring. But telepathy has never worked before so why should it now? I dare myself to call him; if we don't get this impasse between us sorted out soon I don't think there'll be any way back into love.

But its 11pm. Connor'll have gone to bed; he has to get up at 6am to leave for work in Carrick. On the other hand, oh, it isn't that late. I don't let myself think, just press the quick dial button for his number and hold the mobile up to my ear. It goes to answerphone on the second ring. Now I'm sure he's deliberately cut me off. Once again I picture his look of annoyance at the continued texts from Deirdre when she was his girlfriend. Probably is again, for all I know. So. . .

I glance at Mum before I push myself to my feet and tread softly through the doorway into the dining room. Light reaches into here but its' dark out in the hall and I feel my way hesitantly to the downstairs cloakroom. Pushing open the door I switch on the light. The Victorian toilet has a coloured design of roses inside the bowl and an ancient wooden seat. I splash my face with cold water. Staring into my reddened eyes in the mirror above the sink, I wonder what happened to the joy that was in them when I knew Connor loved me.

Wind rattles the back door and I feel trapped. This house isn't mine and I don't think it would make any difference to Mum whether I was here or not. Once again, I think about where I could go if I left, but Ireland seems out of the question now.

Dusty wakes up and starts sniffing around so I take him

out. We walk to the stables across the dark yard, Dusty disappearing into the shadows of the shrubbery along the side of the house to do his business.

I switch on the light in the empty stall to contemplate my latest canvas. It's larger than anything I've done before, an abstract Irish-inspired landscape reminiscent of the Dublin Painters, but my colours have begun to mutate away from blues towards red. Dark charcoal slashes dirty the edges of the colours. The landscape looks angry. I'm leaving Jack B. Yeats behind, finding my own voice through my brush and knife. Influenced partly by Jade and also by a tutor at my new college, I've developed a method of overlaid washes and drips. I add thick areas of paint to this background, which sets the misty spaces between them into stark contrast.

The desire to squeeze out a fresh range of colours, dip my brush into turpentine, and begin painting feverishly is so strong I have to hold my hands behind my back to stop them reaching for a brush.

"Come on, Dusty."

Mum's deeply asleep when I return to the sitting room so I fetch a blanket from the chest upstairs. Dusty follows me through the door leading out of the cosy sitting room, tiptoeing comically. I put my finger on my lips.

"Shhhh, Dusty."

We go up the back staircase, carpeted with a worn brown needlecord. This is my favourite part of the house, an enclosed staircase, small and comforting. The stairs open out onto an L-shaped hallway. Mum's room is in the first leg of this corridor and mine's around the corner. At the end of my part is another staircase with a much plusher carpet. This one leads down into the front hall.

Under the window, just before the bend in the corridor is a wooden chest containing blankets and quilts. I pull out an eiderdown. It smells a bit musty but feels dry. I take it back downstairs, lay it over Mum and she doesn't stir, even when I pull the padded footstool more comfortably under her legs.

She's not really drunk – nothing like I've seen her in the past, but she seems anaesthetised to sound or movement. Her snores rattle, each one catching on a surprised, out-blown breath. I slip my hand down the side of the seat cushion beside her thigh and slide out the photo album as gently as I can.

With the book tucked under my arm I place the curved fireguard in front of the embers in the grate, switch off one of the two lamps in the room and pull the door quietly shut behind Dusty and me.

Dusty flops into his basket next to my bed and I get myself tucked under my quilt.

I've seen pictures of Mum as a teenager before, of course, but most of those were posed with her brother and Uncle Rick in the small back garden of her childhood home in Nottingham, or in the cramped living room there, everyone looking as though they would rather be anywhere else than in that place together.

The first photograph in this album is different from anything I've seen before. It's a picture of Mum, her eyes shining with joy, looking at the camera over her shoulder as she walks away from the photographer towards a tall figure in a pale grey suit. His face is in shadow as he stands waiting for her just out of the spotlight in the middle of a dance floor. Mum's hair is loose apart from a flower clipped to one side of her head. It seems to swing glossily as she half-twirls away from the camera. She looks happy, full of life.

Under the photo is a hand-written caption: *Sebastian and Rebecca. Engagement party, June 13th 1990.*

I strain to see the face of Sebastian, Mum's fiancé: Evelyn's son. But I can't make out his features. I hold the rigid page of the photo album between my finger and thumb, heart thumping. I feel acutely aware that once I've turned the page, everything will change.

Thirty-Four

THE PHOTOGRAPH ON the next page is a close up of the happy couple. It looks to be taken in the same place as the previous picture; flower arrangements in huge bowls with ribbons tied around them pushed up against the walls in the background, fairy lights strung across the ceiling.

Out of focus partygoers look towards the camera behind the loving pair; dancers with out-flung arms are stilled forever in the distant space of the dance floor.

My mother looks beautiful. Her face is so similar to the one I see when I look in the mirror, except there's a poise about her I don't feel I'll ever have; a visible confidence of her rightful place in the world. She looks... the words that come to mind are 'well fed', but I don't mean with food. She gives the impression of having had all her needs met. Like how my half-brothers came across to me when I first saw them. Completely loved and cared for, appropriately cultivated. It's impossible to correlate this image of Mum with the one of her sleeping in the armchair, mouth open, sunken-cheeked, old before she ought to be.

But it's not these notions, the way I feel when I look at my mother's face a lifetime – my lifetime ago, making my head spin, chest tighten up, sweat prickle on my hot face.

It's him. Sebastian.

He's the boy from my dream, the one on the white horse.

I have pressed my head against the chest of my mother's fiancé, I know I have, his chin dug into my shoulder, the sound of his heart against my ear. I remember how his hand cupped the back of my head, his fingers trailed my skin. In turn I positioned my fingertips on each knobble of his spine, divining his strength beneath the muscles and bone.

I could describe precisely the scent of his neck just below his ear, the exact shade of his hair when the light from a pale purple sky glimmered on it.

I can say what it felt like to stand under the hot breath of a horse, this boy's arms around me, and have him speak to me as if he would never love anyone else as much as he loved me.

When I experienced all of those things, I felt the way I somehow know my mother felt at the moment that photograph was taken.

"Oh God. . ."

The sound of my voice dissipates into the dim quiet of my room. I pull my knees up to my chest under the quilt, flex and then curl up my fingers, open my palm again and stare at it as if it could help me understand what's happening. There's no logical explanation for the fact that I know him, that he's mine.

Not my mother's.

There's something completely wrong about this, as if everything has happened backwards. It was me he kissed, me he said he loved; not her.

He can't have been hers; it was me he offered to take to Oblivion.

But my heart sinks even as I'm forced to acknowledge that he changed his mind. He brought me back, told me I was the wrong one. The sensory memory of those unexplained moments are as strong now as when his arms were wrapped around me, the pungent scent of his horse wafting over us in that purple, mystical landscape.

I've never felt more miserable and alone in my life. Jane Grey was right; I made a mistake allowing my mum to persuade me to come and live here.

My relationship with Connor is over; Mum's disappeared into her own past and I'm perched on the edge of a precipice.

I look at my hands and I'm scratching at my arms, red marks appearing on them. My skin feels prickly, heat rising from the inside.

I look at the picture again, ignoring my mother's eyes adoring Sebastian.

Don't look at her, look at me.

It's a college day. I should have got out of bed at 7am, taken Dusty for a walk, settled him in the stables and got my moped out of the garage for the five-mile ride into Leicester. But it's already 8 o'clock and I can't be bothered.

I look at my phone to check the time and see there's a missed call from Connor. If only he'd answered his phone when I wanted to talk to him last night. He left a voicemail this morning at 6am.

"Hi Rebecca, sorry I missed your call darlin'. Would ya believe I had to drive me eejit brother to the emergency department to have his finger sewn back together? He went an' sawed it practically in half the daft eejit. Mam and Dad'd had a drink so it was down to yours truly here to do the drivin'. Anyways, he's fine now, our Riley. Give us a call back at lunchtime if you want? Love ya."

I want to but I can't, I wouldn't know how to talk to him today, not after last night. I have feelings for my mother's dead fiancé; how do I start to deal with that?

From the sound of it, some crows are having a fight right outside my window. Sunlight is filtered blue through the weave of the new linen curtains. It's hot already.

Dusty sits very still with an intense look in his comically round eyes, occasionally a high-pitched whistle of desperation comes out of his nostrils.

"Come on then."

Some things just have to be done. I think of my mum and what she told me about how she once decided to stop living even though her body would carry on.

A burst of adrenaline fires through me.

Oh dear God, her Great Grief was caused by him. Sebastian.

She warned me that I was headed for a Great Grief of my own.

Mum and me, we were the same for so long; sharing favourite songs, TV programmes, food. And now he's come into my consciousness to both unite and divide, making us the same again but splitting us inexorably apart. Is it wrong to have such a strong urge to escape your own mother?

Again I find myself scratching my arms and look down to find a rash on my skin. I hurtle backwards into my illness.

No, I won't let it get me again.

I squat to give Dusty a hug, real and living in my arms, but he wriggles away, desperate for the garden, for relieving himself, freedom.

"Can you save me? Dusty-doo?"

I want to be happy. I'm lucky to live in this place, have a fantastic room, my darling dog. I remind myself I'll soon have my horses, too. It's true that I've no right to be miserable. I nip into the bathroom next door, while Dusty can't help letting out frantic howls waiting for me on the landing.

Still, I decide to use the front staircase instead of the back one. We can let ourselves out of the kitchen door. I don't want to risk the sight of Mum, probably still asleep in that chair, stale in her crumpled clothes, expensive as they might have been.

Barefoot in the sunlit back yard I feel a spark of hope. Air and sunshine make me real again. The paving stones are warm under my feet, there's a strong scent from the carefully-tended roses at the side of the path, their sunset-coloured heads nodding as I brush past them, picking my way carefully. There's a huge laburnum tree, its branches hanging over the corner of the yard like gold chains. The outside tap drips irregularly from the wall of an old brick outhouse. I turn it more tightly. Mr Grahams must have been out early doing some watering. I scan the garden but I can't see him anywhere. Pity, I like talking to him.

I walk under the fanned-out leaves of the horse chestnut tree behind the stables, curl my toes in the dappled grass. The compost heap exhumes a thick scent into the slight heat haze. A bee buzzes past my ear and I am sucked into timelessness. Everything around me this way for generations. It's so calming, tears prick at my eyes. If only I could stay feeling like this.

I'm wearing my nightshirt tucked into a pair of shorts but who cares? I live here; I can take Dusty for a walk in the paddock without caring what anybody thinks, that's the best thing about it.

I meet Mr Grahams pushing a wheelbarrow full of grass cuttings towards the compost heap as I come back through the paddock gate. We stop for a chat.

"You'll be getting chilblains young lady, walking about like that!"

He nods at my bare feet. Putting a hand up to my eyes I can just see a smile tilting up one corner of his mouth, his face mainly silhouetted. His white hair looks like a halo with the sun behind his head. He doesn't seem bothered by my scant attire. I smile.

"In this heat? Actually it's very healing, you know, to walk around barefoot. Metaphysically speaking."

He roars with laughter. That's what I like about him, his energetic displays of emotion. I once saw him cry over a bird injured by a cat; it was thrashing around dragging a bleeding wing and Mr Grahams told me to leave so he could put it out of its misery. But he actually cried.

"'Ere you, you're trying to blind me with science, aren't you? So what d'you mean by that eh?"

"Well you know you have pressure points on your feet? They relate to every part of your body, that's what reflexologists work on when they give you a foot massage."

I'm interrupted by another gale of laughter, but I frown and continue.

"When you walk barefoot you stimulate all those pressure points naturally, putting yourself in direct contact with the earth. It can heal all sorts of things that are wrong with your body."

I look at my feet pensively. I've only just learnt all this stuff from a book I found in the sitting room. "And your mind," I add quickly. I must admit I already feel much better than I did when I woke up. I resolve to do a bit of barefoot walking every day throughout the summer. I'm determined not to sink back into the kind of depression that landed me in hospital at the beginning of the year.

"Eh," says Mr Grahams. "You just watch you don't go stepping on a nail or a thorn then!" He pushes the barrow away, chuckling to himself and shaking his white mane of hair. But I run after him, the grass in the shade of the hedge cool under my feet.

"Mr Grahams?"

He lowers the barrow again, begins tossing out armfuls of grass.

"Yes, chuck?"

"What was Sebastian like?"

A shadow comes over his face, it really does. I glance up sideways but the sun is still shining in the sky.

"I'm sorry he died before you were born, lass."

It seems an odd thing to say in answer to my question. It echoes a comment Mrs Evans made shortly after we moved in, but I can't remember what it was. I wait a moment and then I ask again.

"What was he like?"

"He was a good lad, Sebastian," Mr Grahams says after a while. "A quiet boy; didn't have many friends in the village, a bit 'away with the fairies' I used to think. Your mother was his first real friend."

He kind of chews with his mouth, gazing away into the distance. Then he gives me a long look.

"We spent a lot of time talking as he grew up. You remind me of him, the way you talk about things. He would've been proud of you. Maybe that's why you an' I get on so well together, eh?"

242

I can't help smiling. At least I've made one good friend since I've been here. But again Mr Grahams has said an odd thing, he would've been proud of you. Maybe because I'm Mum's daughter, they associate me with Sebastian.

"What happened to him?"

"Don't you know? Surely she. . ."

He rubs at his chin with a grass-stained finger, examining my face with his green eyes.

"You oughta ask your mother to tell you. Why don't you talk to her about it, lass?"

"She won't," I say. "She's not very well at the moment. I don't want to upset her."

A fly circles my head a few times and ignores me when I brush my hand at it.

"Please, Mr Grahams."

He gives me another penetrating look. Tosses out a few more armfuls of grass, making a new pile next to the full compost heap.

"You've got a right to know, I suppose." Another tattoo of heartbeats lurch painfully in my chest before he speaks again. "It was a riding accident."

He straightens his back, rocks slightly on his feet. I feel the sun burning all down my right side.

"He insisted on having a white stallion he'd seen for his eighteenth birthday," says Mr Grahams in a different voice that seems to me like a special story-telling one. I feel like sitting on the grass with my legs crossed and a blanket shoved up to my nose. But I stay standing.

"Wilful horse, it was," he says. "Very strong. It could be sweet as cherry pie one minute and turn on you the next. I was a younger man then, Rebecca, and I was s'posed to be good with horses, but I was afraid of that horse, I don't mind telling you."

He grasps the handle of the rake leaning against the side of the compost container and starts pushing the pile of grass into shape, close up to the wood.

"Sebastian loved him though, and the horse, Caspian, was generally sweet with your mother. She had a natural way with horses, you know."

He gets a wistful look in his eyes, turning his head to look out towards the trees bordering the paddock. I imagine him picturing Mum the way she looked in those photos. Or maybe he's thinking about that white horse cantering around the paddock, mane and tail flying, hearing the thundering noise of his hooves. I can envisage that white horse exactly; feel his hot breath on my face. I can even remember his sweet, strong smell. I hear Sebastian's voice in my head, *He likes you. He remembers you.*

Mr Grahams turns to me again. "Sebastian wasn't allowed to ride Caspian for six months after they got him. Fetched that horse all the way from Holland they did. They got all sorts of trainers in, horse-whisperers they called them, to work with it. He was a stubborn beast, but eventually he seemed to have settled down. That's when they let Sebastian ride him, and soon enough he was permitted to take him out with your mother riding Tara."

"Tara?"

"Her black mare."

He thinks I ought to know that. Of course, he has no idea of the nature of my relationship with Mum. Or the kind of person she is now. She hardly shows her face anymore, is why.

"Anyway," he says. "It was all right for a good few months, no trouble from Caspian at all. They did make a lovely couple, the two horses. I reckon they were planning to breed them eventually; that was why Sebastian refused to let the stallion be gelded. That was his mistake though."

"What was?"

Mr Grahams finishes raking and brushes the last of the grass off his hands onto the back of his linen trousers, probably part of a good suit once.

"It was days before the wedding. Rebecca didn't oughta 'ave been riding at that point." Under his breath I hear him mutter, "Silly girl."

I wondered why she shouldn't have been riding before the wedding, but I didn't want to break the fairy-tale atmosphere he'd created.

"You couldn't change her mind when she'd made it up about something though. They wanted to go on a last picnic together as an unmarried couple. It was a warm day for September; Sebastian had a rucksack on his back with the picnic in."

The old man pulls a handkerchief from his back pocket and wipes it across his forehead. I clear my throat, shift from foot to foot. Something cold takes root in my stomach. I don't want to hear what comes next but at the same time, I do. I need to hear it.

Days before the wedding.

"The mare'd come into season you see, but nobody had realised; she was a bit early. They weren't meant to go out riding together when the mare was in season, too dangerous. Too unpredictable."

Mr Grahams walks back a few paces and settles onto the low fence around the enclosure beside the grass cuttings. He wipes his forehead again, looking a bit shaky. The cold patch inside me spreads up to my chest.

"Are you OK, Mr Grahams?"

"I'm all right girl. It's upsetting to talk about, that's all. But you ought to know the facts if your mum hasn't told you. It's your history too."

"She hasn't. I don't know anything," I say in a quiet voice.

"Well. The stallion got out of control while they were on their ride, biting at the mare and chasing after her. She was a spirited enough horse herself, was Tara, and she didn't take kindly to it. She took off at top speed towards the forest. Rebecca was thrown but she landed safely. Amazingly, considering. . . But Sebastian. He couldn't rein back his horse. Caspian went galloping after Tara. Sebastian hit his head on a low branch as Caspian crashed into the trees. He was dead by the time the ambulance got anywhere near."

Mr Grahams dabs at his eyes with the folded handkerchief. I stop breathing.

"His father'd gone out looking for them because they were so late. Meant to be having a special family dinner that night, with all the relatives that were visiting for the wedding."

Mr Grahams clears his throat but his voice still comes out croaky.

"Jonathan, Mr Grey, he found your mother in the woods with Sebastian cradled in her lap. She was sitting as still as a statue."

I cough, make myself breathe again. Imagine what it would be like, being alone in the woods. The cracking of branches, the panicked trample of hooves fading into the distance, the inner silence of realisation. Life stopping, there and then.

It's half past nine by the time I return to the house with Dusty. I feed him, and watch him eat, putting teabags into two mugs while I'm waiting for the kettle to boil. Dusty gobbles his food quickly, almost choking on it.

"You are a silly dog," I scold, "Nobody's going to take it away from you, are they?"

I feel strangely numb after everything I've heard. There's a huge tenderness inside me for Sebastian, and for the Rebecca my mother once was, but I feel nothing much for the woman who calls herself Bex and became my mum. I can't relate her to that other Rebecca at all, the one that's more like me.

Dusty burps loudly and patters off through the dining room towards the sitting room where he has a basket. I follow after him, thinking I ought to offer Mum some breakfast since I'm about to get some for myself. I don't know why I imagine she'll still be in exactly the same position in the chair as when I left her last night. Maybe because that's where she can usually be found these days.

She is in the room, but not asleep in the chair. Her hair's all mussed up and I can smell her bad breath as she approaches me furiously.

"What have you done with it?"

"What?" I'm trembling.

This is too big for both of us – not that I borrowed the photo album, but what I discovered from it. She can never know about me and Sebastian. The thing I learnt when I was a child was that nobody must ever sully her Great Grief, her hard-earned treasure that she'd fight anyone to defend.

"My fucking album. You've taken it haven't you? How dare you steal my things?"

She's really screaming now, terrifyingly animated. It's like being trapped in a fairy story, the kind she always told me when I was little, her twisted face that of the wicked witch, revealing her true identity at last.

I press myself against the wall, fingers tracing the patterns in the anaglyptic wallpaper.

"I only wanted to look in it. You never show me any pictures of the past."

Mr Grahams' words come back to me.

"It's my history too." My voice comes out small. I imagine I'm shrinking.

She approaches me, menacing.

"What do you mean by that? It's not your fucking history, it's mine!"

I look around the room and see she's overturned cushions on the sofa and the two armchairs; dragged a whole load of books from the shelves. She's crazy, stamping her feet, pounding the wall with her open palm. It goes through me. Dusty barks hysterically.

"Where fucking is it? Just give it back to me!"

"It's in my room. It's okay; I'll go and get it now. . . "

But I daren't move. I stay with my hand on the doorframe so I don't get trapped inside with her. It takes her a minute to absorb what I've said, then all the air goes out of her.

"Get it," she pleads. She looks harmless now. "Fetch it quickly. I need my pictures."

"I will," I edge forward. "I will. I'll get it now. Don't worry."

"I'll be in there, bring the album in there to me," says my mum.

Then to my astonishment she takes hold of the heavy embroidered rug hanging on the wall, tucked half-behind a bookcase. She tugs at it and pulls it to one side. There's a door behind it, with a copper knob that she turns slowly. She stares at me with hot eyes as if challenging me to stop her. The door scrapes open over a thick grey carpet with swirls etched into it. Inside, it looks as though the room is empty. My stomach drops sickeningly, like when you go over a humped bridge in a car.

It's the grey room. The grey room from my dream, or nightmare, and the painting hanging on the wall in there is 'There is no Night.'

Thirty-Five

Jack

2010

"I CAN'T, DAD."

Her voice sounds as if it's coming from far away. It's the summer holidays and I'm worried about her. She's too isolated. I tried to talk to Bex about her. I insisted on being allowed into the house, that house.

———◦◦◦———

I was shown into the room by an old woman with bleached-blond hair and sun-lamp skin, trying to look like a younger one. She was wearing a velvet leisure suit with the zip of the jacket pulled too far open for comfort. For my comfort anyway. No-one wants to see a wrinkled old chest like that. She looked at me gone-out when I introduced myself as Rebecca's dad. Then she said:

"Whatever you like to call yourself, it's none of my business now Evelyn's gone. I just work here."

What the hell? And I realised this must be the famous 'Mrs Evans' that Rebecca was always on about.

She pushed open a door and stood back, arms folded. Peering in, I saw Bex sitting in a chair, not even turning her head when I entered. I said her name. She ignored me. When my eyes adjusted to the dimness I was shocked. She looked like a zombie: yellow skin, staring eyes. Inanimate. Apparently Rebecca and Mrs Evans, who hovered at the door staring at me as I stared at Bex, have both tried to get her to see a doctor but she refuses.

Anyway I've got to put that image out of my mind for now. My concern is for my daughter. It's not good for her to be entombed, that's the word that comes to mind, in the house where everything went so wrong for her mother.

"Rebecca, this trip has been planned for months," I say to her on the phone.

Edna appears in front of me with a pile of invoices for me to initial. I give her an irritable waft with my hand; go make the tea, or something. She closes the door of the office with a sharp click on her way out. Fuck, it's hot in here. I told Arthur to take the chisel to that jammed window catch. That boy can't do anything without having his hand held.

"Your brothers are looking forward to having you with us," I persist. "You can't back out now."

She doesn't answer.

"What are you doing at the moment?"

I'm afraid she'll cut the conversation short as she has done so often lately.

Rebecca's being sucked back into her mother's grim world of unhappy endings. I need to get her out of that house, before Bex's misery shrivels her heart like it did mine.

Shit, Jack. Focus on what's best for Rebecca.

When I visited the house before, she showed me around the house while her mother dozed in the chair, clutching an old-fashioned photo album to her chest. Rebecca said she wouldn't let go of it.

I wasn't prepared for the weight of sadness that pressed in on me as I walked around the house with Rebecca. I had this odd feeling that the colour was fading out of her. This was the house in which Bex suffered her Great Grief, the tragedy that no-one living, not me, nor her daughter, could ever compete with. Rebecca pulled back a heavy curtain in the sitting room. Bex had remained slumped in the armchair the whole time and didn't seem to notice my presence.

"This is so weird," said Rebecca, her hand closing around a brass knob behind the curtain.

"It's a secret room."

I noticed her hand was trembling as she pushed open the door. Behind it, darkness, not even a window. She flicked on the light. The walls were painted grey.

"Mum sits in here a lot."

A moth-eaten old chair stood close to one wall. Rebecca looked pastier than ever.

"The thing is, Dad, I had a weird dream about a room just like this. Before we even came here. I'm sure I did. It gives me the creeps."

A lighter square on the wall indicated a patch where something had obviously once hung.

"A painting," Rebecca said, noticing me looking. She traced the edge of the pale grey square with the side of her hand.

"This is the weirdest thing. The painting was in my dream too, sort of. You know that lucid feeling I was telling you about?"

"Uhm?" I was distracted by the oppressive greyness of the room. "Sorry, not sure what you mean."

I wanted to get out, felt choked by the airlessness.

She swore under her breath. "You never listen to anything I say."

"That's not fair. . . "

"Don't you even want to know what happened to the painting?" Her arms were rigid at her sides, hands clenched threateningly.

"What's the matter, honey?"

She'd hardened since she went to live there. I tried to stop the thought 'like her mother' from popping into my head.

"Why are you so upset?"

"Mum took a knife to it," said Rebecca. "Mrs Evans arranged for someone to take it away to be repaired."

"This is a really unhealthy environment for you to be in," I said.

Rebecca looked so pale. It reminded me of when I visited her in the hospital; when all those feelings of helplessness came back, along with the guilt that I'd ever let her get into this situation in the first place. We were standing at the window in the crook of the corridor on the first floor, looking out over the paddock where Rebecca's two horses grazed. I should have brought her up myself, not left her with Bex. I was supposed to be the responsible one. It's what I'd pretended to be. At least Bex never pretended. But she did want to keep Rebecca. So I sacrificed my child in the hope she'd be able to save Bex. *You sacrificed her so you could be with Wendy*, the inner me says more truthfully. I tell it to fuck off.

Rebecca regarded me with those seal-like eyes of hers.

"I'm fine, Dad. I love it here, honestly." She had a veil over her eyes when she said it, reminding me so much of her mother when I first knew her.

Sat in my office with the phone pressed against my ear, I try to make my voice firm, but desperate is what I feel. I haven't been this rattled since Rebecca's illness.

"Your ticket's booked. Iris is really looking forward to seeing you."

I hear her breathing.

"I can't, Dad," she says. "You've seen what Mum's like. I can't go away at the moment."

"But Rebecca. . . "

"Hey, sorry, I've got to go now."

It sounds as if she's moving. I hear the soft thud of feet on carpet and then what must be the back door being opened.

Another girl's excited voice saying, "It looks like there might be a thunderstorm this afternoon, we'd better get a move-on."

"Talk to you later, Dad," Rebecca says breathily.

The call disconnects.

—◦—

1993

We packed as much of our stuff as we could in the van alongside some boxes of stock. Calling round at my parents' before driving to Skegness that night I felt more excited about a fresh start with Bex and Rebecca than sad at leaving my home.

"Here are the lock-up keys, Dad. Sorry to leave you in the lurch like this. Is it okay if I keep what's in the van? I'll need to set up a new stall as soon as I can get a spot on the market there."

Dad was fine about it.

"About time you expanded the family business, a new leaf and all that. You can finally start putting some of your own ideas into practice without me holding you back." He laughed and then used a coughing fit to explain away the wetness in his eyes.

Mum was furious, also distraught at the thought of being separated from her granddaughter, but when I told her that the crazy couple who used to be Bex's parents-in-law had appeared and were trying to take the baby away (I had to embellish the story a bit), she couldn't give me the caravan key fast enough.

"I'll be over to visit next weekend," she promised. "And of course I won't tell anyone where you've gone, no, nobody, not even Bex's family."

She said the last part with a satisfied straightening of her mouth, making a zipping gesture with her finger and thumb.

She couldn't stand Bex's mum.

"You're my hero, Jack," said Bex. Her cheeks were still flushed from our earlier lovemaking. And yes, it had felt like love. I was still tingling, full of hope for our new life.

She gave my mum a kiss on the cheek, hitched our sleeping daughter more securely onto her shoulder, a canvas bag stuffed with food that Mum had given her clutched in her spare hand. She turned for a last look into my parents' living room. A wistful expression came over her face but then it was as if a drawstring had been tightened around it. Her face hardened.

"Come on then. We'd better get off. See you Beryl, Jim. See you soon, bye for now."

She was all determination and action again.

We lived in the caravan for the rest of the summer and for the first months of winter. In January we moved into a one-bedroomed flat. Bex was disappointed that it wasn't bigger but my business hadn't taken off as well as I'd hoped and our budget was tight. I tried to stay positive.

"Look, see? The bedroom having two windows means we can section part of it off for Rebecca. Then she can have some privacy and so can we."

Bex gave me a withering look.

"She's eight months old, Jack. She doesn't need privacy."

But I did.

Rebecca had slept in our bed since we left Nottingham. Each night she snuggled between us. Bex and I hadn't had sex since then. My bright-cheeked, hopeful girl of that night had disappeared pretty soon after we left, masked again by Bex's customary melancholy.

It would get better, I told myself. She was the mother of my child, I just had to cherish her, make her well again. One day, she'd get over Sebastian, stop being so sad. She had to.

Thirty-Six

Rebecca

I UNCLICK THE fastener and pull the helmet off my head. My hair's all sticky. Sliding my hand along the wooden top of the stall, I'm thinking as usual of Sebastian. He's been in my head ever since I saw the photograph.

I'm sure he's in the house. I catch glimpses of him in the corridor and once I felt his sleeve brush against my bare arm. At night I wait for him in bed but nothing happens. I want that feeling back again. *Forget about her, Sebastian, I want to be the one. Take me to Oblivion.*

Here in the stables I imagine the white stallion pawing the concrete floor angrily; hear his snort and feel his hot breath. He once lived in this stall.

Mr Grahams had said he was scared of that horse, but he liked me in the dream, Caspian did.

"He remembers you."

Topaz nudges me impatiently. His hooves ring on the stones. Darkness hovers, the atmosphere's oppressive. A storm is beginning; or it's a scream brewing up inside me, could be either.

Sophie and I work in silence. She arrived later than usual because her auntie wanted her for an extra afternoon at the corner shop. I finish grooming Topaz and we wait for Bo to finish her feed. She's a much slower eater than Topaz.

By the time we've let them out an artificial night's already pulling in. Wind ruffles the trees surrounding the paddock, spooking the horses. Then it's as if someone's fired a starting pistol, both of them take off at the same time, their eyes wild, manes and tails streaming. It's not their usual happy gallop of freedom.

They seem scared.

Sophie and I look at each other, no doubt thinking the same thing, *Bugger.* I rub my finger on the fence, jump as a splinter stabs under the nail, Bloody hell. I try to pinch the splinter out but it's in too far, I'll need a needle. I turn my attention back to the horses, say what we're both thinking.

"Maybe we should bring them back inside?"

Sophie agrees. So we have to start all over again, load in some fresh straw, fill their hay nets, give them water.

Sophie's developed a special whistle that Bo responds to, but I'm left standing there yelling.

"Topaz, come on, come on."

I call him at the top of my voice while he continues his wind-spooked dance around the paddock.

I left Dusty in the house with Mum, thinking he'd be good company for her. It's past the time Mrs Evans will have gone home.

I hear the whimpering as soon as I push open the kitchen door.

"Dusty, where are you?"

He howls.

I open the downstairs doors one by one. He's not in the kitchen or the back hallway or the sitting room or her weird grey room that makes my stomach clench. The howling's not coming from the dining room either.

"Dusty?"

I open the door into the front hall and he's there.

"Oh my God, Dusty,"

He's crying because of Mum. She lies, oddly crumpled at the bottom of the stairs. You wouldn't think a fully-grown person could make a shape like that. Her head's jammed against the skirting board and she has a violent purple bruise on her cheek. A gargling noise comes out of her throat. She's bitten her tongue.

I have a horrid visualisation of her teeth snapping shut as her jaw hits the bottom step. Blood soaks into the carpet.

Oh my God. Do I move her or leave her where she is?

"Mum!"

The air around us seems to vibrate.

I could swear someone, with a flash of bright hair, is hovering at the edges of my vision. I catch a whiff of a poignantly familiar scent; boy mixed with the tang of horse. That could be coming off my own clothes, the horse bit anyway. But I'm certain it's not, though when I turn my head to look there's no-one there.

My own breathing sounds too loud in my head. I reach for my phone in the pocket of my jodhpurs, manage to locate the 9 and press it three times. With my other hand I try to comfort Mum.

Sebastian, I wish you were here.

Was it was Mum thinking that or was it me? I can't tell.

"Let me come and fetch you, you can't stay in that big house all alone."

"No, Dad."

I can hardly speak. My muscles have gone rigid, elbows juddering against my body like that stupid chicken dance we used to do at parties.

I'm in the lobby of Leicester Royal Infirmary. A woman with a bandaged foot sits hunched up in a wheelchair, crying. There's a man wearing a shirt and tie and a bright green stethoscope round his neck, standing over her, arguing with another man who could be either her husband or her son.

People hurry past me in both directions and the automatic door keeps sliding open and shut. I want to close my eyes and hide.

A large woman carrying a flushed-faced child with golden curls barges past me calling: "I need a doctor, now!"

I have to put my hand over my ear so I can hear what Dad's saying.

"It's too much for you to cope with alone. Have a break with us while she's in hospital."

I bite my lip, picture Dad and Wendy's house in Nottingham, the wide hallway, the peach-coloured living room with those comfy brown sofas and my two little brothers bashing each other with cushions. I haven't seen them for weeks.

How simple everything seemed when I was there. I wish I could go back, but I can't. I have Dusty and Topaz and Bo to think about.

One of the paramedics was kind enough to let me bring Dusty in the ambulance even though it was against the rules. He's being looked after in their office right now. But I've got to get back for the horses' morning feed.

"The boys are missing you," Dad says softly. His voice has gone all weird. My throat closes up.

I suppose Mr Grahams and Sophie could manage.

"It's an easy journey from Nottingham to Leicester by train," Dad continues.

I breathe again.

"You'll be able to visit your mother every day."

"Okay, thanks... but I'll need..."

Before I have a chance to say to *go home first and collect some things for Dusty and me*, a nurse is at my shoulder, putting her hand on my arm.

"Hang on a minute Dad..."

"Your mother's awake, she's asking for you, getting quite upset I'm afraid." The nurse gently presses my arm.

For a bitter moment I think of the night I woke up surrounded by my own vomit on a hospital bathroom floor. How I cried for my mother then, but she didn't come.

258

A nasty part of me pictures an alternative reality to this one in which my mum hasn't woken up at all; the nurse has come out here to give me a different piece of news.

But the nurse is making beckoning movements, turning on her heel to hurry back the way she came, and I'm impelled to follow.

"Sorry Dad, I've got to go."

"I woke up and wondered where you were," says Mum. "Don't leave me again, ducky."

I can't shake the feeling she's been invaded by a body-snatcher. I don't recognise her at all.

Nurses and a doctor stand watching us. I'm in some kind of freak show. Mum gives a wan smile, which turns into a grimace when it reaches the right side of her face.

"Ow. Can't you give me anything for the pain, Doctor? It hurts even to smile at my daughter here."

"I'm afraid we've already given you the maximum possible dose of analgesic, Mrs Grey. It should begin to take effect soon. What I wanted to talk to you about was something else entirely."

A crafty look comes over her face.

"I could go private, you know."

She tries to give me a wink but I look the other way. I'm not colluding anymore. Now I know she's not going to die the only thing I can think about is Dusty.

"Mum, I need to go and check on. . . "

"Could you wait a moment please, Miss Grey?"

Mum mutters a stream of words but all I catch is: "That bloody dog, it's all you think about, isn't it?"

"Would you sit down please?" says the doctor. "I need to talk to you and your mother together."

Numbly, I take the pink upholstered chair at the side of the bed.

I'll never escape now.

I wish I could do that thing again when part of me splits off and goes somewhere else. I want to go away and play with my dog. I want to go home and ride my horses. Or talk to Lady Jane Grey: she'd say something profound and meaningful.

I'd be all right at Greys Mount, with cheerful Mrs Evans coming in, Mr Grahams to chat to in the garden and in the stables. I want to be there. I need to be convinced that I've just brushed against an arm clothed in crisp white cotton in the hallway; seen the flash of sunlight on a head of blond hair. I want the excited feeling it gives me in my stomach.

Yes, I can finally think of Greys Mount as home, especially without Mum there. I know that sounds awful, but it's true. I want to go home. I don't want to be rescued by my dad.

"Well, what is it, Doctor?"

Mum's hand snakes out like claws to fasten around my wrist. Hansel and Gretel comes to mind like it did in the caravan that time. I shift in my seat.

"As you know we've done some blood tests and taken you up for a scan, and I'm afraid I've got some bad news about your liver, Mrs Grey."

There's a pause, presumably for us to take the news in.

"Have you been having any pain recently? Maybe you've had some dizziness or blackouts? May I ask if you consider yourself a heavy drinker?"

I look at Mum's face and she looks back at me. And I get what was making her look so alien.

It occurs to me that I haven't seen her in daylight for quite a long time. In the small sitting room with the curtains pulled across, or in that horrible poky room she loves so much, I've been thinking how grey her skin looks. But now I see her under the stark lights of the hospital, I realise the tone that's taken over the normal colour of her flesh is not grey at all, it's yellow.

A day later, things have suddenly sped up. My recollections of the days leading up to now are static images.

Mum sits with the photo album on her lap; that swelling of her stomach I'd noticed, now explained by the doctor as water

retention due to her liver not functioning properly. She's smiling
with vacant eyes in the little grey room.

Her eyesight has been slowly failing, that's another sign. She always seemed to be staring at nothing. And I've learned that her mental absences are also due to complications of liver dysfunction.

I focus on other pictures in my mind.

The sunlit vista of Bradgate Park stretches around me, its huge boulders and crooked trees drawn in vivid contrast to the white bright sky. Lady Jane Grey's family home outlined in broken red brick against a landscape of bracken, the burnished red-brown of Topaz's shoulders in front of me, the groomed silk of his black mane. I see Sophie's round-cheeked smile to my right as we ride side by side on the bridleways of Bradgate. Dusty's comical look of surprise when I play hide-and-seek with him in the paddock, me suddenly jumping out from behind a tree.

But in the here and now the images of my life are blurred by urgency, confusion, disbelief. The trudge of time has reached a pinnacle. Mum's seriously ill. Deathly ill. I can't take it in.

It's horrible and stuffy in the hospital. I can't breathe. Red blotches appear on my too-hot skin. I tear at the neck of my t-shirt. I'm being choked.

"I want to go home."

Mum surprises me. I thought she'd have enjoyed the attention she's getting here at the hospital. But she clings onto my wrist. She begs me with her yellowed eyes.

"Please, Rebecca. You can look after me can't you? Make them let me go home. I want to go back to Greys Mount." She's crying like a child. I should feel for her but I can't. It's all gone.

I'm horrible; an awful daughter.

I don't want to look after her on my own.

"I need to be near. . . him."

She's begging me.

Rage.

I feel rage.

261

He's not yours anymore.

With the purple bruise covering half her face, her tinged skin, her yellow-whited eyes search for mine. I pull my hand away.

"I have a plot at the cemetery, next to him. Mr Johnson, Adam, he has all the papers. He knows what to do. Please, let me."

Let her what, *die?*

Her breath is fetid. He wouldn't want her now anyway, Sebastian. I'm the one who looks like she did when he was in love with her. I've even let my hair grow longer than it's been for years. I realise now why she always encouraged me to keep it short. She was jealous of me.

I love your hair.

His lips against my ear.

It didn't work, Mum. It didn't stop him loving me. He loved my hair short; he said so.

"Miss Grey."

The doctor walks into the room, flanked by a couple of lesser white-coats.

He gives me a practised smile, lowers his eyes to the folder at the end of her bed.

"Your mother has been asking if she can be discharged. There's really no reason why she shouldn't be, in a couple of days. We just want to do some more tests first, see if we can establish the extent of the damage. We could then send her home with pain relief and some other medication, a special drink called lactulose she will need to take every day. We can also give you a low-protein diet sheet to follow. If you think you could manage? Is there anyone at home to help you look after her?"

Mum sniffs, spits phlegm into a bunched-up tissue. She aims it at the bin beside her bed but misses. It sits there on the floor, greenish contents making me sick.

"She can manage by herself, can't you, Rebecca? We don't need anyone else Doctor, never have, we've always looked after each other."

I stand wringing my hands. The doctor waits for my response. He probably thinks I'm a terrible daughter, and I suppose he's right. I think hard.

There's Mrs Evans and Mr Grahams, but I couldn't ask him to do anything in the house. There's Jackie who does Mum's ironing. Or, maybe I could hire a nurse to stay at the house. We've got the bloody money.

After all, I've got my horses to look after and Dusty to take for regular walks. I can't do everything on my own.

The doctor's still looking at me. So are his students and the nurse who's taking Mum's blood pressure. Mum has her sunken eyes fixed on my face. The room holds its breath; even the bleeping machines seem to take a pause.

I lick my lips, dredge out a voice. "Would you be able to tell me how to hire a private nurse?"

———⊸⊂———

"Dusty."

This morning Mrs Evans offered to look after him. She took him back to her sister's when she'd finished cleaning Greys Mount. The two women have obviously doted on him; he looks fat and smug. When I reach out my arms he darts playfully behind Mrs Evans' legs.

Mrs Evans nods her head for my jacket, which I've just shrugged out of. It's almost as stiflingly hot in this tiny sitting room as it is in the hospital.

"It's my sister," she whispers behind the shield of her gold-ringed hand, "She feels the cold terribly."

I notice that her purple nail varnish needs reapplying.

She says in a louder voice: "I don't like the look of those dark shadows around your eyes, young lady, sit down and have a cup of tea."

Her sister comes trundling in with a tea trolley on wheels, nodding and smiling, wearing one of those floral fold-around aprons you see on films about the 1960's. The sister's hair is completely white, delicate as cobwebs.

"Now, tell us all about it."

I'm crying. They must think I'm useless. The words I should really say are frozen inside me in a block of ice.

Mum's going to die, quite soon.

"She'll be home in a day or two," I substitute. "The hospital's helping me organise a nurse to live in. I need to get a room ready for her."

The smiling sister passes me a spotless handkerchief.

"Thank you."

I mustn't fill it with snot so I dab my eyes instead. I pull out a ragged piece of tissue from the hospital toilets for my nose. Dusty craws into my lap, looks around sheepishly to see if he's going to get told off for breaking furniture rules.

Mrs Evans pats my hand.

"You've got enough on your plate already. Leave the nurse's room to me; I'll make it lovely for her. You're doing the right thing, Rebecca."

In the front hallway of Greys Mount I can still see a stain of blood on the carpet, though Mrs Evans has obviously done her best to remove it.

It's my second night alone.

I bend forward, arms pinned across my waist. In the hall mirror I see the face of a girl I used to know, drained of colour. I thought I'd left her behind back in March. How can everything have gone so wrong again?

It occurs to me that I could have invited Sophie to stay at the house; offer her a room of her own, to live in.

But not the orange room. There's one other spare bedroom besides the one the nurse will have. It's small, papered in pale green with an antique iron bed in it. The floor's painted white like mine. We could get her a rug.

I pull out my mobile, scan the list of contacts; put it away again. It's late, Sophie's done enough today.

I go and check that the front gate's properly locked. It's the type you need a code to open, but I can also lock it manually with a key.

Back inside, I make a sandwich and take it up to my room. After that I have a long bath. I'm reading Rebecca. Dusty lies on the bathroom floor with his head on his paws. The room's full of steam. When I stand up, dizzy, I wipe the mirror and stare into it. I don't know what I'm looking for – her? She was all I had once, Mum, and she spent my whole life saying that about me. But it wasn't true.

There was always Sebastian.

I could ransack her room if I wanted, turn it upside down, find those other photo albums. I'd be able to feed off images of her past, the girl that looked just like me. I could be her, see myself in the arms of Sebastian. But I can't touch her things now she's not here.

Those words echo hollowly in my head.

Now she's not here.

I have a plot at the cemetery, next to him.

I shake so hard my elbow flies out and knocks against the doorframe, sending a tingle right up to my shoulder. Ah, that hurt.

It's all right, I'm here.

That voice, my first love. My arms fold against my own body as he places his around me, comforting. I close my eyes and sink into him, smell the familiar scent of boy and horse.

Are you Rebecca?

I am.

It's all right, I love you.

I love you too.

Thirty-Seven

Jack

2010

IT'S MY FIRST day back at work since I returned from the fortnight in Ireland and I'm called straight down to the workshop to test-drive the working model of our adaptable swimming pool.

Doorphenalia contracts the actual builds of our projects out to Jeff and Adam Cartwright, the sons in Cartwright & Sons. Funnily enough, their dad started out on a market stall like mine.

The lads have unloaded the model at the back of the warehouse that is attached to our showroom.

The model is open-fronted, so it shouldn't feel claustrophobic, but it does. I go cold when I get in, but I ignore the feeling and nod at Jeff.

He pushes the lever and the floor starts to rise. It moves on a perfectly level trajectory. I walk from one side of the gridded metal platform to the other and the balance remains steady. It's all good.

Jeff and Adam are laughing at me. The floor's still rising, the ceiling's coming closer.

It starts to freak me out.

"Stop it," I say.

I find myself covering my head with my arms.

267

"Turn the bloody thing off. I mean it. Stop it, turn it off."

How fucking dare they take the piss out of me?

I can't believe how shaken I am. Before they've had a chance to bring the floor down again I lower myself into a sitting position and slide off it, drop to the ground. There's an oil stain on my trousers. Sweat prickles the back of my neck.

Adam attempts to give me a friendly pat on the back as I try to shove past.

"Sorry mate," he says. "It was only a joke, like."

I shrug away from his hand and nudge past the pair of them.

"Fuck off."

"He's not usually this touchy," I hear Adam say to Jeff.

I climb back up the steps to the office, slam the door behind me. I'm not. What the fuck's wrong with me?

Her. She's home from the hospital. Rebecca says the prognosis isn't good.

———◦◦◦———

1994

We spent another Christmas in the one-bedroomed flat, and then another spring and another summer.

Now two years old, Rebecca was obsessed by dogs and begged us to let her have one, but it wouldn't have been fair in the flat so we got her a kitten instead.

She named it Matilda after her favourite rag doll. It slept in her cot with her, curled up against her back.

Bex took Rebecca to a parent and toddler group three mornings a week, on the health visitor's recommendation. She was keeping a close eye on Bex, had also introduced her to a volunteer from an organisation called Home-Start.

Margie, the volunteer, was in her thirties and her own children were almost grown up. The health visitor explained over and over again that Margie wasn't a social worker; Bex's biggest fear was that Rebecca would be taken away from her.

"I can see you've been suffering from depression," the health visitor said.

I felt guilty but I didn't know why. I was doing my best. Margie was often still at the flat when I arrived home after packing up the market stall for the night.

Bex was drinking again. She was sober in the mornings; the only reason I was prepared to leave Rebecca with her when I went out to work. I think she started on the alcohol shortly before I arrived home, because she knew I'd be back soon to take care of Rebecca. I could never be late. The sad thing was, she became more like the old Bex. I was so fucking turned on by her, but scared at the same time. Scared of the sexual hold she had over me. I knew I ought to do something about the situation.

I'd resolve to confess my worries about her drinking to the health visitor, or to Margie. But then Bex would come out of the bathroom wrapped in her towelling dressing gown and open it to reveal the pink softness underneath. Her body still intoxicated me. Her breath would smell of the whisky or gin she'd been drinking in the bath and I'd have to turn my face away. But my hands would find her, every inch of her, and hold on.

I could believe again that she loved me, all soft and pliable as she was. She'd fold herself into my arms; pull me into the bedroom, now divided by a thick curtain. We would make love.

I kind of hoped she would get pregnant again and couldn't help wondering if that was what she was after. Why else would she turn back to me after such a long time?

But she didn't get pregnant.

Summer became autumn. Then it was winter. Mum and Dad came over to Skegness for Christmas and slept in their caravan for a few nights. We all went for a walk on the bleak, wind-ravaged beach and I pretended we were a happy family.

"Look Mummy," Rebecca said excitedly.

We followed the direction of her pointing finger.

"It's a seal!"

The seal regarded us impassively from the pebbles at the edge of the sea. Grit blew up into our eyes.

"Isn't she a clever girl?" said Mum. "Fancy her knowing what a seal is."

"We see them all the time, don't we, Popkins?"

Bex tugged gently on the pom-pom of Rebecca's hat, a knitted present from Mum. I watched Bex closely. She is a good mother, I thought, changing my mind again. Rebecca squealed and stamped her feet. Bex grabbed her hand and they ran off together towards the edge of the sea, but the seal turned and plopped into the water before they could reach it.

Mum and Dad exchanged smiles. I shivered, and hugged myself.

Dad died. It was just after Rebecca's third birthday, a terrible shock to us all. Mum sobbed on the phone.

"It isn't right. Nobody should die that young without at least a bit of warning."

"Bex," I said. "We're going to have to move back to Nottingham. We can't leave Mum there by herself."

"You know we can't do that, Jack."

Bex was brushing Rebecca's hair, tying it into pigtails ready for nursery. Rebecca squirmed and Bex tapped her lightly with the back of the hairbrush.

"Stand still, Miss Ants-in-your-pants."

Rebecca giggled, but at the same time stiffened. I didn't register her moment of wariness until later, too busy thinking about my mum. Bex met my eyes.

"We can't risk Jonathan and Evelyn finding us again."

"It's been three fucking years," I said. I'd forgotten why we'd moved to Skegness in the first place. "Why would they bother tracking you down now? You're nothing to do with them anymore."

"I know, but. . . "

She sucked in her lower lip. Then her mouth lifted at the edges. Brightness came into her eyes.

"Why don't you ask Beryl to move over here? It'll be awful for her, staying in the house without Jim. She could move into the caravan for the summer while we help her look for a house, for all of us, if you like. She'd love having full-time access to Rebecca. We can't stay in this poky flat forever."

It seemed a workable solution. We put it to Mum, and she wasn't against it. But in the end the decision in favour of Nottingham was made by Dad's Will. It turned out that, unbeknownst to Mum even, he'd recently invested in a small warehouse and office with a two-bedroomed flat above the premises. It had been left to me. Apparently the progress of the paperwork to transfer it into my name was underway at the time of Dad's heart attack. I couldn't believe he'd bought it without consulting me. He'd assumed we'd be happy to move back to Nottingham.

Among his papers Mum discovered a notebook with various designs of 'Portman and Son' scribbled all over it. At the bottom of one of the pages he'd written *'Doorphenalia'*.

So we had to go back to Nottingham.

"Why don't you go on ahead and get the flat decorated and furnished?" suggested Bex, changing tack. "Get your new business set up over there."

Rebecca was nearly four by then.

"Us two can move into the caravan for the time being so we don't have to pay the rent on this flat. Why disturb Rebecca's nursery routine before we have to?"

She made it sound so reasonable. The flat above the business premises in Nottingham was in a dilapidated state, after all. But she could have moved into the house with Mum, got Rebecca settled into a new nursery school from there.

Bex wound her arms around my neck when she saw the doubt in my eyes.

"It won't be for long, Jack, will it?"

The new business had another investor. Apparently he had given Dad a loan to start up his first market stall and Dad had accepted his further offer to invest in *Doorphenalia*.

I had to remind myself that although the building would legally belong to me, Dad had been planning for us to go into business together. So I was stuck with Bill Whitnail for the time being.

Bill had told me on the phone that he wouldn't want an actual involvement, only a return on his money. We arranged to meet at the warehouse on my second day back in Nottingham. I'd spent the night at Mum's and was full of a good breakfast. I paced what seemed at the time to be an enormous amount of floor space, my excitement at owning such a place increasing. Maybe Bex would finally love me properly; even marry me now I was a man of property.

In the surprisingly well-lit warehouse, I felt heady with the potential of my future.

I went upstairs and planned how I'd start clearing out the rooms of the flat, currently cluttered with someone else's left-behind furniture, as soon as possible. I wanted my woman and my child there with me. I couldn't help fretting about Bex, left alone with our daughter, but she seemed to be in control of her drinking and I was certain she wouldn't put Rebecca in danger.

"Hello?" A feminine voice called out into the empty cavern below, echoing up through gaps in the floorboards of the flat. I'd have to get a new floor laid before Rebecca could move in.

Who the hell was it? The large metal door at the front of the building clanged shut below and footsteps echoed in the empty space.

I felt nervous. I took the enclosed internal staircase down to a lobby shared by the warehouse and the flat. I shut the flat door behind me, making sure I had the Yale key in my pocket.

Pushing open the side door into the warehouse I got my first glimpse of Wendy.

My first thought was *oh, fuck*.

It must have been some kind of premonition.

She stared straight at me, her mouth slack. I noticed how full and pink her lips were. Her blue eyes had an unnatural glitter, like a brand-new doll.

The unexplained knowledge that this young woman was going to become obsessed with me hit me full force. It would definitely happen; she was looking at me in exactly the way I'd looked at Bex the first time I saw her. I wasn't going to stand a chance, just as Bex didn't.

She'll wear me down, I thought. *So what's the point of resisting?*

Bex and Rebecca were erased from my brain just like that. I let myself relax as my eyes wandered over the blonde's body, resting on the very generous curves of her hips and breasts. She seemed both sensuous and innocent. I wondered how old she was.

"Hi," she said. "My dad sent me to introduce myself. Bill did, I mean. I'm Wendy. He says I can get my work experience in the office. I'll be your secretary."

A rush went through me. The girl with golden hair took a few steps towards me. She put out her smooth white hand.

"You're Jack, right? I'm competent with a word processor and everything. And I've got A level Maths. Dad'll be the one who pays me so you don't have to worry about that."

I shrugged my jacket off and held it over my left arm so it obscured my crotch, then took the hand she was still holding out to me with my right.

"Pleased to meet you, Wendy." I coughed and made an effort to deepen my voice, then tried again. "Yeah, I'm Jack."

———◦●◦———

2010

Mrs Evans, that bloody woman with the crocodile skin, has opened the door. She's wearing what looks like a towelling beach dress, the sort of thing that goes over a swimsuit. It's

273

bright pink, strapless. She has flip-flops on her feet, and painted toenails.

" I don't have to let you in at all." She bars the doorframe with her chicken-wing arm.

"I'm Rebecca's father. I need to see my daughter."

She laughs. "Not really, you're not, whatever you may call yourself."

She's said something like that to me before. What the hell does she mean? I shove my foot forward so she won't be able to close the door.

"I'm Rebecca's father," I say again.

Maybe she's suffering from dementia; I should be patient with her.

She repeats: "Oh no, you're not."

"Dad," says Rebecca from the staircase behind Mrs Evans.

The old woman glances round. She leans forward towards me. "If you're her father," she sort of growl-whispers, "How come she was born before you ever met her mother?"

Rebecca didn't hear her say that. It makes no sense at all but I'm dazed by the suggestion nevertheless. The old woman shuffles away.

Another girl appears, I didn't see from where. Her healthy country glow makes Rebecca elfish in comparison.

"This is Sophie," Rebecca says. "She looks after Bo. You know, the other pony. Are you coming out to see them?" Then she looks anxious. "You should have called before you came. Sophie and I were just going for a ride."

She's wearing jodhpurs and a polo shirt. With her helmet clasped in her hand, she gets a defensive look on her face.

"Mum's asleep, but the nurse is there, so it's all right for me to leave her."

Before she leaves I persuade her to take me upstairs to see Bex. She grumbles because of having to take her boots off and then put them back on again.

I give her a nudge.

"I need you to smuggle me past Lily-the-Pink."

She laughs. "Mrs Evans is all right, you know. She's just taken against you for some reason. But anyway, I'm not sure. Mum's seriously ill. You can't upset her."

I promise that I only want to make my peace with her mother. Rebecca gets me clearance with the nurse.

"This is my dad."

I wonder if Mrs Evans has told the nurse anything to the contrary, mad old bat.

"Bex," I whisper.

She looks fucking awful. I never expected her to look that bad.

"Bex."

The nurse has gone for a cup of tea.

"Bex. . . "

She stirs. Her arm goes up over her face. She rubs her eyes with a curled fist. They open slowly and the whites of them are as yellow as her skin. I'm filled with awe.

This is Death, looking out at me.

She makes a noise like a crow, twice. Then: "Hey up, Jack."

I swallow. "Hey up."

"What d'you want?"

"I dunno." I really don't. My mind's gone blank. This has been a long time coming. Fuck, it has. She's been killing herself for all the years I've known her, but I can't believe she's gonna die. Not be gone for good.

"Come on," she croaks. "Don't try and kid a kidder. What've you really come for?"

"Fuck, Bex," I find myself saying. "How could you do this to yourself?"

She's little more than a skeleton in the bed. This creature was once the witch, disguised as a princess; that cast a spell on me.

Her eyes appear to bulge in their sunken sockets.

"You know why," she says quietly. "I was never supposed to be alive. Not since--"

"Yeah, I know." I want her to shut up now. It'll be the same old story.

Not since the sainted Sebastian.

I swallow again, this time bitterness. My body folds into the chair at her bedside. A kettle whistles downstairs. A shout ricochets outside the window, there's a throb in the ground of horses' hooves. But I don't move. My hands are jammed between my knees. I've been sitting here forever.

Bex seems to come back from somewhere. She coughs, more of a rattle in her chest.

"Spit it out. You didn't come to empathise with my situation."

She strains to raise her head from the pillow. I lean forward, thinking I should help but too awkward to touch her. She manages to push the pillow into shape behind her head, breathes noisily. She looks me full in the face.

"What've they said to you, Mrs Evans and them? It's time she knew the truth anyway... Rebecca... You'll be the one that has to tell her. But not until after. You can tell her after I'm gone."

"Is she mine?" It's all I can think of to ask.

It's the only thing I want to know. I need it to be true that what I felt for Bex did result in Rebecca.

"Of course she is, you dork. You're her dad. It's not about that. It's about the other Rebecca. The first one I had."

The first one she had.

The silver 'X' above her belly-button marked the spot. I realise that now, but I never wanted to acknowledge it. He got there before me in everything, Sebastian.

Bex's eyelids have fallen closed. Now they flutter open again. She blows air out through her lips; then manages more words.

"That's what I want you to tell her about, after I'm gone."

Thirty-Eight

Rebecca

WEARING FLORESCENT WAISTCOATS and colourful caps over our helmets, Sophie and I walk our horses along the bridle path into the woods behind the paddock. Where the path narrows, leaves from overhanging branches brush against my face. Sun tickles the skin exposed by gaps on the backs of my gloves. I'm in a suspended state, imagining Sebastian and my mother riding this same route.

We break out of the woods into sunshine. A breeze blows up from nowhere. Cantering across a field we move down to the track running alongside the reservoir. The air here is cool and damp. After we emerge from the tree-tunnelled lane at the end of the track we trot home along Bradgate Road. I give Topaz a reassuring pat when he startles at a car that doesn't slow down enough. Sweat drenches the back of my neck; it feels muggy again. My scalp itches under the helmet. I'm always nervous riding on the main road.

We re-enter the village from the opposite end that we started from; coming back into Greys Mount through the iron gates. Sophie reaches over to punch in the code.

We smile at each other as we lay our saddles over the stands. I don't know how to broach the subject of offering her a room but I'm saved from the decision by her looking at me funny a few times. She clears her throat.

"Have I done something to upset you?"

Oh no, I hadn't realised she was feeling uncomfortable.

"No, of course not, what do you mean?"

"I don't know; you just seem odd towards me."

I clear my own throat, nervous.

"Well, there is something, but I don't know how to put it."

The worry that spreads over her face makes me launch straight in.

"I was wondering if you wanted to move into a spare room here. There's so much space and I thought it would make it easier for you to help look after the horses. It would also make me feel better about you paying to ride Bo. Could we call that money your rent? After all, you shouldn't have to pay to do all this work. God, look around you, you can see we don't need the money. I never expected to find myself in this position, honestly."

I stop short of saying *I was once as poor as you.*

She shuffles her feet.

"What do you think?" I ask. "I hope I haven't embarrassed you. I didn't mean to. If you want to know the truth I'm. . . well it gets a bit lonely living here."

She's staring at me. I must tell her the truth.

"My mum's really ill. I mean, seriously ill. It's bad. I should have told you that. It's probably not a good idea to ask you to move in."

She must think I'm a total idiot. I've dropped Topaz's bridle. My knees click when I bend to gather it up. We've still got to groom the horses and get them turned out. I shouldn't leave Mum for too long. Sophie stands with Bo's bridle over her arms, staring at me, biting her bottom lip. Her face changes like clouds are scudding over it. She smiles.

"I think it's a great idea, I'd love to, if you're really sure? It would be amazing to live in this house and yeah, I could help you."

A week later and I can't believe how much Mum's changed. Her skin's completely yellow now and her eyes have sunken further. She's got a thing called 'hepatorenal syndrome', it means that because of liver cirrhosis her kidneys are failing. She refuses to go back into hospital, and she'll never recover from it. She's planning to die here at home. My tummy flutters with panic. A lot of the time I can't swallow properly; my mouth is always dry.

I get up early every day to tend the horses with Sophie. I throw a ball for Dusty in the paddock while the horses are eating. The only time I feel truly relaxed is when we're out riding. I can forget everything then, air sliding over my face, my mind drifting. The rhythm of my rise and fall when we trot is effortless. I give myself in to the sway of Topaz beneath me when we amble, the creak of the saddle, the leather reins between my fingers. The weather continues to be hot. When the rain falls it's always a relief.

Sophie's moved her stuff into the room next-but-one to mine, separated by the bathroom. Not the orange room, thank God.

Her family have worked out with Mrs Evans and Mr Graham that they'll provide fresh meat for our freezer. She's got family all over the village, in different businesses. I wonder what it would be like to be part of a big family like hers and then I'm shocked to remember that I have Dad and the boys. There's also Wendy and Iris. And Connor felt like my family for a while too. I did have all that, but I feel cut-off from it now.

Anyway, here in this house we've accumulated a family of sorts.

Mrs Evans and Mr Graham are the grandparents. Sophie and I are the sisters. We also have Jackie who does Mum's ironing and Brenda-the-nurse, they're the aunties.

Mum's friend Diane from Skegness visited. But she was more trouble than she was worth, crying all the time. I've tried to contact Uncle Dave but he's gone off on another finding-himself trip. Uncle Rick says he'll bring Nana over next week.

Thirty-Nine

SOMETHING WAKES ME up, a movement of some kind. It must be the middle of the night because it's inky-dark. Dusty isn't barking, so it can't be anything bad. I stretch and turn over, fingers slipping automatically under the pillow. I keep the photo of Sebastian under there, the close-up of Mum and him that was taken at their engagement party. And, this is bad but I can't help it – I pretend that Mum in the picture is me. In a way it makes me feel closer to Mum.

Let me be her. Let now be then.

And let Sebastian never have died. It would all have been so beautiful.

There's that movement again.

A hand presses gently on my shoulder. Warmth floods me like my mum's arms when I was little.

"*Rebecca, wake up, sweetheart.*"

It's a long time since she called me that.

"*Mum?*"

She shouldn't be out of bed. I sit up quickly.

"*Wake up sleepy-head, there's somewhere I want to take you.*"

Her voice is light, as if she's smiling. This is too weird.

Her long hair swings across the back of my hand. It's silky and it smells clean. I take a handful and press my nose to it like I used to.

She laughs out loud, and I don't have to draw back from her breath. It smells as sweet as her hair.

"Mum?"

"Come on. Shhhh."

In the dim light from the crack in the curtains I see she has a finger to her lips. She stands upright, holds herself straight. She shows no signs of pain.

"Come on, slowcoach."

Dusty stands up and stretches in his basket when I get out of bed.

"Make him stay there, Rebecca; he can't come with us. I'm sorry."

I close my bedroom door. We instinctively avoid the creaking floorboards in the corridor, going past Sophie's room and then Brenda's. I've no idea where Mum is taking me but a sense of fun bubbles up. It's so long since we did anything together and Mum seems really well. Maybe the doctors were wrong after all.

She takes me down the back staircase, the part of the house I used to like best when we first came here. It's as familiar as the freckles on the backs of my hands, as if I've lived here forever. I feel warm and relaxed; it's suddenly perfectly normal to get up in the middle of the night and go off on some sort of mystery tour.

She stops at the bottom on the tiled floor of the corridor. Thanks to the quarter moon, faint light sketches the contours of her face. She looks young again, her skin filled out, not sunken into the hollows of her cheeks. She's wearing a lacy white nightdress that I've never seen before, long, almost to the ground.

A sense of unreality pervades all my movements, but excitement rises in my stomach, flutters like butterflies.

Hurry, hurry.

"Open the door, Mum."

"Are you sure?"

She's breathing rapidly and I am too. My stomach keeps swooping like I'm going to be sick, but I know it's just the anticipation.

At last.

He's coming, it's in the air, the way the molecules swirl; I can see it in Mum's eyes.

"Hug for your old Mum?"

She used to say that to me when I was small.

She feels like her again, the one who used to read me all those stories, tell me I was the most beautiful girl in the world. I scratch the top of my leg under my pyjama shorts, something's just bitten me; I hear the buzzing whine as it goes past my ear.

"Don't let the little buggers bite," says Mum and we both laugh.

I'm taller than her now, resting my chin on her shoulder.

"OK, it's time."

I kind of know what she means, though I couldn't put it into words. But it definitely is time.

We've got to go.

We enter the sitting room and she pushes back the curtain obscuring the door to the grey room. A rush of familiarity hits me. I – she, used to play with Sebastian in here. That's what this room is. No wonder she's been so fond of it since we moved into the house. I stroke her arm, pleased to feel how much plumper it is now, healthy and strong.

"You're all better."

She's like someone my own age. A tiny part of me thinks that's not fair.

We move into the room and sit in the two armchairs. I can't help tapping my fingers on the arms of mine, getting impatient.

Hurry, hurry.

I even start rocking back and forwards on the edge of the chair but Mum tells me to stop it. I'm like a fidgety child.

"Be still, Rebecca, you never were a patient girl."

Was I not?

It's light enough in here, in this grey room. Mum's skin has returned to its normal colour. Better, in fact. She has roses in her cheeks. That's what she used to say to me about mine. Her eyes shine. She's looking at the wall where I know the window will appear, and it does.

The landscape materialises, ah yes. The pleasure I feel is almost pain. This landscape is so dear and familiar, I know it

283

by heart. I want to go out in it so badly. The purple hills loom in the distance, the coarse, bluish grass in the foreground is so tangible I want to feel it between my bare toes. Ah. I've waited for this moment so long. Tears of relief water my face and I can see them on Mum's too. We reach across the gap between the armchairs and take hold of each other's hands. Mum gives mine a squeeze.

A new wave of excitement crashes against a harbour wall in my tummy.

The light in the landscape changes: red, pink, blue. . . purple darkening to a deep indigo. There is a rumble in the distance. Mum and I tense.

But we are distracted by the opening of the door. A grey-haired woman comes in carrying a tray. It's Evelyn. She moves in front of us, something robotic in her actions.

"Hello, Rebecca dear, oh hello Rebecca, how lovely to see you both."

She leans towards us with the tray and we accept a cup each.

"Thank you."

"Thank you so much."

I'm happy to see Evelyn again, but she can't seem to meet our eyes, or maybe she doesn't want to.

"You're very welcome, dears. He'll be here soon."

He will.

Evelyn turns and walks out of the room again with the empty tray.

We sip our tea. I wince as it burns my bottom lip. Mum drinks hers more carefully, holding the cup with her little finger raised like a lady.

Then it happens. We both see Sebastian at the same time, uncoiling from a reclining position in the bottom-left hand corner of the painting. The landscape I mean; the real landscape. God, it's really him. Sebastian!

He stretches, beyond the window, puts two fingers between his lips and whistles. He's facing away from us, his shoulder-length blond hair lifting in a breeze. He wears a loose white

cotton shirt which billows around his body, cut-off jeans expos-
ing his strong tanned legs, and his feet are bare. I know what
he's waiting for. The thundering sound we heard earlier is get-
ting louder; the horse's hooves on the hard ground. It's coming.

I drink the last of the hot tea, it scalds me but I don't care.
Mum has already finished hers. We look at each other and both
put our cups on the floor, under our chairs.

We lean forward in our seats, poised as if at the beginning of
a race.

Prickles of sweat have broken out on my brow. I put up my
arm to wipe them away. Mum's skin looks flushed, too. I'm
confused, enjoying the new closeness with Mum but at the same
time afraid she'll take away from me the only thing I want. Why
is she here?

The horse is in view, galloping towards us. My heart gallops
in rhythm. Intensity builds, almost unbearable.

I want you, I want you.

I've stopped looking at Mum. She's the other Rebecca. It's
not fair that she looks the same age as me; it's supposed to be
my turn now.

He is turning, so we can see his face. The horse nuzzles into
his hands, breathing hot breaths, letting out a snort. The look in
its eye is wild but the boy bends his neck and breathes into the
horses' nostrils and it calms, still pawing its front left hoof. It
settles, while he rests his hand on its neck, talking to it in a low
voice. We hear the rumble of his gentling tone until the horse is
completely still.

The boy puts out the flat of his hand to the horse, telling it
to wait. It tosses its head once but remains in place on the
tussocky ground just outside the window.

He is coming.

I let out a long breath. I won't look at Mum. The boy, Sebas-
tian, my boy, slides back the huge window letting the landscape
breathe into the room. We're touched by a pinkish glow, settling
on our skin and hair. I've leapt up, hopping from foot to foot. I'm
so excited that he is here in the flesh at last.

"Sebastian."

And yes, he comes straight towards me; he seems as excited as I am.

This is it, now; he's come to me, wrapping his arms around me as he did before.

"Rebecca, I've missed you so much. Have you missed me?"

"Oh God, Sebastian, more than I can say."

My ear is against his chest, I can hear the pounding of his heart. I smell the familiar, intoxicating mixture of horse and boy, a scent I'll remember for the rest of my life. Held in his arms like this, his finger tracing the line of my cheek; it's the nicest feeling I could ever imagine. I want to stay like this.

Out of the corner of my eye I see that Mum has crumpled into her armchair. Her skin has yellowed and loosened on her bones, her eyes sunken in her face. Her limp brown hair straggles around hollowed cheeks.

Sebastian cups the back of my head in one of his big hands, tilting my chin back with the curled forefinger of the other.

"I love your hair like this, Rebecca, it suits you, my love; you're so beautiful."

But I'm worried about the puzzled look in his eyes. It shouldn't be there. I hold him tighter against me with linked hands at his back, grinding my hips into his.

"Rebecca?"

"Sebastian. You too. . . "

"Me too?"

"You too are beautiful."

Don't look at her.

Unlinking my fingers I pull his head closer to mine, trailing my lips just barely over his, hovering before the kiss. Then I plunge forward, sucking and drawing in his lower one. At the same time I circle each nodule of his spine with a fingertip, from neck to base. He's stroking my back with his hands but he breaks away and leans back to study my face.

"I love it when you do that, Rebecca, I always have done."

"I know you do. I've waited forever for this day."

"I know, my darling. I've come to take you to Oblivion."

But we're both aware there's something wrong, terribly wrong. From her armchair in the corner Mum lets out a long moan.

Sebastian stiffens in the circle of my repossessing arms. His eyes change as he takes another look at my face. A frown dents his forehead.

"Rebecca. . ."

"No."

"Rebecca, I am so sorry."

"No!"

"Rebecca, I can't take you to Oblivion, you're not the right one."

"I am. I'm the right Rebecca. Take me, Sebastian, please, I promise I'll be the right one for you, I promise. Please take me."

But he's already loosening my arms from his waist. Gently removing my fingers from his wrists as I try to grab him. He holds me away by my hands. His eyes are impenetrably blue, dazzling like the sky in ice as they gaze at me for a second longer. His blond hair sweeps forward as he moves away, past me.

"There she is. My Rebecca. Rebecca darling."

He's murmuring over my mother in the chair. Anger boils in my blood. Mum's breath comes strangely from her throat, creating a gravelly noise I can't bear to listen to.

She tricked me. Cheated me.

"Rebecca, my dearest love."

Sebastian leans over her, scoops her weak body up in his arms. Disgustingly, she's wet herself. The smell burns my nostrils. Tears streak her ravaged cheeks; her mouth hangs open.

How can he choose her over me?

She sounds like she's choking.

I want to scream and rage, but I stand, silent and immobile. I watch him carry her over to the window with more tenderness than I'd ever imagined possible. I follow, tugging at his shirt, but he's no longer aware of me.

Mum's head lolls in his arms, her sunken eyes seek me out.

No, I won't look at her!

287

"Rebecca." It's a crow's caw. Not a human voice at all. "Rebecca, you are the most beautiful girl in the world. My baby."

No. No.

She tries to move her lower jaw upwards but it falls open again. Her eyes go cloudy.

"No, Mum!"

He carries her out into the landscape and somehow I can't get out of that room, even though I can feel the air on my face; hear the snapping static of the pink and purple atmosphere.

A warm wind stirs the horse's mane. He stamps his hoof and snorts a hot breath. I didn't see how, but Sebastian has managed to get my mother and himself onto the back of the huge horse. He holds Mum in front of him, cradles her body in the broad span of his arms. His face is bent over Mum's, kissing her dry lips.

He gives a command to the horse and it swerves its powerful body around on two hooves, pointing itself into the landscape.

"There's a storm coming," I somehow hear Sebastian whisper.

It's only at that moment I notice the deep gash on the left side of his head, what looks like fresh blood trickling out of it, coagulating in his hair.

Then with a kicking up of dust and a thundering of hooves on the dry ground, they are gone.

They are gone, my boy, his horse and my mum, and there's only me left in the little grey room, all closed up now.

Forty

Jack

To: Mr P. Clithero,
Psychiatric Consultant,
Honey Tree Private Hospital,
Leicester

Jack Portman
Doorphenalia
Palmer Building,
Eastside Estate,
Woodside Close,
Nottingham

19 August 2010
REF: Rebecca Grey

Dear Mr Clithero,

I am writing, as you suggested, with as much information about Rebecca as possible. I hope this helps you to find a way of getting through to her and making her better again.

First, let me point out that until just before the end, I had no idea how ill Rebecca's mother actually was. From the small amount of information my daughter gave me I had been satisfied with a nurse in the house to do the caring duties, and a friend of her own age who had recently moved in. Rebecca should not have had an overburden of responsibility on her young shoulders. But I miscalculated the situation, I admit it.

My daughter is a bright, resilient girl with a great talent for Art. Last year she became ill with an escalating series of ailments which eventually hospitalised her. Although she seemed to make a good recovery, I believe it left her quite frail.

She has also been forced to move home several times due to her mother's alcoholism. Ms Grey, Rebecca's mother, refused to accept any help from me in providing a home for our daughter. I have to admit that communication between us was very poor, accusatory on both sides, and I suppose I must take my full share of responsibility for my daughter's messed-up childhood. Neither the behaviour of her mother nor I has helped Rebecca. It was not until she turned sixteen that I began to have regular contact with her again.

My relationship with Ms Grey broke when Rebecca was four. After that my situation was regretfully too complicated to accommodate her needs and so I can only honestly say that I have known her properly for the past two years. But since her severe illness, which ended in the early spring of this year, I believe we have become quite close and she is now well integrated into my second family. My wife and I and our two young sons would be very happy to have Rebecca come and live with us once she is well enough.

I know that throughout her young life, Rebecca felt responsible for her alcoholic mother. She chose to return to her mother's care, or rather, to return and care for her mother when she was old enough, even after being settled in a stable foster-family. I should have taken her in myself when the Social Services got involved, but my wife had recently suffered a miscarriage and did not feel able to have Rebecca at that time. And the second time she was delicate with the pregnancy of our twins, or getting used to being a mother. Ms Grey's alcoholism has been an enormous strain on Rebecca over the past year in particular.

As you already know, the nurse who was caring for Ms Grey, Brenda Withers, woke Rebecca up at about midnight on Tuesday 10th of August. She had already notified Ms Grey's health-providing team. Rebecca was taken to her mother's bedside and was present as she drew her final breath. At about 3am, an hour after her mother's death, Rebecca went back to bed or so the nurse believed. But in the morning the members of her household could not find her. The house was searched and it was the housekeeper Mrs Evans along with Rebecca's friend Sophie who finally discovered her in a tiny room hidden by a curtained door. A doctor was called to the house and Rebecca was given sedation.

At her mother's funeral six days later, which I attended to give support to my daughter, Rebecca was not much better. In the church she was silent but at the cemetery she could not seem to keep still. She kept pacing over to the grave next to her mother's, which belongs to Ms Grey's former husband. Every few moments Rebecca kept screaming, "It should have been me. I was yours." It was very distressing for all present, as you can imagine.

You know the rest; she was referred to your facility by an emergency medical team that same afternoon. I know you are treating her with Diazepam at the moment but I hope very much she will not have to be on this medication for long. I think as much Art Therapy as possible, as you suggested, may be the way in to her troubled mind.

I beg you to keep me informed and let me know of any tiny progress, however insignificant it may seem. For quick correspondence, my email address is below.

Yours Sincerely,

Jack Portman
Jack@Doorphenalia.com

P.S. I'll be bringing Rebecca's brothers in to visit her at the weekend. Also, I am sending on some of Rebecca's sketchbooks in case they are of any use to you.

Rebecca

The symptoms of my illness return: the rash covering my body and the headache pressing at the back of my skull. I long for sleep and the possibility of seeing Mum again. I'd tell her I don't mind about Sebastian. I should never have competed with her. Maybe it was my fault that she died.

I claw at my arms, leave ugly scratches on the skin.

The nurses encourage me to wear cotton gloves like a baby but I can't bear the fabric at my wrists.

At the begining I felt as if I would be trapped in the grey room forever but the walls have begun to open out and the ceiling has lifted. I draw huge landscapes, smudge red chalk into hard ink lines. I draw a figure, me, over and over again, trying to negotiate its way through the coloured fog.

Time passes; I don't keep track of it. Sometime, maybe three months later, I tell Dad I think I'm ready to go home, but that doesn't feel like it should be Greys Mount anymore. "You'll come to us, of course," he says. "When you're strong enough." Wendy nods in the background. The twins bring me their drawings and I can't stop crying.

Iris comes and raises an eyebrow as she does every time she visits. Finally, I agree to see Connor. He stands in front of me, shoulders slumped, and I want to poke him in the back and make him stand up straight like he always used to.

There's a faint scar on his cheek. I find out afterwards that it was me. He came to see me at the beginning and I caught his face with my fingernail, screaming at him that he wasn't the right one.

"I'm sorry," I tell him later.

"You could give Deirdre a run for her money with that temper of yours, to be sure," he says. And for some reason that makes me feel pleased.

Forty-One

Rebecca

County Leitrim, Ireland, July 2013

IT'S RAINING HARD, but that's not unusual. Apparently it's been the wettest summer on record. Topaz hates the feeling of his hooves squidging into the ground with every step he takes. He walks like a prissy girl, lifting each hoof disdainfully. I'm thinking of keeping him in the concrete yard until the ground hardens a bit. Dev, that's Connor's old pony that he's had since he was a baby, thinks Topaz is a real wimp. Dev comes splishing through the puddles towards Topaz, tortures him by nipping his bottom. But Dev was born and bred here and he's a hardy type, much more than Topaz is. Generally though, those two get along together like a grouchy old couple.

My eyes go back to my painting. It's a commission for a local landowner, a view of his farm from the side of a mountain, looking down on the landscape.

My angry reds of three years ago have softened to purples and browns mingled with splashes of the vivid greens of this country I now call home. I take a palette knife, and using the very tip, lay in a narrow line of black, just a bit of delineation for the roof of Mr McConnell's farmhouse. I've been given permission by him to include this painting in my first solo exhibition at Sarah O'Toole's gallery. Underneath, a notice will say 'from the collection of Martin McConnell'. It's likely to encour-

293

age more sales, Sarah tells me.

Connor's coming across the yard with a mug of tea, holding one hand over the top to shelter the hot liquid from the rain. He knows I can make my own in the kitchenette off my studio but he likes to bring me one during his lunch break.

"How're you, my love?"

Dusty jumps up at the sound of Connor's voice. What a traitor, I'm sure he loves Connor more than me.

"Ahhh, you're making me spill the tea yeh mad pooch!"

Connor's wet hair drips on my face as he bends to kiss me, but I warm up inside. He grins as I dab the end of his nose with a blob of ultramarine paint.

"Can't improve on perfection, much as you might try," he boasts.

He still says the same kind of cocky things as he did when I first met him.

"Anyways, I came out here to bring you this; you left it inside again, eejit."

I start to take my mobile phone from him, noticing there's a missed call from Sophie.

"Oops. Hold onto it for me a minute, will you?"

Too late I've remembered I need to wash my hands; paint is already smeared on the phone.

"I'm hoping she's got some good news for me."

"You're referring to the Greys Mount Riding School, no doubt, m'lady?"

"Yep." I'm so excited. "It's ringing now."

I smile at Connor; the ultramarine paint on his nose is almost the same colour as his eyes. He moves behind me, slides his arms around my body, cradling the small swell of my belly in his work-worn hands. I must remember to encourage him to moisturise even though he thinks it's not manly. I keep telling him he needs to soften them up before I'll allow him to handle our baby.

While I wait for Sophie to answer – she's like me, she puts her phone down and walks away from it – I remember that Iris is coming over tonight, bringing us a casserole that we'll eat together.

Iris thinks I can't cook.

"Ach, I know you can, niece, of course I do. It's just that we've got to make sure the little one in here gets all the correct nourishment, don't we?"

She knew I was pregnant before I did; says she can always tell.

"It's a look women get about them. I helped deliver our Connor here you know. Don't know what Sarah would have done without me. You just make sure you call me when the time comes for this one's entrance."

"Hmmm. That's not for a while yet, Iris; I'll think about it."

I'm planning on a hospital birth.

"And I got an email from your father yesterday, Rebecca, with a video of that wee Megan of theirs. Only just a year old and tearing around already. I bet you can't wait to see them all when they come over in the autumn, eh?"

Yep. Dad, Wendy, Bobby, Joshua and baby Megan are all coming here to visit. They've already got a family room booked at the Ramada Hotel.

My baby's going to be a girl too, I know it is; I can feel it somehow. I haven't told Connor yet, but I'd like to call her Eve. Evelyn Iris, probably.

Rain patters on my studio roof as Sophie's phone rings on and on. Connor's still standing behind me, his chin fitted neatly into the hollow between my neck and shoulder. His hands make rhythmic circles on my belly. Time has stopped, and if it has to, this is as good a point as any for that to happen.

The dialling tone cuts itself out but I know the drill, I press redial and it's not long before she answers.

"Hi, Sophie? Yes, did you pass as well? Oh that's brilliant, such good news. So we're on then, yayy!"

Sophie has qualified as a riding instructor. She'll be running our riding school at Greys Mount.

"Did Jade get back to you?"

Jade has finished her second year of a Fine Art degree at De Montford University. She's keeping her horses at Greys Mount, allowing them to be used by the riding school, old Jonah especially. Tetra will only be offered to experienced riders because apparently he's still a bit unpredictable.

Jade's going to work at the new stables with Sophie at the weekends; she's also just passed her IGEQ instructor's passport.

"And how are Mrs Evans – sorry, Linda and Granddad getting on, have they been out on another date yet?"

Sophie and I roar with laughter. The old – odd – couple fight like cat and dog now they're sharing the house I gifted to them both, but we reckon they'll be getting married before long. Linda Evans' dotty old sister died last year, with a smile on her face apparently, and that's when Linda agreed to move into Greys Mount. Sophie lives there too with Mr Grahams.

Because he's her Granddad, he's also become mine by association. They were all so kind to me when I was ill.

When I came out of hospital I transferred Bo's papers into Sophie's name so she officially owns her now.

There'll always be plenty of room for Connor and me to stay at Greys Mount if we want to visit Newtown Linford. But I've kept away from it so far; I don't think I'm ready to face those memories just yet. Linda Evans and Bob Grahams have promised to look after the graves for me--

"Hey, what's with the sad eyes, lady?"

Sophie and I have finished our phone conversation but I'm still holding the phone in my hand, staring at it blankly. Connor comes around to my front, peering at me with concern from under his black curly fringe. He traces a finger under one of my eyes.

"Have you been painting on your skin or are those violet shadows natural to your pale Englishness, beautiful woman?"

Suddenly I can feel her beside me: Mum. The brush of her long hair against my face. I blow on it from the side of my mouth and she moves away; she never liked me breathing on her.

There were times when she made me feel like the most beautiful girl in the world. But it's Connor who holds me tightly now, and I shudder in his arms.

The doctors explained to me that it can take years to go through the process of bereavement, and Connor is always here. For me. My grip on him tightens.

Connor is real, he is mine, and I love him all the more for coming back to me after the dream was over.

———◦◦◦———

I meet her not long before my baby is due to be born: my older sister. Dad had wanted to tell me about her after Mum died; he'd only just found out himself that Mum had given Sebastian's baby away during her Great Grief. But I was too ill to take on board information like that for a long time.

Mum's first daughter comes on the ferry in the autumn, with the rest of my family. Her name is Catriona now, but she was once named Rebecca like me.

A jolt of recognition goes through me when I see her, and I remember a dark shadow at my shoulder just after I was ill.

"I think I've always known about you."

I've realised this, too late.

She's a year and a half older than me, taller, with lighter hair than mine. Sebastian's influence, I suppose. But her eyes are similar to mine and Mum's.

It's hard not to be bitter at what I missed out on for all those years. I was a lonely child, and yet she was in the world all along. It wasn't fair to her, either. I feel slightly ashamed at the memory of Mum telling me I was the most beautiful girl in her eyes, the only one. I'd have been happy to have been half as important.

"My mother, my mama, I mean," my sister tells me, "is from an Italian family. So I get to spend time in Florence. Your dad found it hard to trace me because I've been working at a museum there for the past year. May I, please?"

I allow her to lay her hand on the mound of my belly. Eve is getting restless in there although she still has over two months to wait before she can come out.

"My niece, I can't believe it," says Catriona. She looks at me with glittering eyes. "I always wanted a sister."

Catriona and I, we could have had each other.

I tell her all about our mother, leaving out the bad parts for now, and explain how deeply Bex loved Sebastian.

"I have a photograph of them both together," I say. "You can have it."

After all, it rightfully belongs to her: the first daughter named Rebecca.

Acknowledgements

Thanks to Phil for being my partner, and to our lovely Luna and Pixie, rescue dogs and constant companions. (Not forgetting Pheoby, the van-travelling cat!) Thanks to my children for being a massive inspiration in my writing and art; they continue to be so now that they've all grown up.

Thanks to Sara-Jayne Slack and Fiona Campbell for their excellent editing and to Jane Dixon-Smith for the amazing new cover.

Thanks to Ali Edgley for being the first reader of this book and offering her opinion on an early version of the manuscript. Also to Judith Williamson (RIP, my friend) and Gordon Hall for even earlier readings.

A special acknowledgement goes to Helen and Ian Butland of Doorstuff (www.doorstuff.co.uk) for the inspiration for Jack's work (and obsession with hinges.) I find it really funny how Ian and Helen know everything about anything to do with doors – just ask!

To Terry Tyler, writer and Twitter inspiration, for her valued endorsement of Another Rebecca and the lovely Sharon Booth who thrills me with her reaction to Another Rebecca and my other stories.

Thanks to The Book Club (TBC), Book Connectors and Writers, Authors and Readers on Facebook for providing so much fun, serious debate and information about readerly and authorly stuff.

Bradgate Park, where Rebecca meets Lady Jane Grey in the book, is a place I've visited every year with my family whilst at a summer camp in Leicestershire.

RIP Geoff Bainbridge (1948 – 2013), who first took us there.

And thanks to the writers of all the historical novels I've read in the past for engaging my interest in the Tudors and in Lady Jane Grey and her ilk.

Other novels by Tracey Scott-Townsend:

The Last Time We Saw Marion

Inspired Quill 2014

Meeting author Callum Wilde is the catalyst that turns Mari-anne Fairchild's fragile sense of identity on its head, evoking demons that will haunt two families.

'This is a haunting read, enriched by its references to uneasy mother/daughter relationships, to uncertainties around existence... The plot is strongly and carefully crafted with one mystery lay-ered upon another. The settings are well chosen to embody this shifting so that the storyline never lacks atmosphere.'
Rosalind Minett, Goodreads

'It's like no other story I've ever read. A ghost story with a living phantom; a heartbreaking tale of grief, separation, obses-sion, devastation; a story of spirit, family, love.'
Sharon Booth Goodreads

'Life. Death. Does reincarnation exist? Do memories of our past bubble under the surface of our consciousness? This novel certainly made me consider my answers to these questions.'
Claire Hill, Goodreads.

Of His Bones

(sequel to The Last Time We Saw Marion)
Inspired Quill 2017

Of His Bones explores uncertainties around existence, identity and predestination. The characters must come to terms with events in the past that continue to echo in their present, and resolve unfinished issues. Eventually, two families are able to become a coherent whole through a painful progress of interactions which involves losses as well as gains for all of them.

'Tracey Scott-Townsend crafted a haunting, emotional tale of complicated and difficult relationships within families and how much past events can mark the future.'
Magdalena, Goodreads

'A fabulously haunting, atmospheric tale that I couldn't put down.'
Ange, Goodreads

'The story kept me gripped from the start and kept me interested throughout. Highly recommended and I will be reading more from Tracey.'
Kerry, Goodreads

The Eliza Doll

Wild Pressed Books 2016

It can be lonely on the road. Ellie has two companions: her dog, Jack, and the mysterious Eliza who turns up in the most unexpected places. At every encounter with Eliza, Ellie feels as if she's standing again in the aching cold of a waterfall in Iceland, the sound of crashing water filling her with dread. Ellie can't change the past. But is it really too late to rectify the bad thing she did when her third child was a baby?

'Wow. I finished this book and sat and held it for a moment, breath stopped. It was extraordinary. So many layers. So patiently building up to a devastating reveal, one that wasn't tricky or gimmicky, but beautiful, raw, painful and heartbreaking.'
Louise, Goodreads

'Ellie's character is both compelling and enigmatic in her earlier years and her continual strength resonates throughout. Raw emotion and traumatic events give the book gravity and presence, whilst the descriptions in Iceland and relationships between some of the characters tenderise it perfectly.'
Debra, Goodreads

'Vivid characters, some beautiful description particularly of Iceland, which is such a powerful presence, almost like another character, and Ellie is a wonderful creation.'
Ali, Goodreads

About the Author

Tracey is the author of four novels and is also a poet. She has performed at Hull's Freedom Festival and in many local open mic settings. She won an Apples and Snakes commission for Deranged Poetesses: 'Maidens' at ARC Stockton in March 2018.

As a Visual Artist, Tracey's narrative work utilises digital photography and moving image as a starting point. Drawings, mixed media paintings and delicate 3D work made from materials such as tissue paper and muslin, (and now the Apple Pencil) are inspired by the emotions of her own experiences and perceptions.

She has a Fine Art MA (University of Lincoln) and a BA Hons Visual Studies (Humberside Polytechnic) She has exhibited throughout the UK (as Tracey Scott) and initiated several independent artist led projects with diverse groups of people within the community, schools and residential homes.

Lightning Source UK Ltd.
Milton Keynes UK
UKHW042142070719
345743UK00001B/1/P